BLACK
SCIENCE

COLLECTION DESIGN: JEFF POWELL

IMAGE COMICS, INC.

Robert Kirkman – Chief Operating Officer
Erik Larsen – Chief Financial Officer
Todd McFarlane – President
Marc Silvestri – Chief Executive Officer
Jim Valentino – Vice President

Eric Stephenson – Publisher/Chief Creative Officer
Corey Hart – Director of Sales
Jeff Boison – Director of Publishing Planning & Book Trade Sales
Chris Ross – Director of Digital Sales
Jeff Stang – Director of Specialty Sales
Kat Salazar – Director of PR & Marketing
Drew Gill – Art Director

BLACK SCIENCE VOLUME 8: LATER THAN YOU THINK. First Printing. October 2018. Published by Image Comics, Inc. Office of publication: 2701 NW Vaughn Street, Suite 780, Portland, Oregon 97210. Copyright © 2018 Rick Remender and Matteo Scalera. All rights reserved. Originally published in single magazine form as BLACK SCIENCE #35-38. BLACK SCIENCE™ (including all prominent characters featured herein), its logo and all character likenesses are trademarks of Rick Remender and Matteo Scalera, unless otherwise noted. Image Comics® and its logos are registered trademarks of Image Comics, Inc. No part of this publication may be reproduced or transmitted, in any form or by any means (except for short excerpts for review purposes) without the express written permission of Image Comics, Inc. All names, characters, events and locales in this publication are entirely fictional. Any resemblance to actual persons (living or dead), events or places, without satiric intent, is coincidental. For information regarding the CPSIA on this printed material call: 203-595-3636 and provide reference #RICH-815027. PRINTED IN THE U.S.A. For international rights inquiries, contact: foreignlicensing@imagecomics.com.

GIANT

RICK REMENDER
WRITER

MATTEO SCALERA
ARTIST

MORENO DINISIO
COLORS

RUS WOOTON
LETTERING + LOGO DESIGN

SEBASTIAN GIRNER
EDITOR

BLACK SCIENCE CREATED BY
RICK REMENDER & MATTEO SCALERA

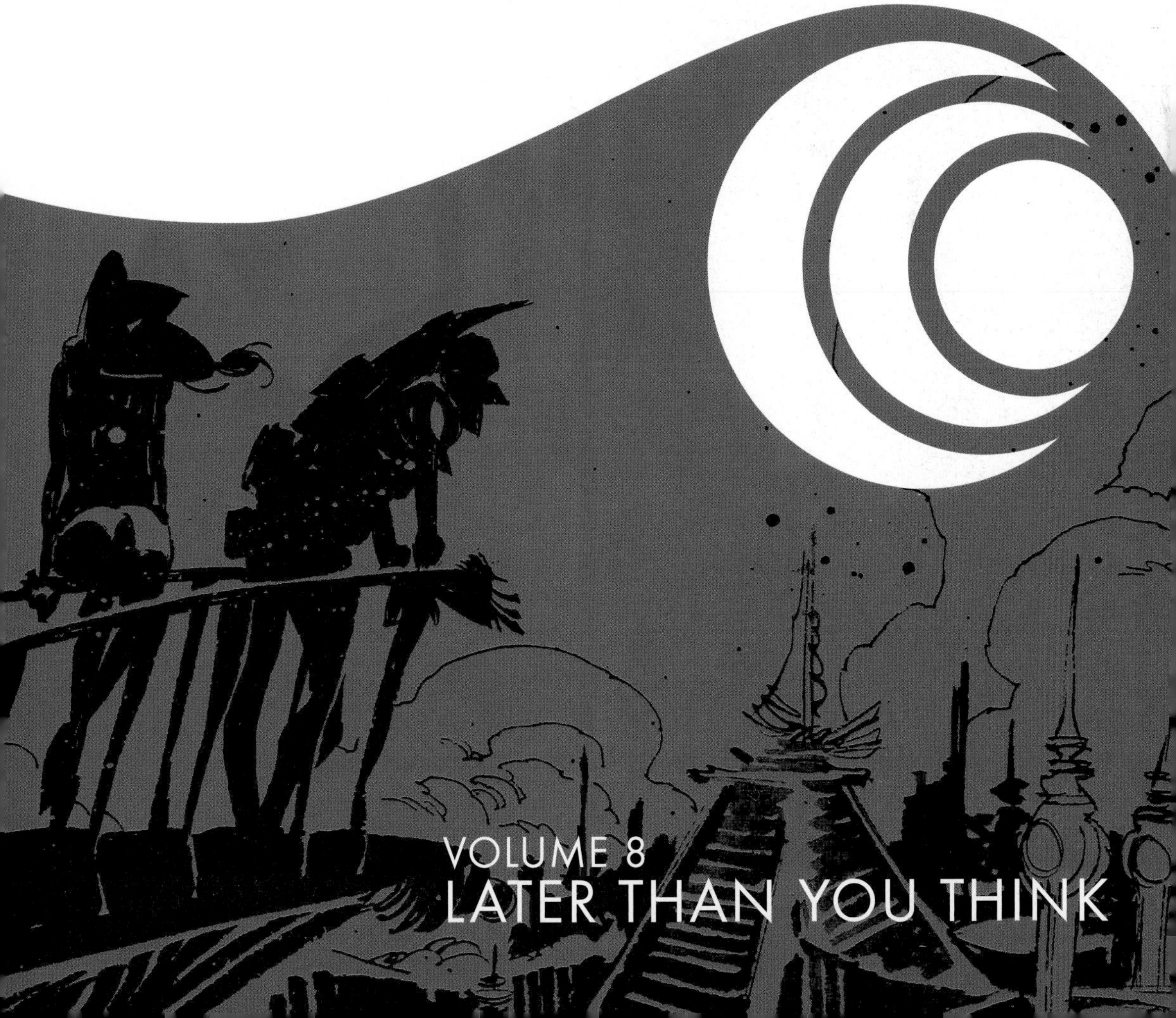

VOLUME 8
LATER THAN YOU THINK

35

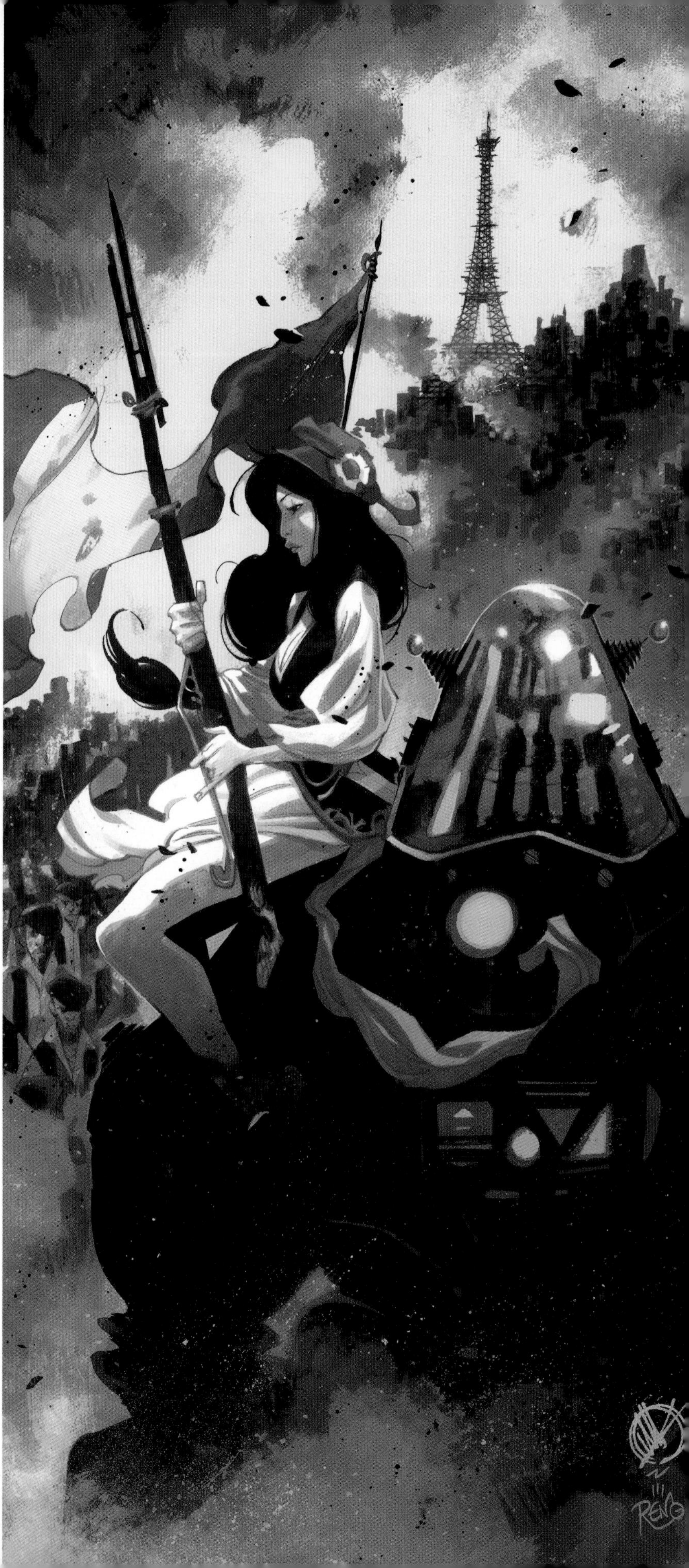

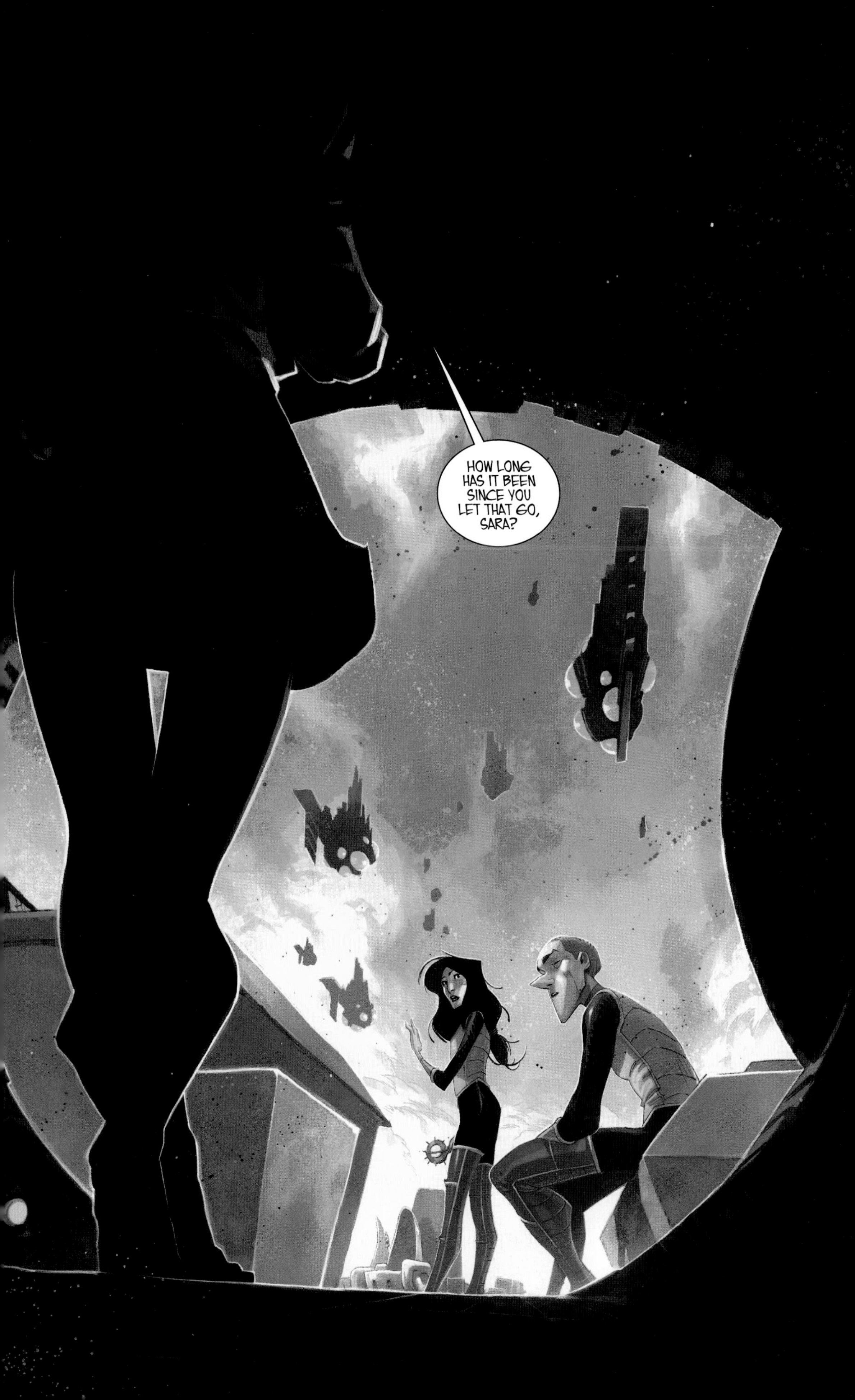
HOW LONG HAS IT BEEN SINCE YOU LET THAT GO, SARA?

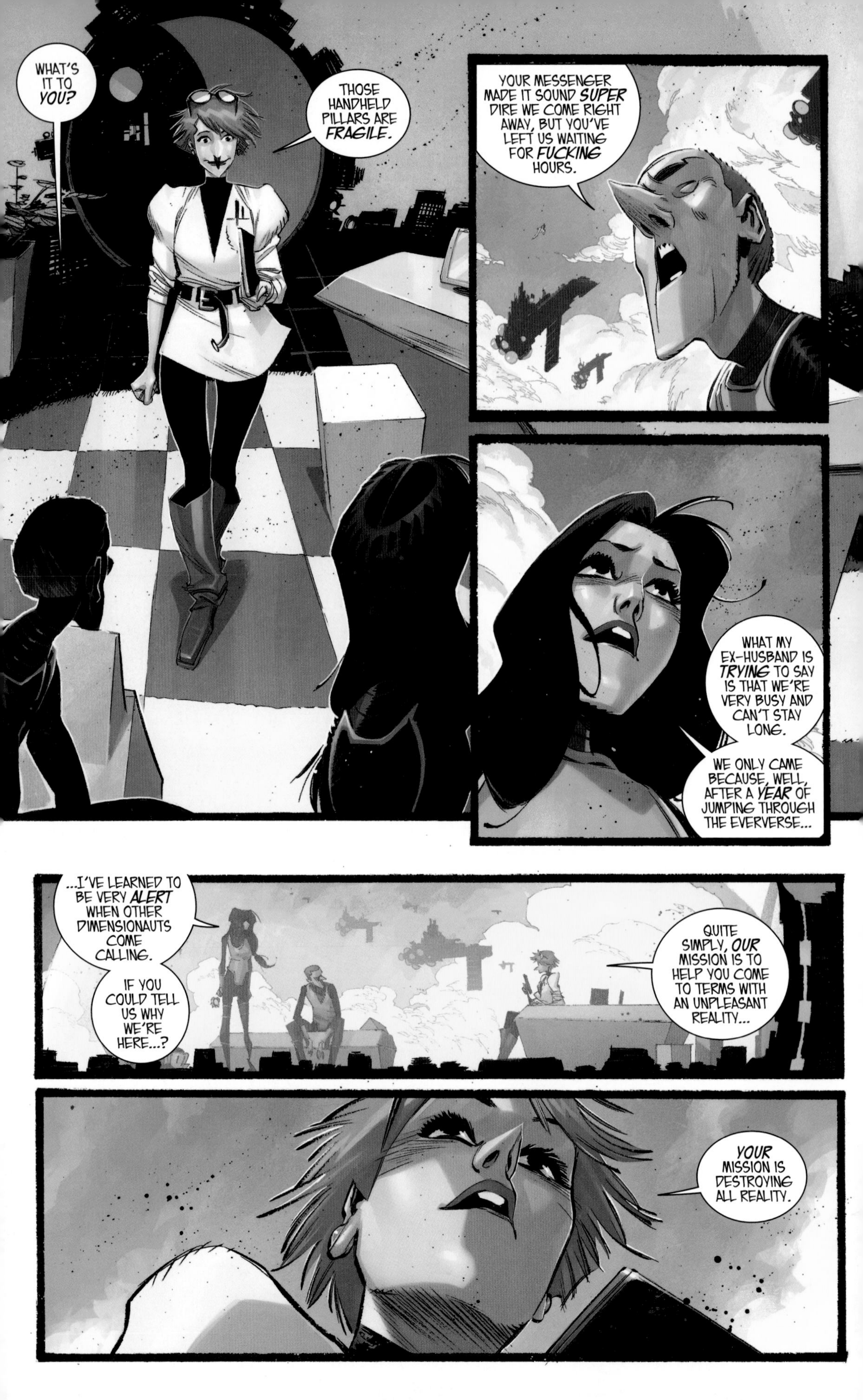
WHAT'S IT TO YOU?
THOSE HANDHELD PILLARS ARE FRAGILE.
YOUR MESSENGER MADE IT SOUND SUPER DIRE WE COME RIGHT AWAY, BUT YOU'VE LEFT US WAITING FOR FUCKING HOURS.
WHAT MY EX-HUSBAND IS TRYING TO SAY IS THAT WE'RE VERY BUSY AND CAN'T STAY LONG.
WE ONLY CAME BECAUSE, WELL, AFTER A YEAR OF JUMPING THROUGH THE EVERVERSE...
...I'VE LEARNED TO BE VERY ALERT WHEN OTHER DIMENSIONAUTS COME CALLING.
IF YOU COULD TELL US WHY WE'RE HERE...?
QUITE SIMPLY, OUR MISSION IS TO HELP YOU COME TO TERMS WITH AN UNPLEASANT REALITY...
YOUR MISSION IS DESTROYING ALL REALITY.

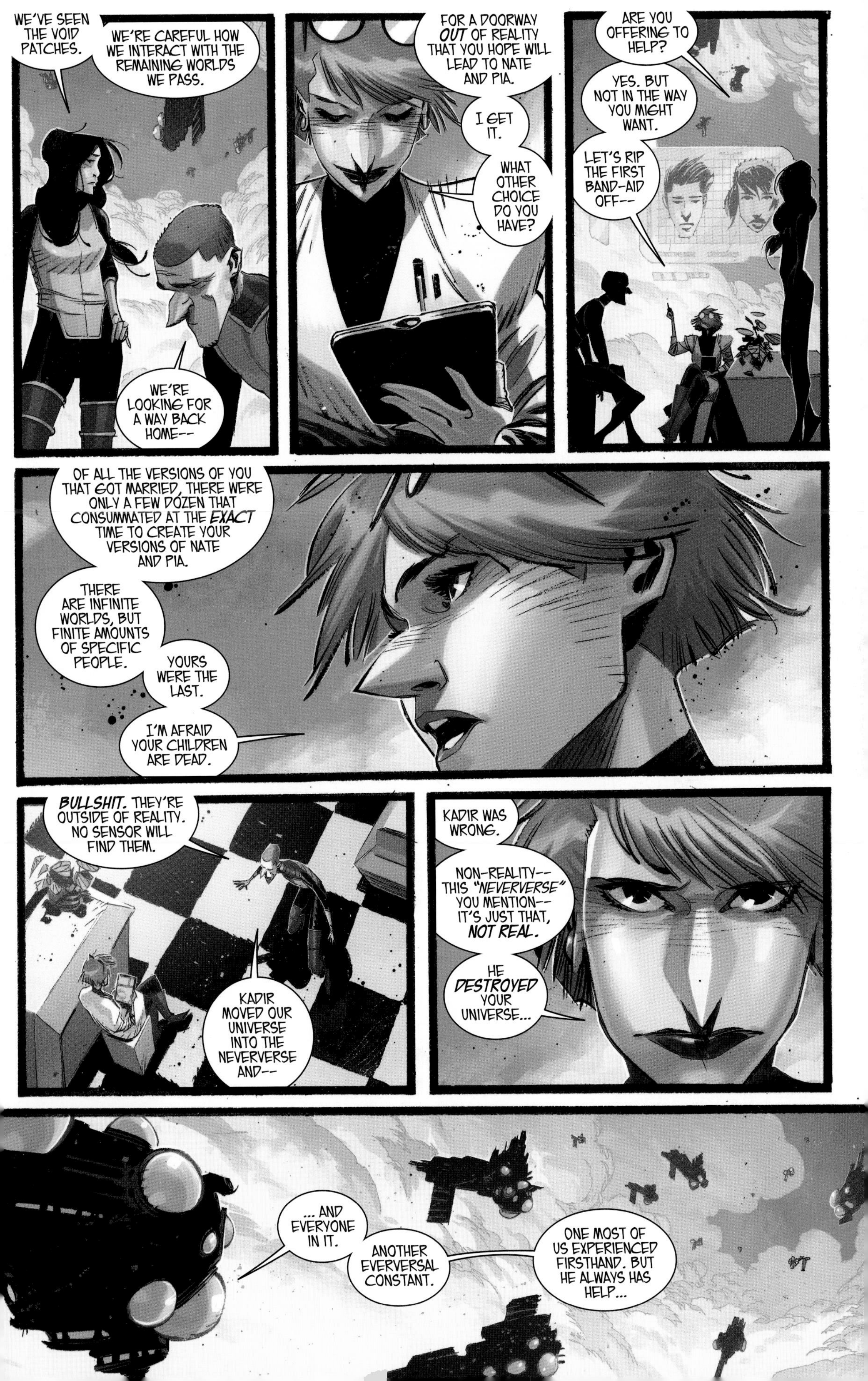
WE'VE SEEN THE VOID PATCHES.
WE'RE CAREFUL HOW WE INTERACT WITH THE REMAINING WORLDS WE PASS.
WE'RE LOOKING FOR A WAY BACK HOME--
FOR A DOORWAY OUT OF REALITY THAT YOU HOPE WILL LEAD TO NATE AND PIA.
I GET IT.
WHAT OTHER CHOICE DO YOU HAVE?
ARE YOU OFFERING TO HELP?
YES. BUT NOT IN THE WAY YOU MIGHT WANT.
LET'S RIP THE FIRST BAND-AID OFF--
OF ALL THE VERSIONS OF YOU THAT GOT MARRIED, THERE WERE ONLY A FEW DOZEN THAT CONSUMMATED AT THE EXACT TIME TO CREATE YOUR VERSIONS OF NATE AND PIA.
THERE ARE INFINITE WORLDS, BUT FINITE AMOUNTS OF SPECIFIC PEOPLE.
YOURS WERE THE LAST.
I'M AFRAID YOUR CHILDREN ARE DEAD.
BULLSHIT. THEY'RE OUTSIDE OF REALITY. NO SENSOR WILL FIND THEM.
KADIR MOVED OUR UNIVERSE INTO THE NEVERVERSE AND--
KADIR WAS WRONG.
NON-REALITY-- THIS "NEVERVERSE" YOU MENTION-- IT'S JUST THAT, NOT REAL.
HE DESTROYED YOUR UNIVERSE...
... AND EVERYONE IN IT.
ANOTHER EVERVERSAL CONSTANT.
ONE MOST OF US EXPERIENCED FIRSTHAND. BUT HE ALWAYS HAS HELP...

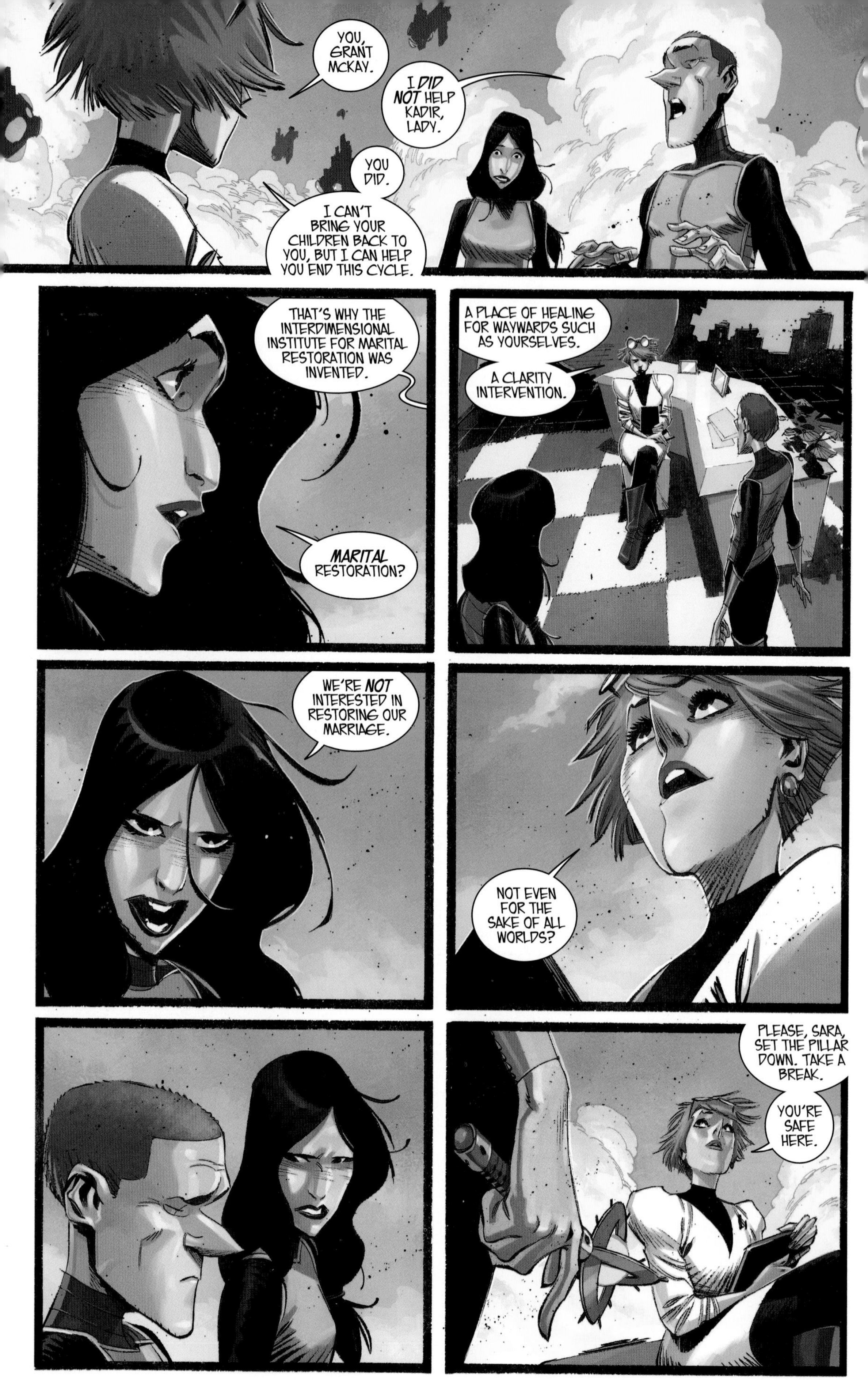
YOU, GRANT MCKAY.
I *DID NOT* HELP KADIR, LADY.
YOU DID.
I CAN'T BRING YOUR CHILDREN BACK TO YOU, BUT I CAN HELP YOU END THIS CYCLE.
THAT'S WHY THE INTERDIMENSIONAL INSTITUTE FOR MARITAL RESTORATION WAS INVENTED.
MARITAL RESTORATION?
A PLACE OF HEALING FOR WAYWARDS SUCH AS YOURSELVES.
A CLARITY INTERVENTION.
WE'RE *NOT* INTERESTED IN RESTORING OUR MARRIAGE.
NOT EVEN FOR THE SAKE OF ALL WORLDS?
PLEASE, SARA, SET THE PILLAR DOWN. TAKE A BREAK.
YOU'RE SAFE HERE.

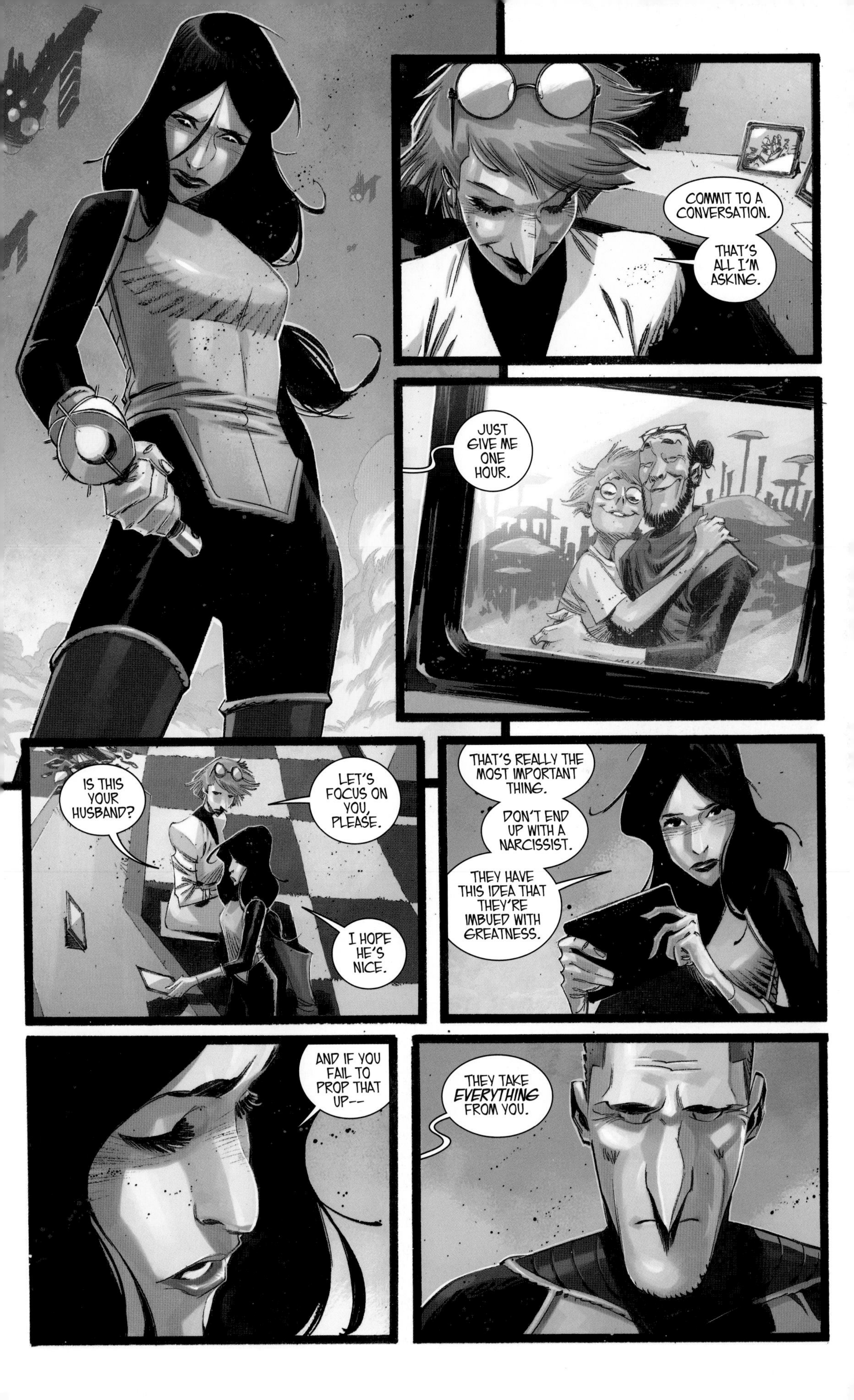
COMMIT TO A CONVERSATION.
THAT'S ALL I'M ASKING.
JUST GIVE ME ONE HOUR.
IS THIS YOUR HUSBAND?
LET'S FOCUS ON YOU, PLEASE.
I HOPE HE'S NICE.
THAT'S REALLY THE MOST IMPORTANT THING.
DON'T END UP WITH A NARCISSIST.
THEY HAVE THIS IDEA THAT THEY'RE IMBUED WITH GREATNESS.
AND IF YOU FAIL TO PROP THAT UP--
THEY TAKE *EVERYTHING* FROM YOU.

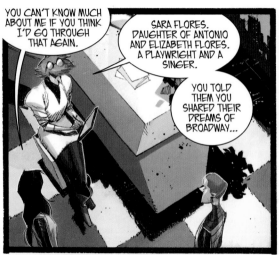

YOU CAN'T KNOW MUCH ABOUT ME IF YOU THINK I'D GO THROUGH THAT AGAIN.

SARA FLORES. DAUGHTER OF ANTONIO AND ELIZABETH FLORES. A PLAYWRIGHT AND A SINGER.

YOU TOLD THEM YOU SHARED THEIR DREAMS OF BROADWAY...

BUT THEY NEVER FOUND TIME TO TAKE YOU TO THAT ACTING CLASS.

WOULDN'T TAKE THE TIME OUT OF THEIR OWN PURSUITS TO HELP YOU WITH YOURS.

YOU WERE NEVER THE PRIORITY, YOU WERE TAUGHT TO MAKE OTHERS THE PRIORITY.

TO NEVER STAND IN THE WAY OR BE A HINDRANCE TO THEIR DESIRES.

YOU IMAGINED THEY'D LOVE YOU FOR IT AND RECIPROCATE.

WHEN IT CAME TIME TO FIND A HUSBAND YOU LOOKED FOR SOMEONE WHO WOULD CONTINUE THIS DYNAMIC.

BUT, UNLIKE YOUR PARENTS, GRANT'S NOT A NARCISSIST.

HE'S A CHILD OF ABUSE MIMICKING HIS WRETCHED MOTHER'S BEHAVIOR.

HE DOESN'T TRUST ANY AUTHORITY TO PROTECT HIM, SO HE CONTROLS.

HE WAS ABANDONED, SO HE ABANDONS.

THANK YOU, BUT I'M FAMILIAR WITH THE DAMAGE OF GRANT MCKAY.

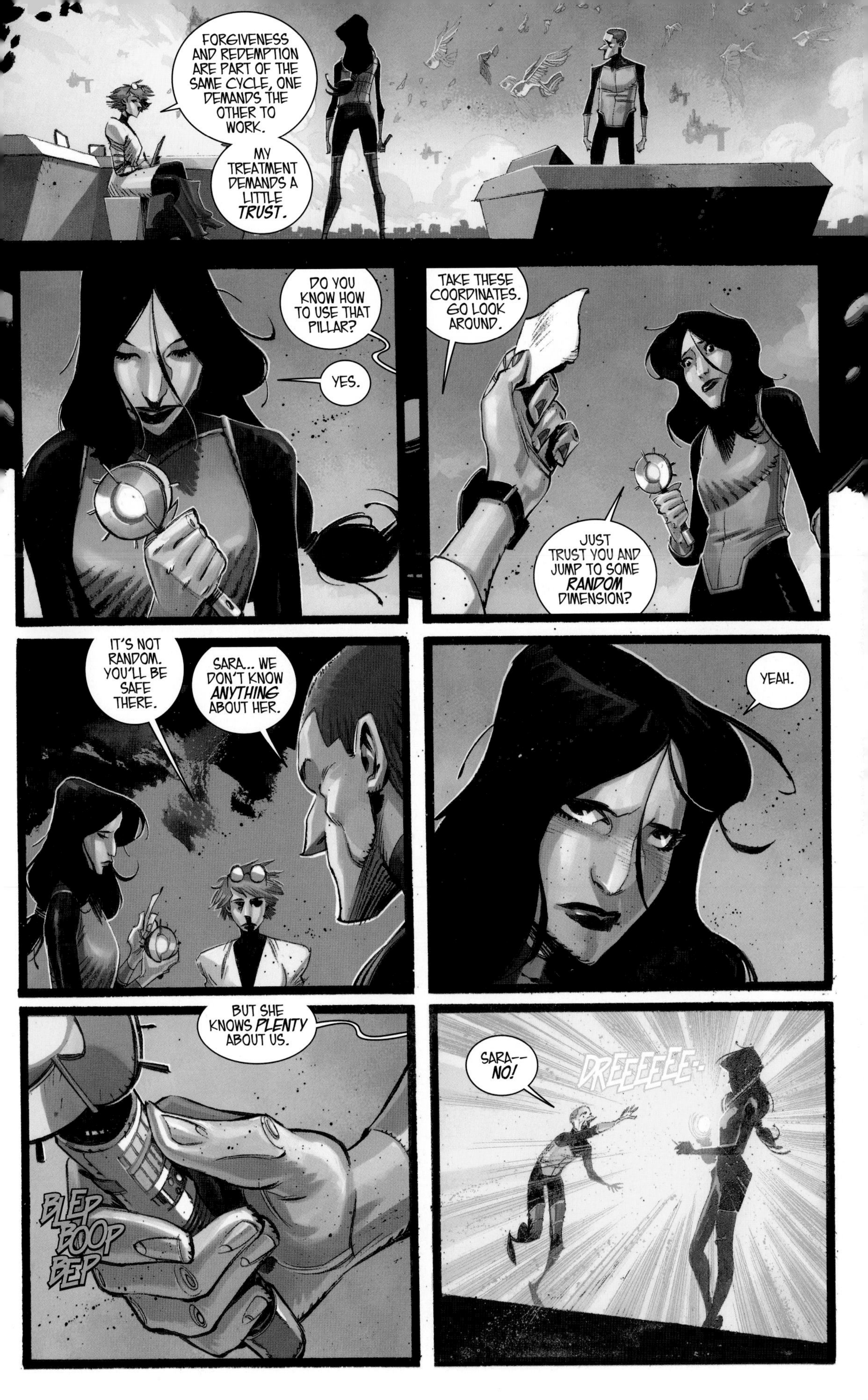
FORGIVENESS AND REDEMPTION ARE PART OF THE SAME CYCLE, ONE DEMANDS THE OTHER TO WORK.
MY TREATMENT DEMANDS A LITTLE *TRUST*.
DO YOU KNOW HOW TO USE THAT PILLAR?
YES.
TAKE THESE COORDINATES. GO LOOK AROUND.
JUST TRUST YOU AND JUMP TO SOME *RANDOM* DIMENSION?
IT'S NOT RANDOM. YOU'LL BE SAFE THERE.
SARA... WE DON'T KNOW *ANYTHING* ABOUT HER.
YEAH.
BUT SHE KNOWS *PLENTY* ABOUT US.
BLEP BOOP BEP
SARA-- *NO!*
DREEEEEE-

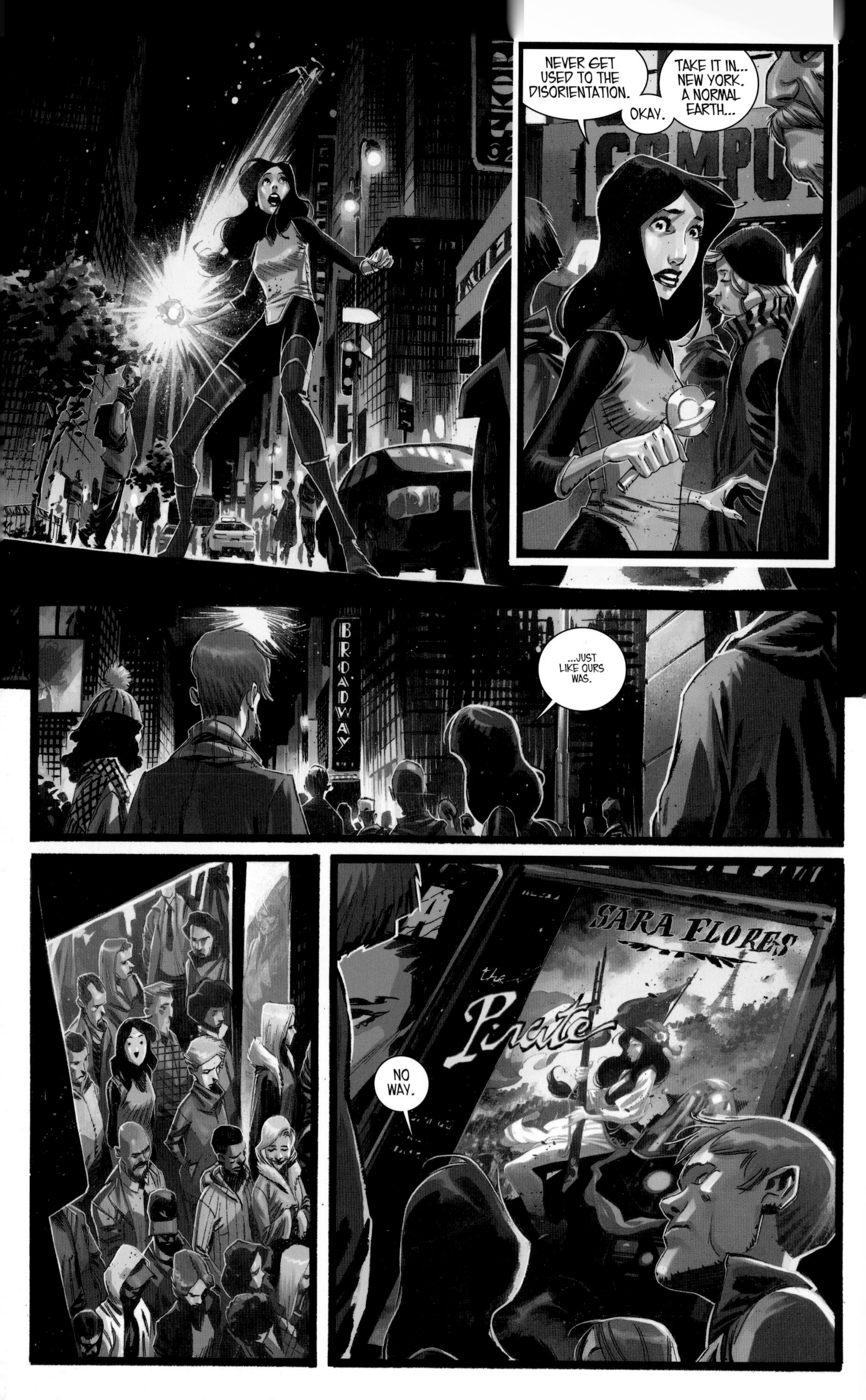
NEVER GET USED TO THE DISORIENTATION.
OKAY.
TAKE IT IN... NEW YORK. A NORMAL EARTH...
BROADWAY
...JUST LIKE OURS WAS.
SARA FLORES
NO WAY.

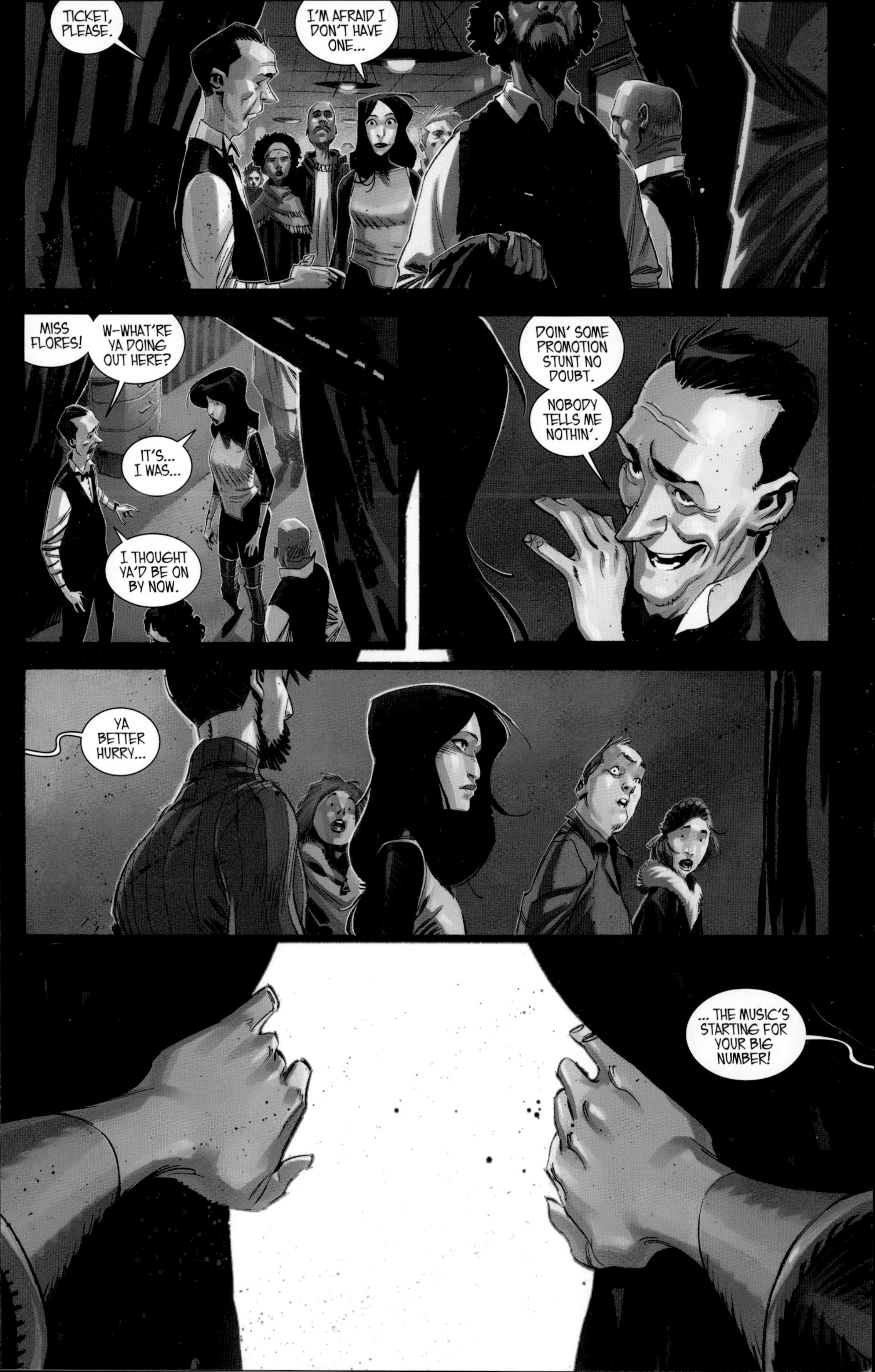
TICKET, PLEASE.
I'M AFRAID I DON'T HAVE ONE...
MISS FLORES!
W-WHAT'RE YA DOING OUT HERE?
IT'S... I WAS...
I THOUGHT YA'D BE ON BY NOW.
DOIN' SOME PROMOTION STUNT NO DOUBT.
NOBODY TELLS ME NOTHIN'.
YA BETTER HURRY...
... THE MUSIC'S STARTING FOR YOUR BIG NUMBER!

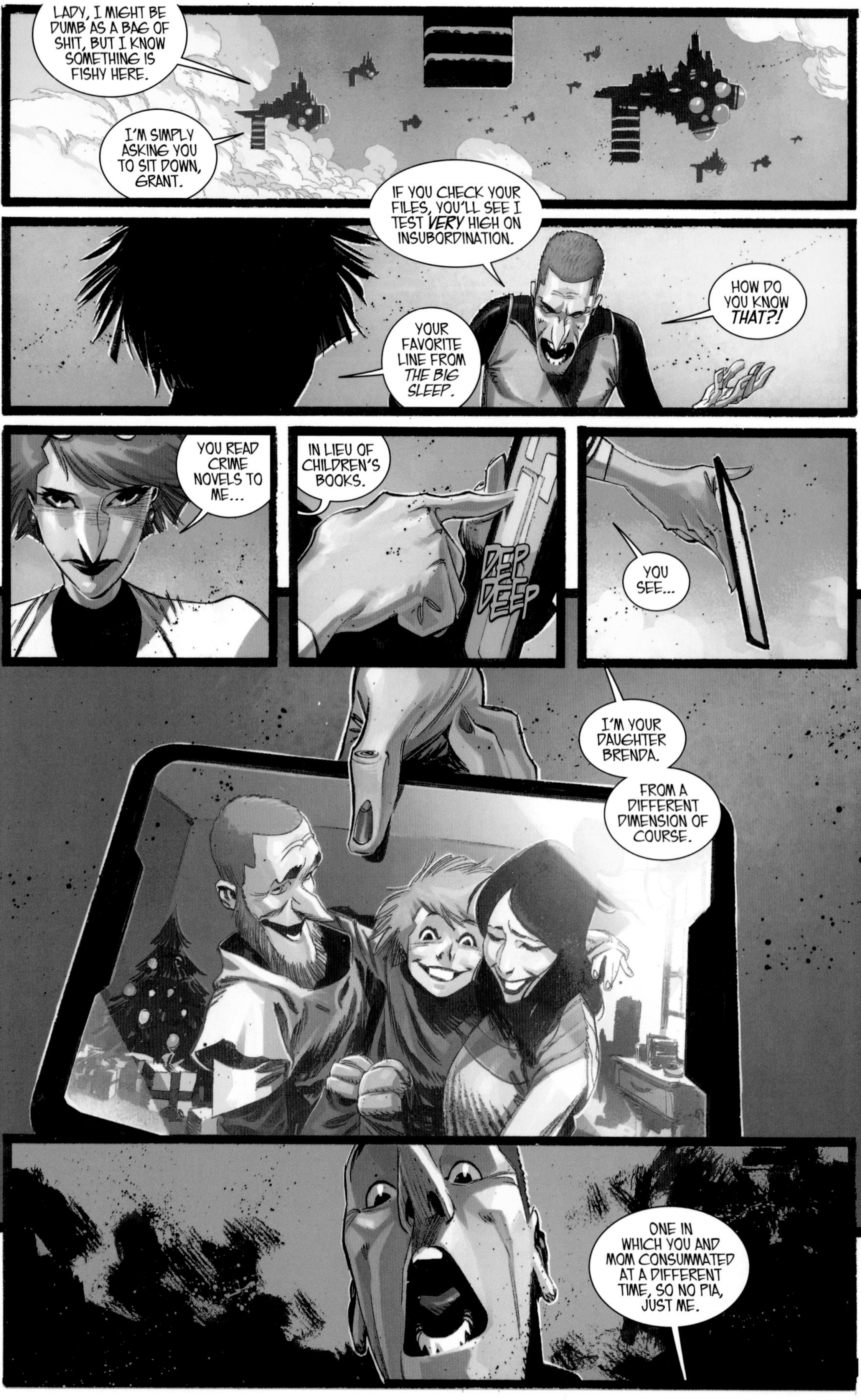
LADY, I MIGHT BE DUMB AS A BAG OF SHIT, BUT I KNOW SOMETHING IS FISHY HERE.
I'M SIMPLY ASKING YOU TO SIT DOWN, GRANT.
IF YOU CHECK YOUR FILES, YOU'LL SEE I TEST VERY HIGH ON INSUBORDINATION.
YOUR FAVORITE LINE FROM THE BIG SLEEP.
HOW DO YOU KNOW THAT?!
YOU READ CRIME NOVELS TO ME...
IN LIEU OF CHILDREN'S BOOKS.
DEEP DEEP
YOU SEE...
I'M YOUR DAUGHTER BRENDA.
FROM A DIFFERENT DIMENSION OF COURSE.
ONE IN WHICH YOU AND MOM CONSUMMATED AT A DIFFERENT TIME, SO NO PIA, JUST ME.

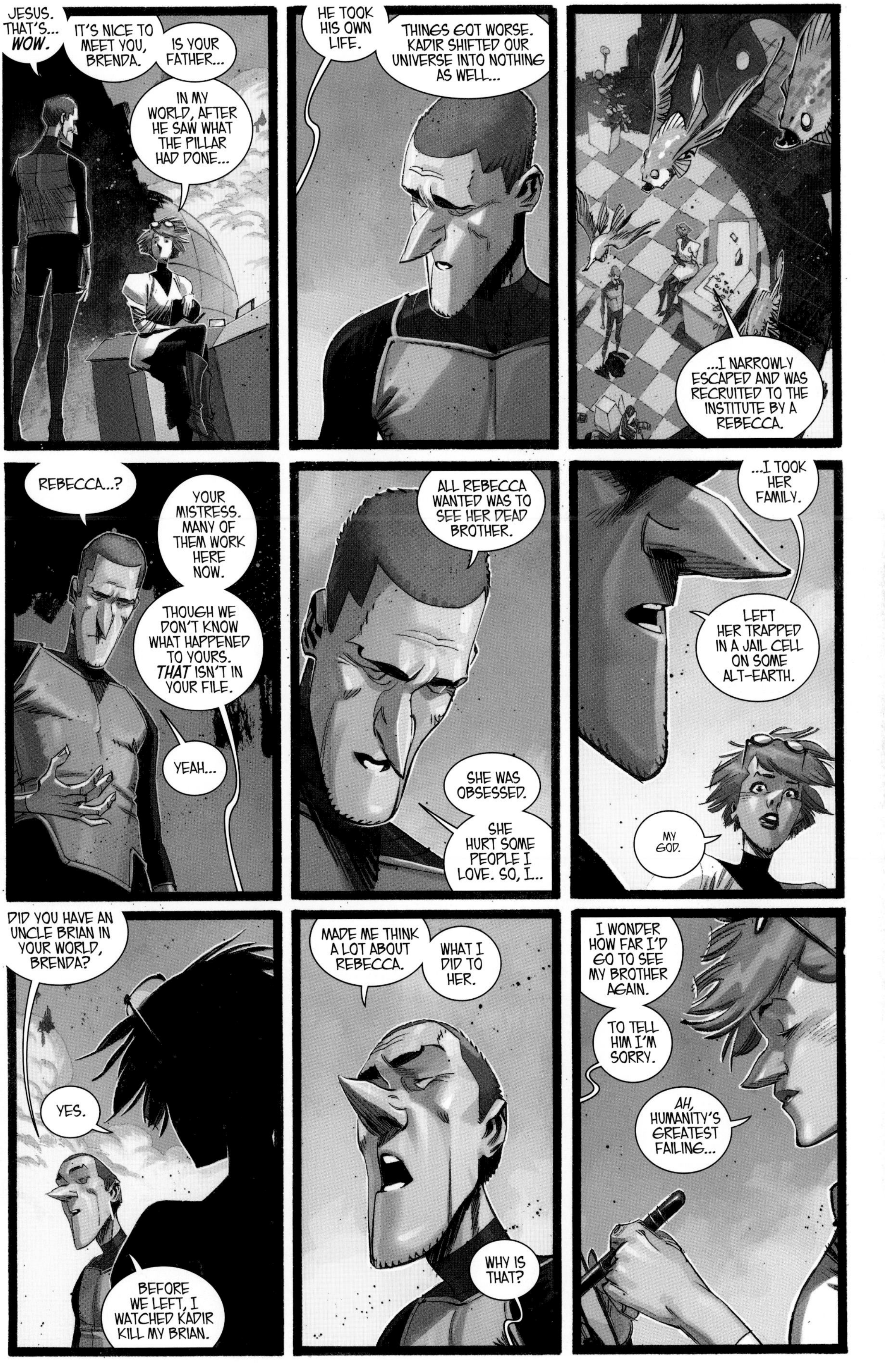

JESUS. THAT'S... WOW.
IT'S NICE TO MEET YOU, BRENDA.
IS YOUR FATHER...
IN MY WORLD, AFTER HE SAW WHAT THE PILLAR HAD DONE...
HE TOOK HIS OWN LIFE.
THINGS GOT WORSE. KADIR SHIFTED OUR UNIVERSE INTO NOTHING AS WELL...
...I NARROWLY ESCAPED AND WAS RECRUITED TO THE INSTITUTE BY A REBECCA.
REBECCA...?
YOUR MISTRESS. MANY OF THEM WORK HERE NOW.
THOUGH WE DON'T KNOW WHAT HAPPENED TO YOURS. THAT ISN'T IN YOUR FILE.
YEAH...
ALL REBECCA WANTED WAS TO SEE HER DEAD BROTHER.
SHE WAS OBSESSED.
SHE HURT SOME PEOPLE I LOVE. SO, I...
...I TOOK HER FAMILY.
LEFT HER TRAPPED IN A JAIL CELL ON SOME ALT-EARTH.
MY GOD.
DID YOU HAVE AN UNCLE BRIAN IN YOUR WORLD, BRENDA?
YES.
BEFORE WE LEFT, I WATCHED KADIR KILL MY BRIAN.
MADE ME THINK A LOT ABOUT REBECCA.
WHAT I DID TO HER.
WHY IS THAT?
I WONDER HOW FAR I'D GO TO SEE MY BROTHER AGAIN.
TO TELL HIM I'M SORRY.
AH, HUMANITY'S GREATEST FAILING...

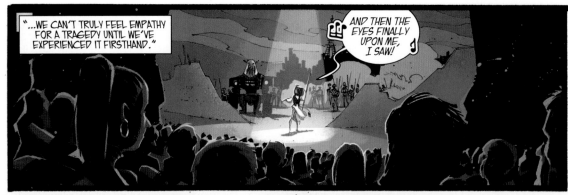

"...WE CAN'T TRULY FEEL EMPATHY FOR A TRAGEDY UNTIL WE'VE EXPERIENCED IT FIRSTHAND."

AND THEN THE EYES FINALLY UPON ME, I SAW!

THERE'S A CORE TO EVERYTHING ELSE, WHY NOT ONE INSIDE OF US?

WHAT IF THERE IS A SOUL?

CLAP CLAP CLAP CLAP CLAP CLAP CLAP CLAP CLAP CLAP CLAP CLAP CLAP

SHE'S AMAZING.

CLAP CLAP CLAP CLAP CLAP CLAP CLAP

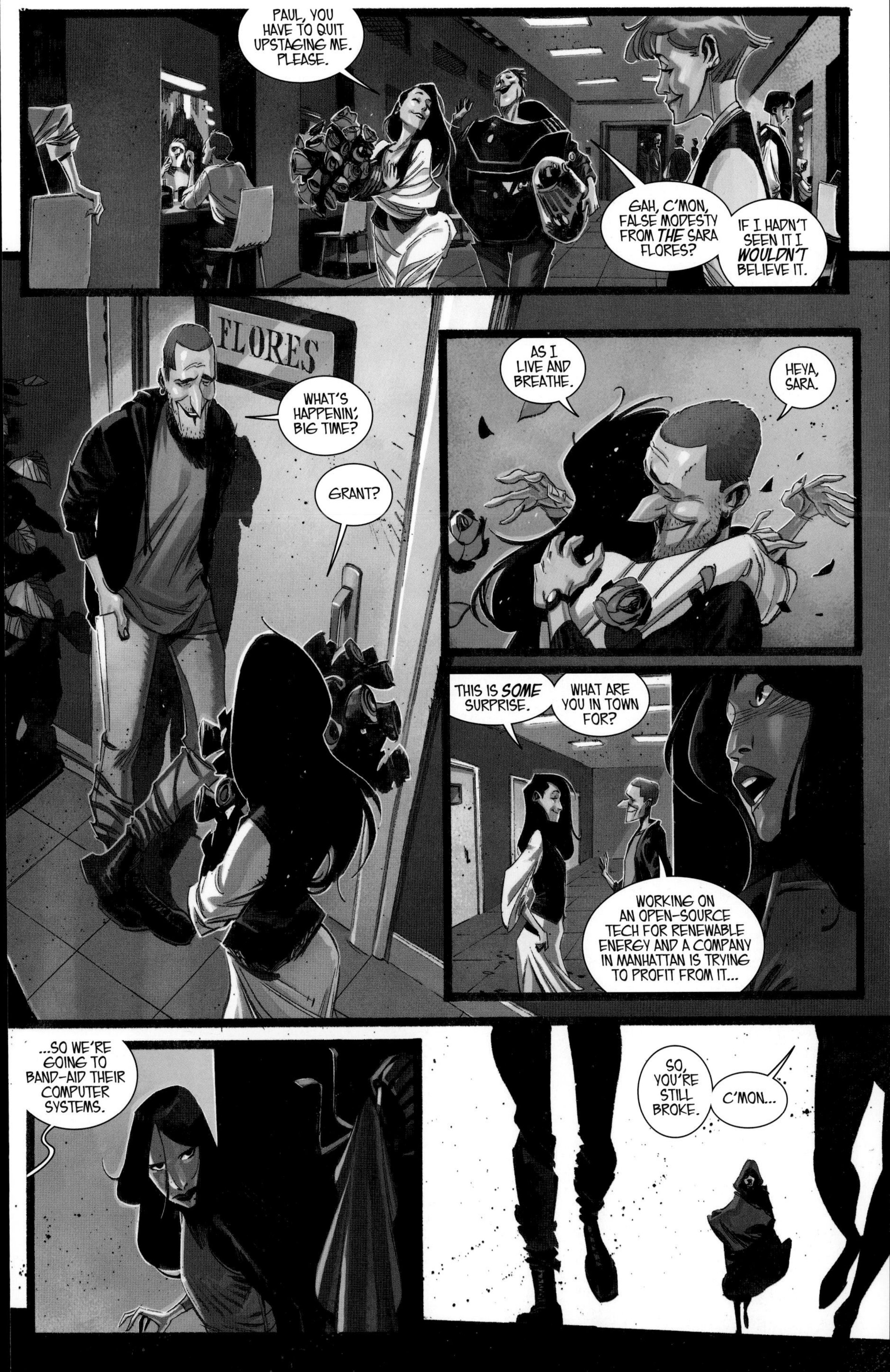
PAUL, YOU HAVE TO QUIT UPSTAGING ME. PLEASE.
GAH, C'MON, FALSE MODESTY FROM THE SARA FLORES?
IF I HADN'T SEEN IT I WOULDN'T BELIEVE IT.
FLORES
WHAT'S HAPPENIN', BIG TIME?
GRANT?
AS I LIVE AND BREATHE.
HEYA, SARA.
THIS IS SOME SURPRISE.
WHAT ARE YOU IN TOWN FOR?
WORKING ON AN OPEN-SOURCE TECH FOR RENEWABLE ENERGY AND A COMPANY IN MANHATTAN IS TRYING TO PROFIT FROM IT...
...SO WE'RE GOING TO BAND-AID THEIR COMPUTER SYSTEMS.
SO, YOU'RE STILL BROKE.
C'MON...

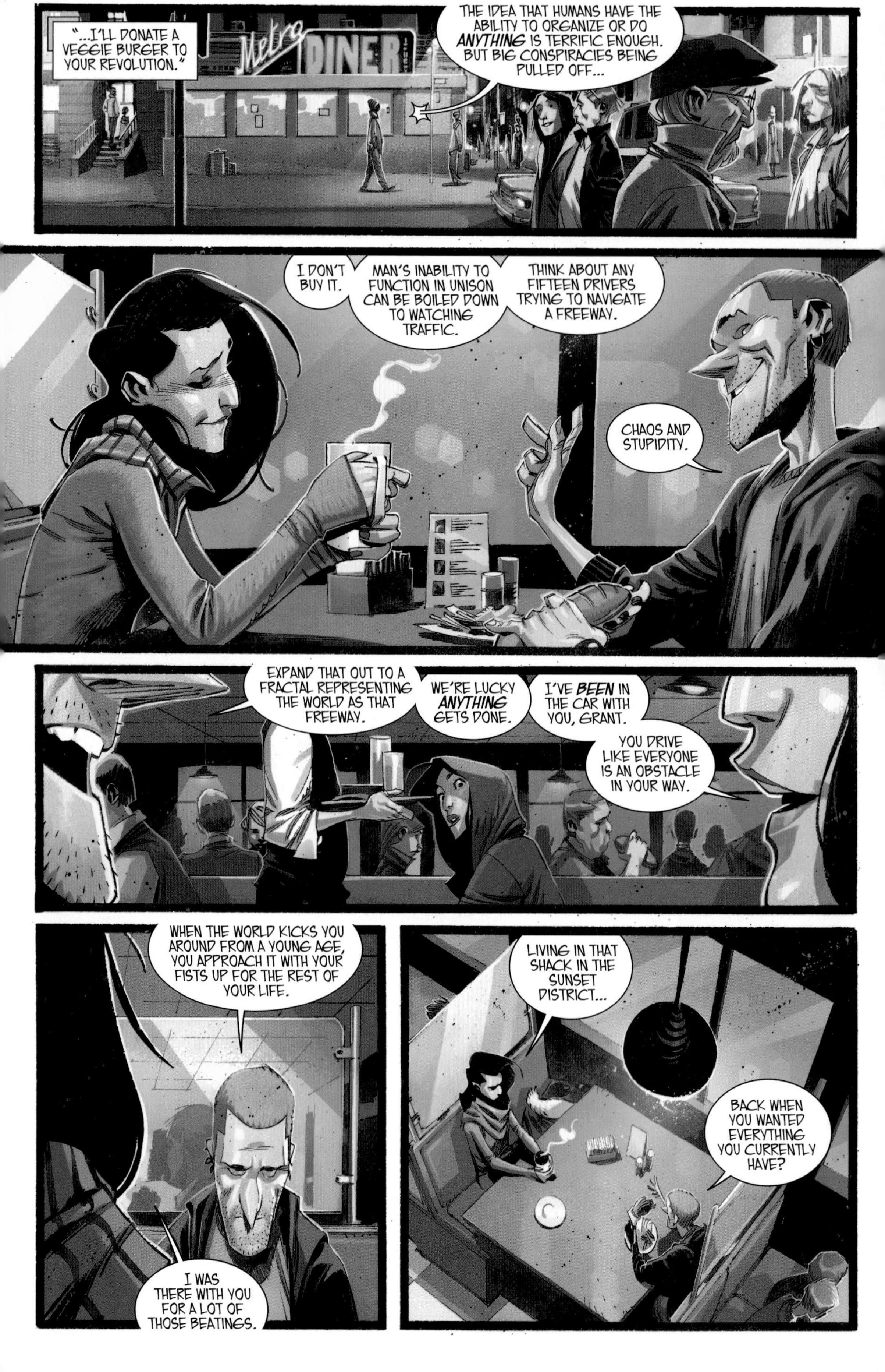
"...I'LL DONATE A VEGGIE BURGER TO YOUR REVOLUTION."
Metro DINER
THE IDEA THAT HUMANS HAVE THE ABILITY TO ORGANIZE OR DO *ANYTHING* IS TERRIFIC ENOUGH. BUT BIG CONSPIRACIES BEING PULLED OFF...
I DON'T BUY IT.
MAN'S INABILITY TO FUNCTION IN UNISON CAN BE BOILED DOWN TO WATCHING TRAFFIC.
THINK ABOUT ANY FIFTEEN DRIVERS TRYING TO NAVIGATE A FREEWAY.
CHAOS AND STUPIDITY.
EXPAND THAT OUT TO A FRACTAL REPRESENTING THE WORLD AS THAT FREEWAY.
WE'RE LUCKY *ANYTHING* GETS DONE.
I'VE *BEEN* IN THE CAR WITH YOU, GRANT.
YOU DRIVE LIKE EVERYONE IS AN OBSTACLE IN YOUR WAY.
WHEN THE WORLD KICKS YOU AROUND FROM A YOUNG AGE, YOU APPROACH IT WITH YOUR FISTS UP FOR THE REST OF YOUR LIFE.
I WAS THERE WITH YOU FOR A LOT OF THOSE BEATINGS.
LIVING IN THAT SHACK IN THE SUNSET DISTRICT...
BACK WHEN YOU WANTED EVERYTHING YOU CURRENTLY HAVE?

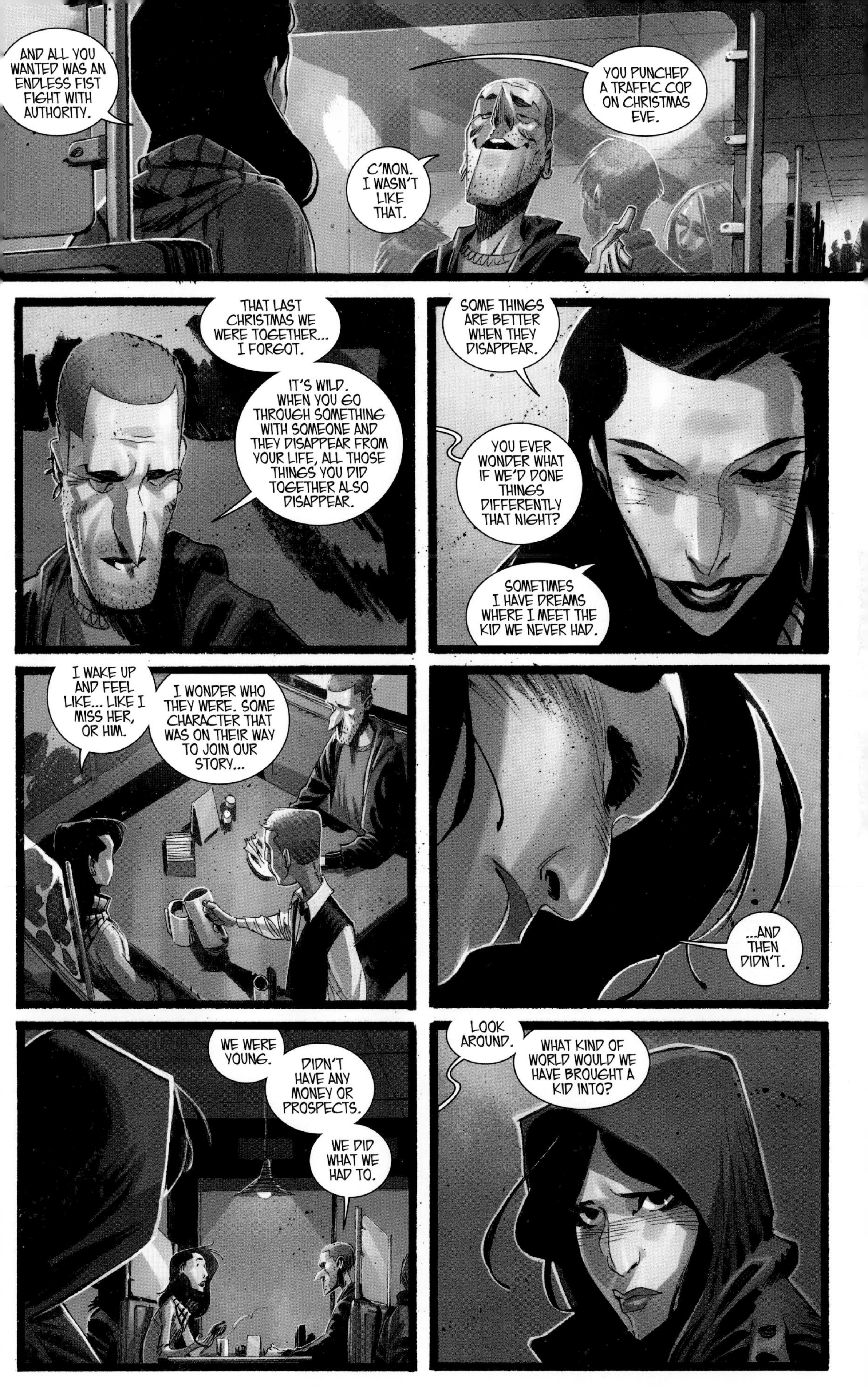
AND ALL YOU WANTED WAS AN ENDLESS FIST FIGHT WITH AUTHORITY.
YOU PUNCHED A TRAFFIC COP ON CHRISTMAS EVE.
C'MON. I WASN'T LIKE THAT.
THAT LAST CHRISTMAS WE WERE TOGETHER... I FORGOT.
IT'S WILD. WHEN YOU GO THROUGH SOMETHING WITH SOMEONE AND THEY DISAPPEAR FROM YOUR LIFE, ALL THOSE THINGS YOU DID TOGETHER ALSO DISAPPEAR.
SOME THINGS ARE BETTER WHEN THEY DISAPPEAR.
YOU EVER WONDER WHAT IF WE'D DONE THINGS DIFFERENTLY THAT NIGHT?
SOMETIMES I HAVE DREAMS WHERE I MEET THE KID WE NEVER HAD.
I WAKE UP AND FEEL LIKE... LIKE I MISS HER, OR HIM.
I WONDER WHO THEY WERE. SOME CHARACTER THAT WAS ON THEIR WAY TO JOIN OUR STORY...
...AND THEN DIDN'T.
WE WERE YOUNG.
DIDN'T HAVE ANY MONEY OR PROSPECTS.
WE DID WHAT WE HAD TO.
LOOK AROUND.
WHAT KIND OF WORLD WOULD WE HAVE BROUGHT A KID INTO?

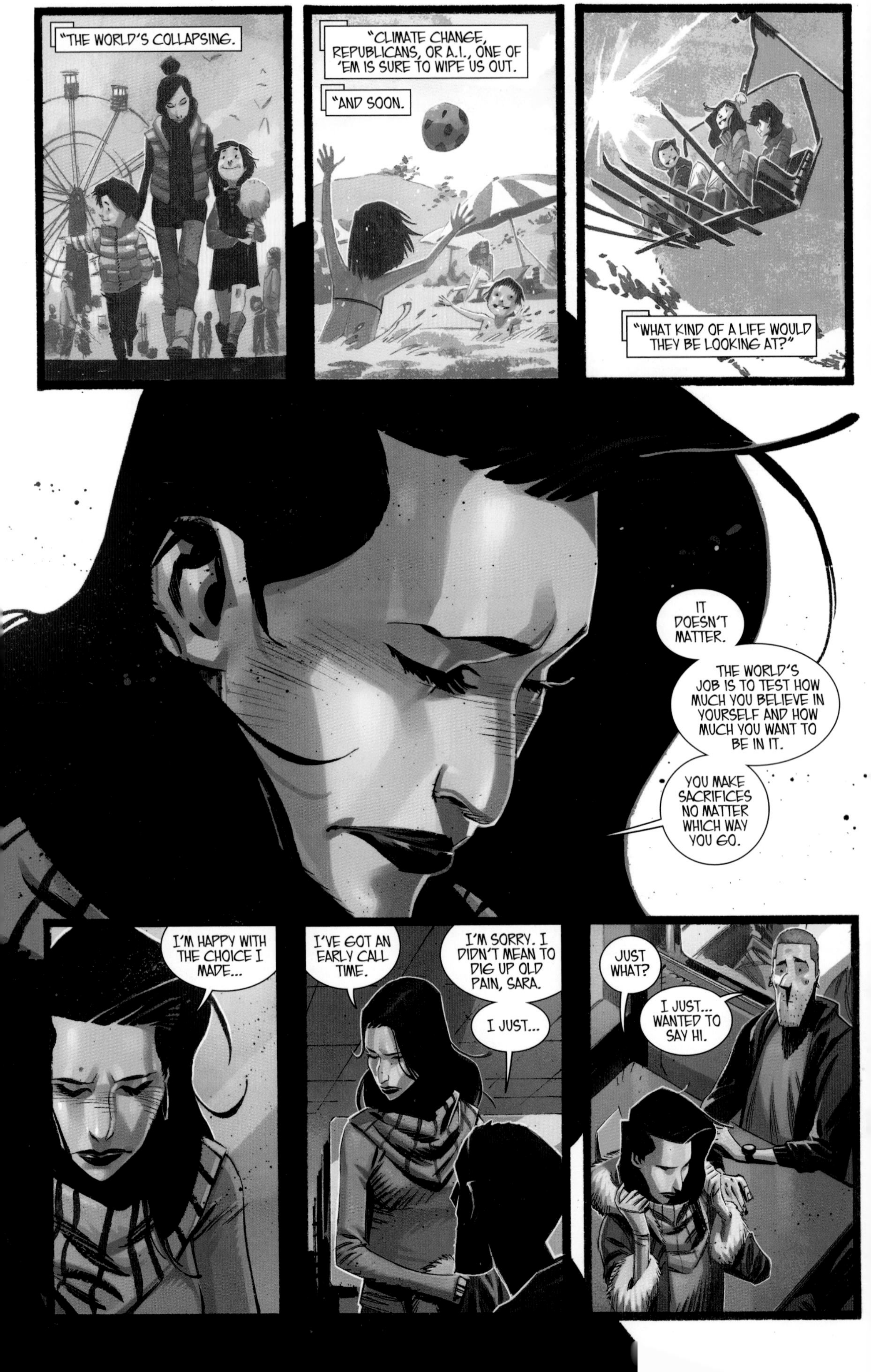
"THE WORLD'S COLLAPSING.
"CLIMATE CHANGE, REPUBLICANS, OR A.I., ONE OF 'EM IS SURE TO WIPE US OUT.
"AND SOON.
"WHAT KIND OF A LIFE WOULD THEY BE LOOKING AT?"
IT DOESN'T MATTER.
THE WORLD'S JOB IS TO TEST HOW MUCH YOU BELIEVE IN YOURSELF AND HOW MUCH YOU WANT TO BE IN IT.
YOU MAKE SACRIFICES NO MATTER WHICH WAY YOU GO.
I'M HAPPY WITH THE CHOICE I MADE...
I'VE GOT AN EARLY CALL TIME.
I'M SORRY. I DIDN'T MEAN TO DIG UP OLD PAIN, SARA.
I JUST...
JUST WHAT?
I JUST... WANTED TO SAY HI.

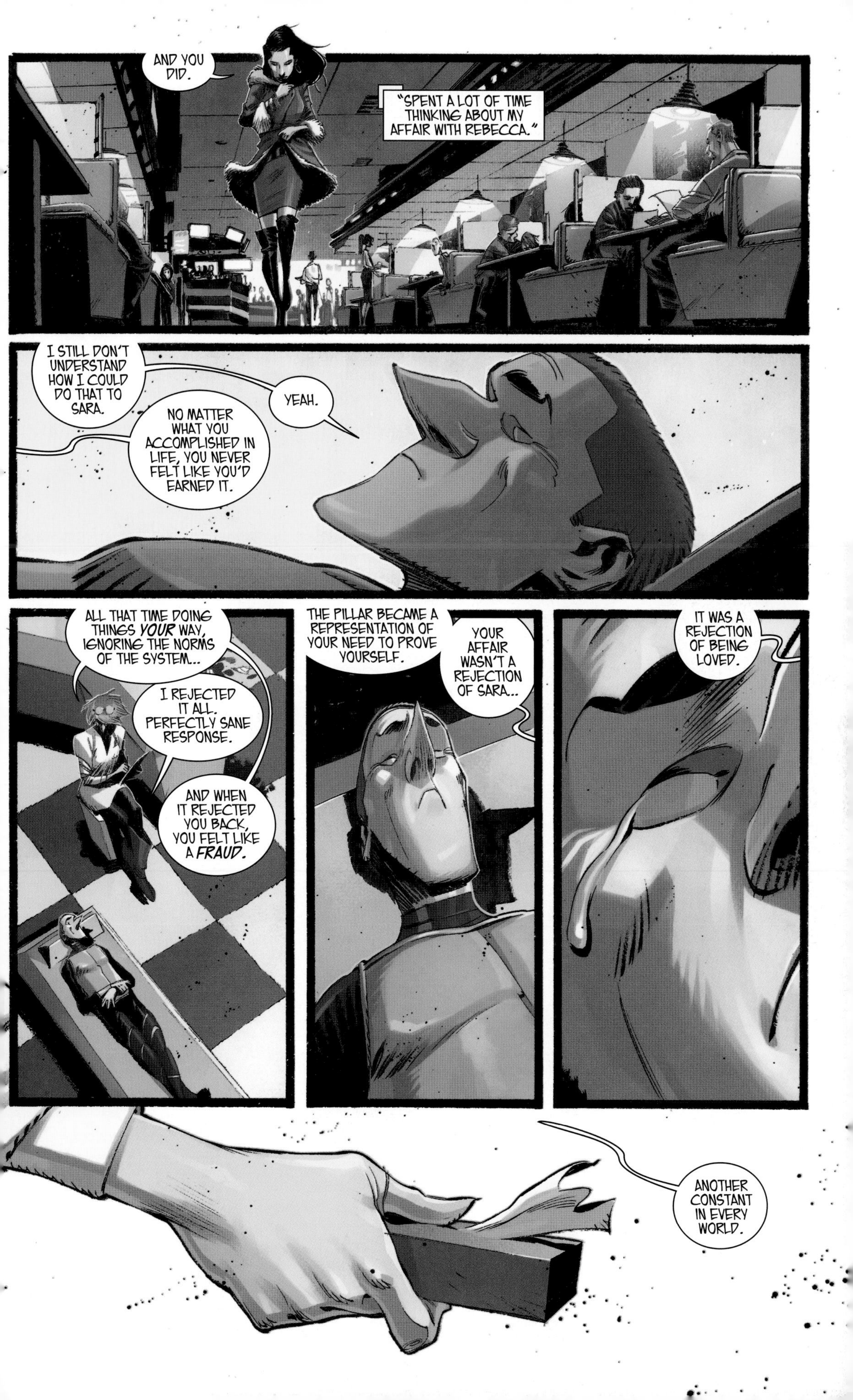
AND YOU DID.
"SPENT A LOT OF TIME THINKING ABOUT MY AFFAIR WITH REBECCA."
I STILL DON'T UNDERSTAND HOW I COULD DO THAT TO SARA.
YEAH.
NO MATTER WHAT YOU ACCOMPLISHED IN LIFE, YOU NEVER FELT LIKE YOU'D EARNED IT.
ALL THAT TIME DOING THINGS YOUR WAY, IGNORING THE NORMS OF THE SYSTEM...
I REJECTED IT ALL. PERFECTLY SANE RESPONSE.
AND WHEN IT REJECTED YOU BACK, YOU FELT LIKE A FRAUD.
THE PILLAR BECAME A REPRESENTATION OF YOUR NEED TO PROVE YOURSELF.
YOUR AFFAIR WASN'T A REJECTION OF SARA...
IT WAS A REJECTION OF BEING LOVED.
ANOTHER CONSTANT IN EVERY WORLD.

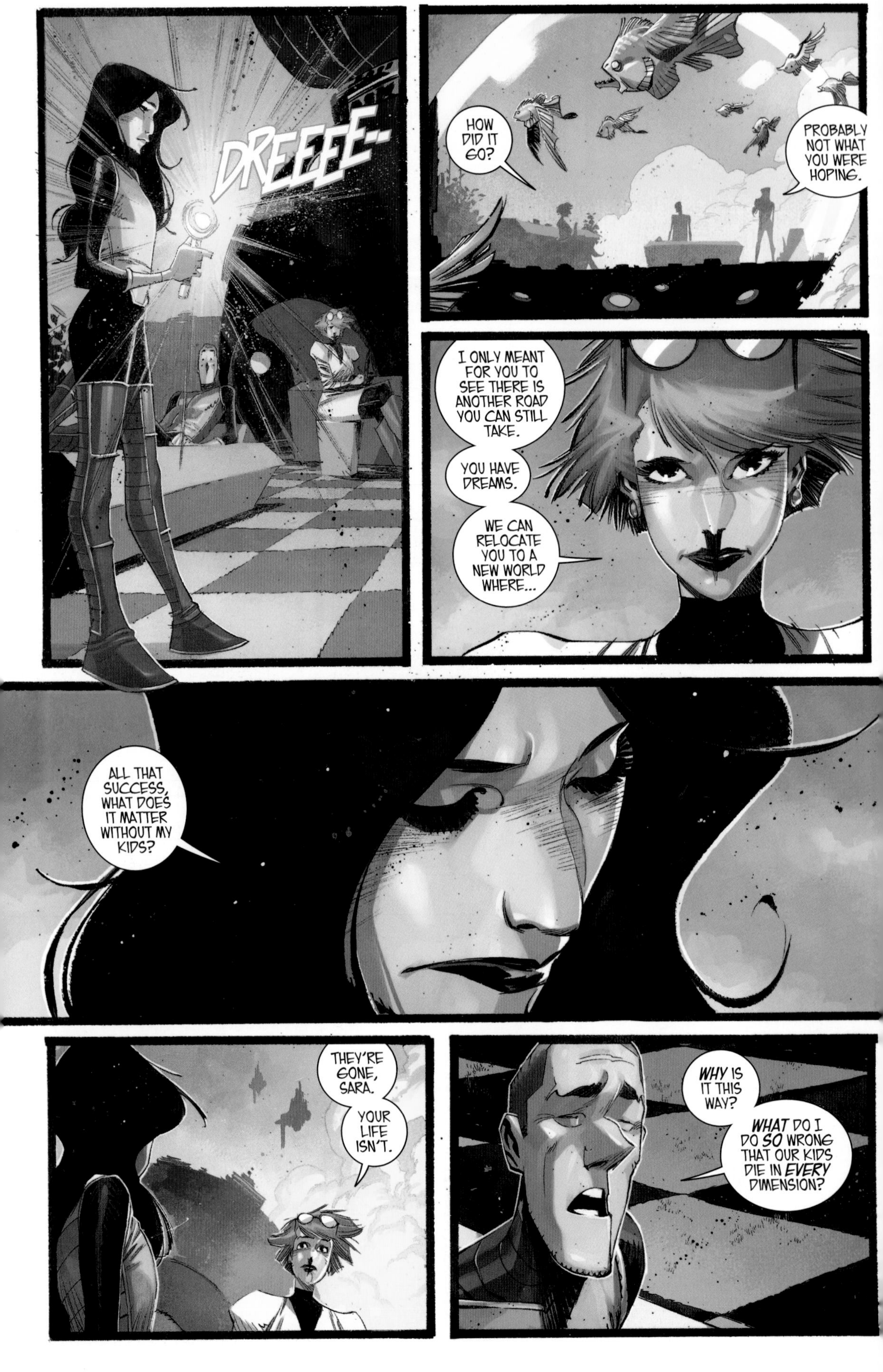
DREEEE--
HOW DID IT GO?
PROBABLY NOT WHAT YOU WERE HOPING.
I ONLY MEANT FOR YOU TO SEE THERE IS ANOTHER ROAD YOU CAN STILL TAKE.
YOU HAVE DREAMS.
WE CAN RELOCATE YOU TO A NEW WORLD WHERE...
ALL THAT SUCCESS, WHAT DOES IT MATTER WITHOUT MY KIDS?
THEY'RE GONE, SARA.
YOUR LIFE ISN'T.
WHY IS IT THIS WAY?
WHAT DO I DO SO WRONG THAT OUR KIDS DIE IN EVERY DIMENSION?

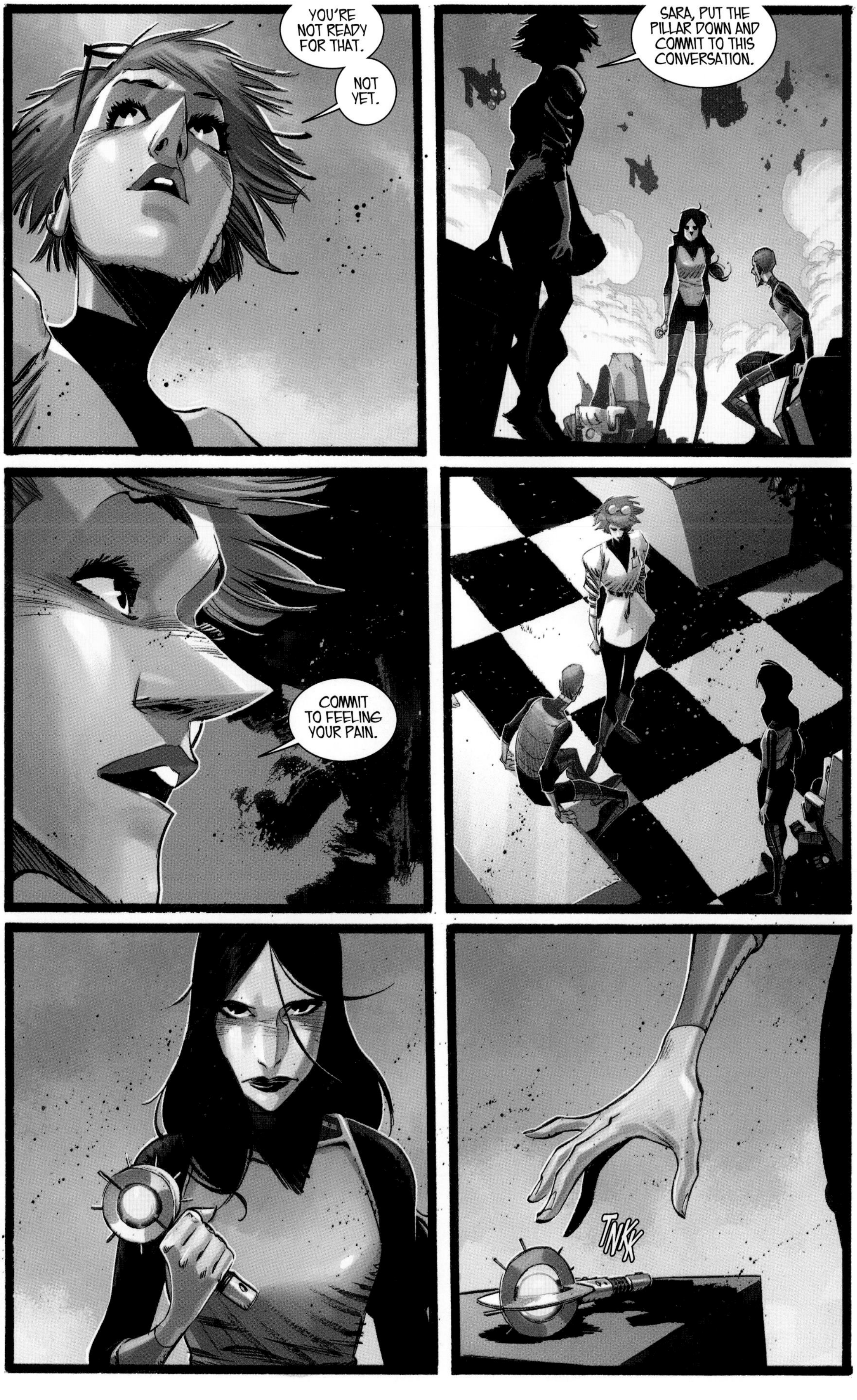
YOU'RE NOT READY FOR THAT.
NOT YET.
SARA, PUT THE PILLAR DOWN AND COMMIT TO THIS CONVERSATION.
COMMIT TO FEELING YOUR PAIN.
TNKK

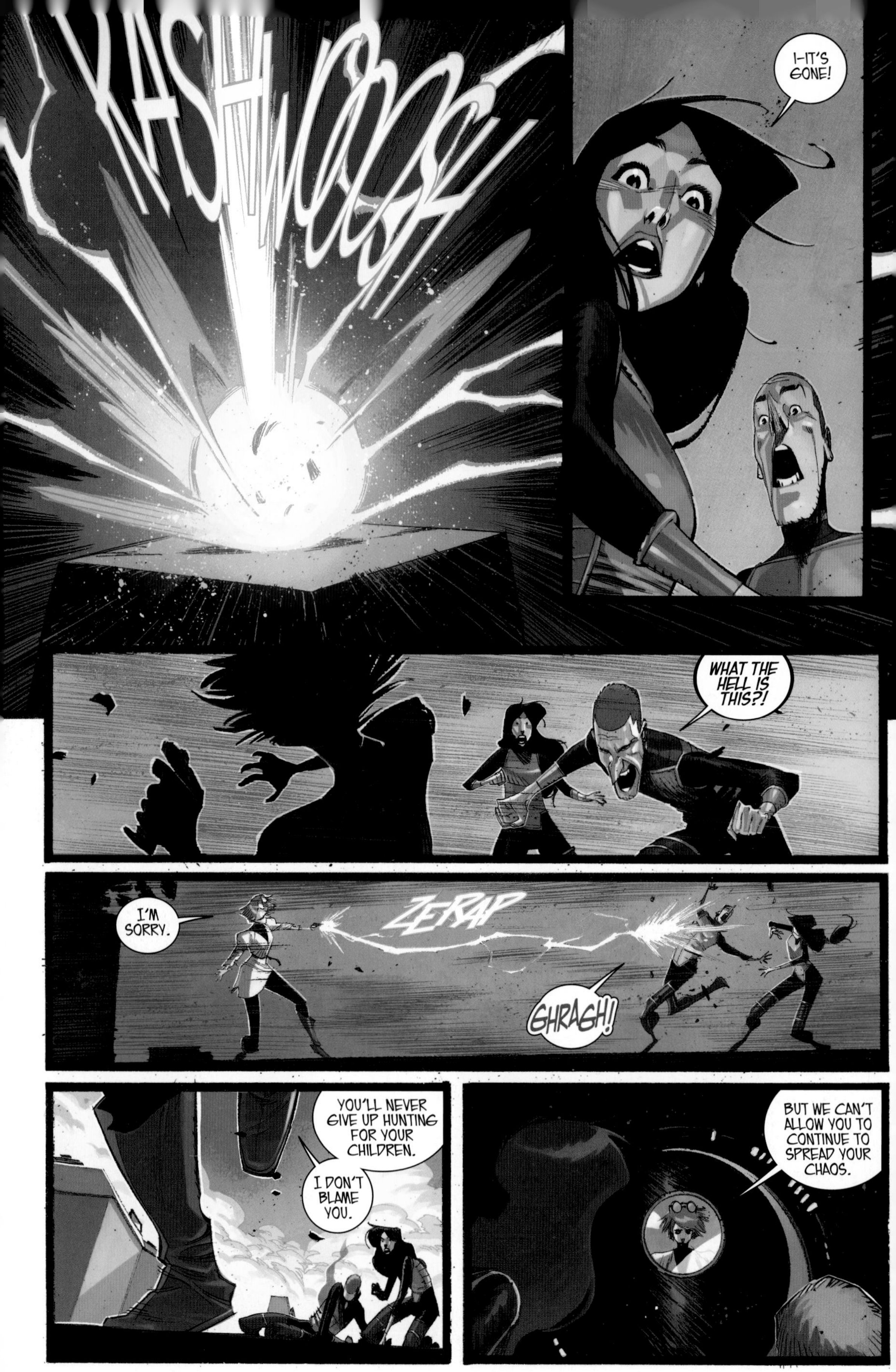
KASHWOOOSH
I-IT'S GONE!
WHAT THE HELL IS THIS?!
I'M SORRY.
ZZERAP
GHRAGH!
YOU'LL NEVER GIVE UP HUNTING FOR YOUR CHILDREN.
I DON'T BLAME YOU.
BUT WE CAN'T ALLOW YOU TO CONTINUE TO SPREAD YOUR CHAOS.

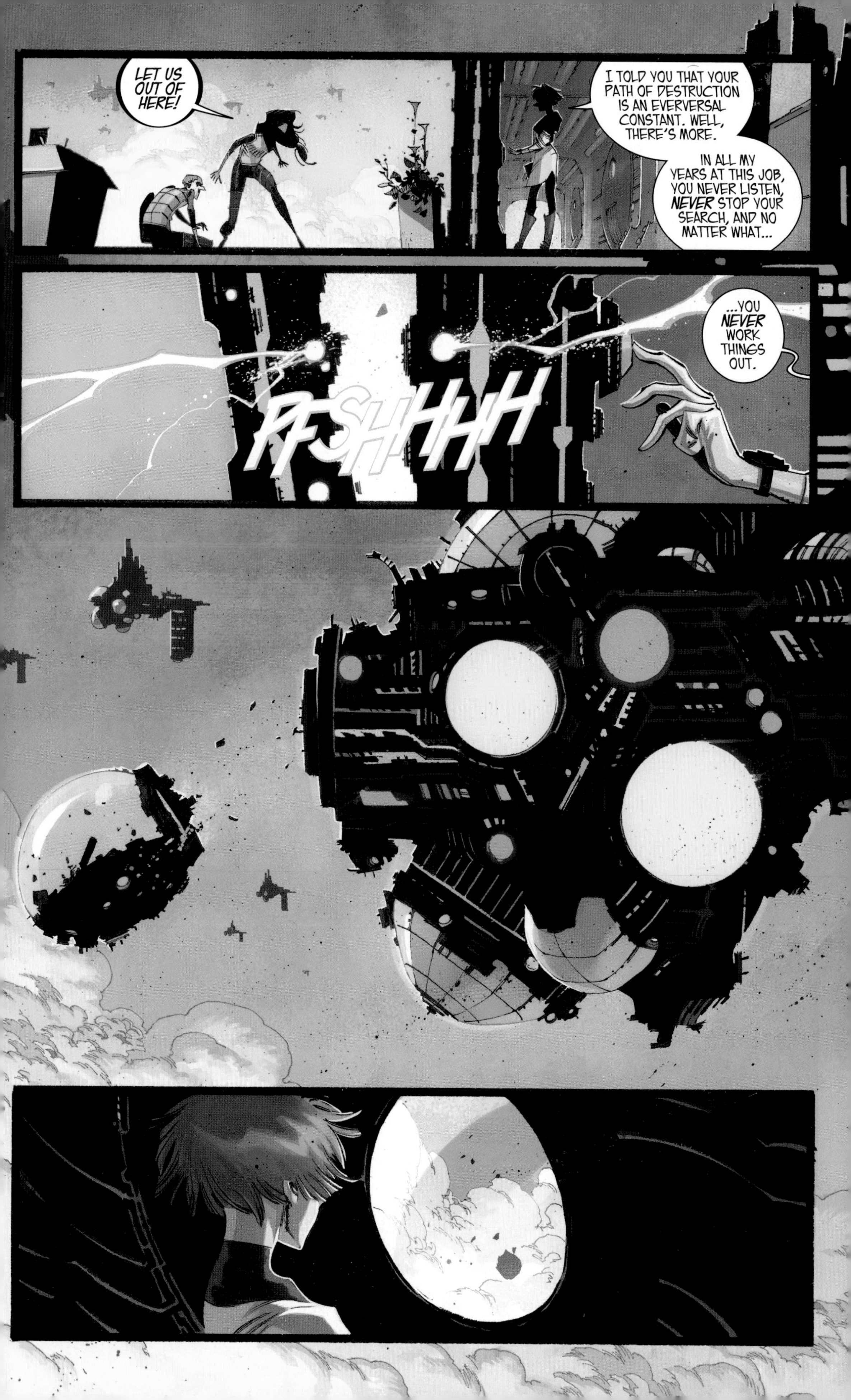
LET US OUT OF HERE!
I TOLD YOU THAT YOUR PATH OF DESTRUCTION IS AN EVERVERSAL CONSTANT. WELL, THERE'S MORE.
IN ALL MY YEARS AT THIS JOB, YOU NEVER LISTEN, NEVER STOP YOUR SEARCH, AND NO MATTER WHAT...
PFSHHHH
...YOU NEVER WORK THINGS OUT.

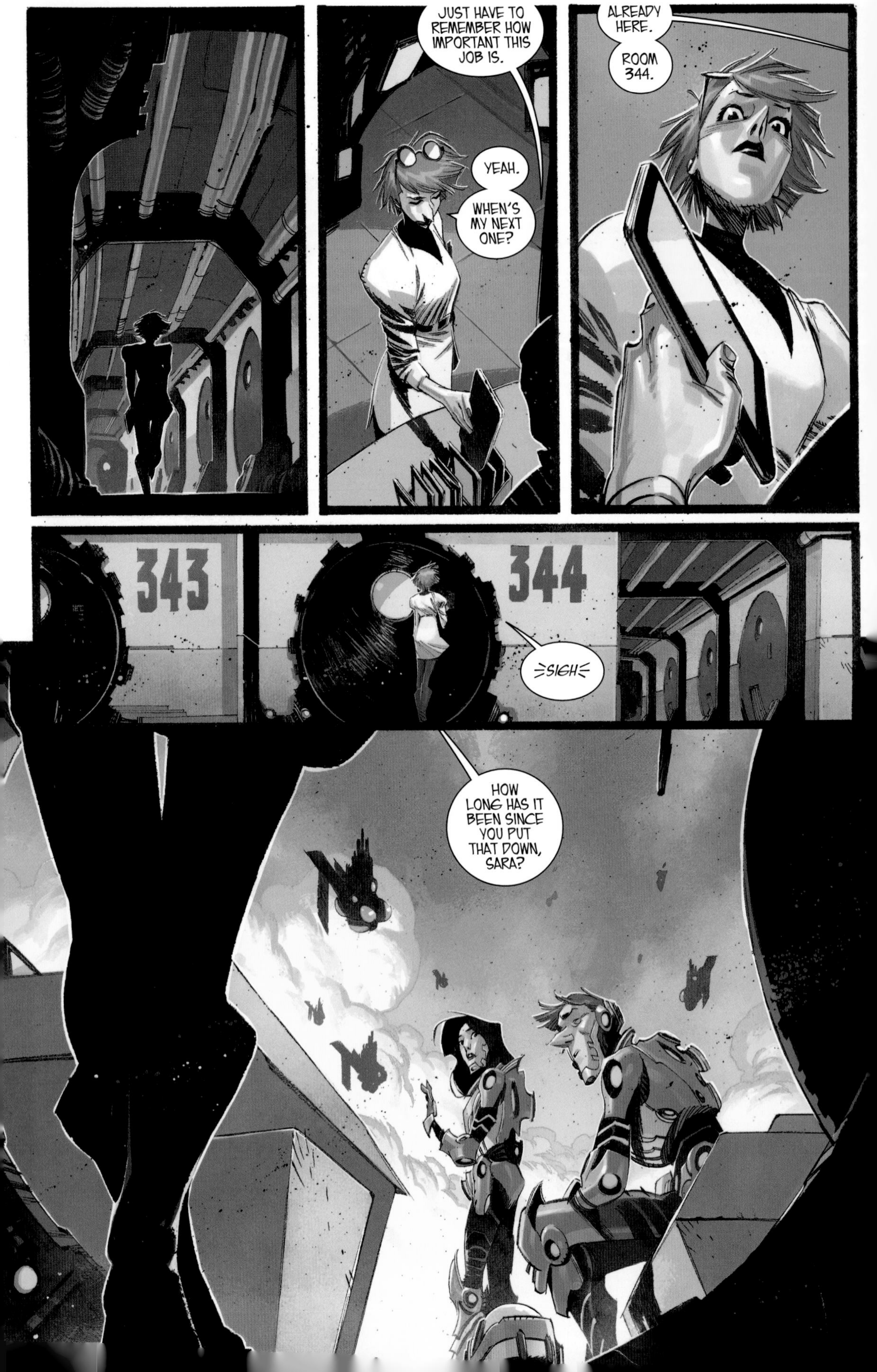
JUST HAVE TO REMEMBER HOW IMPORTANT THIS JOB IS.
YEAH.
WHEN'S MY NEXT ONE?
ALREADY HERE.
ROOM 344.
343
344
=SIGH=
HOW LONG HAS IT BEEN SINCE YOU PUT THAT DOWN, SARA?

36

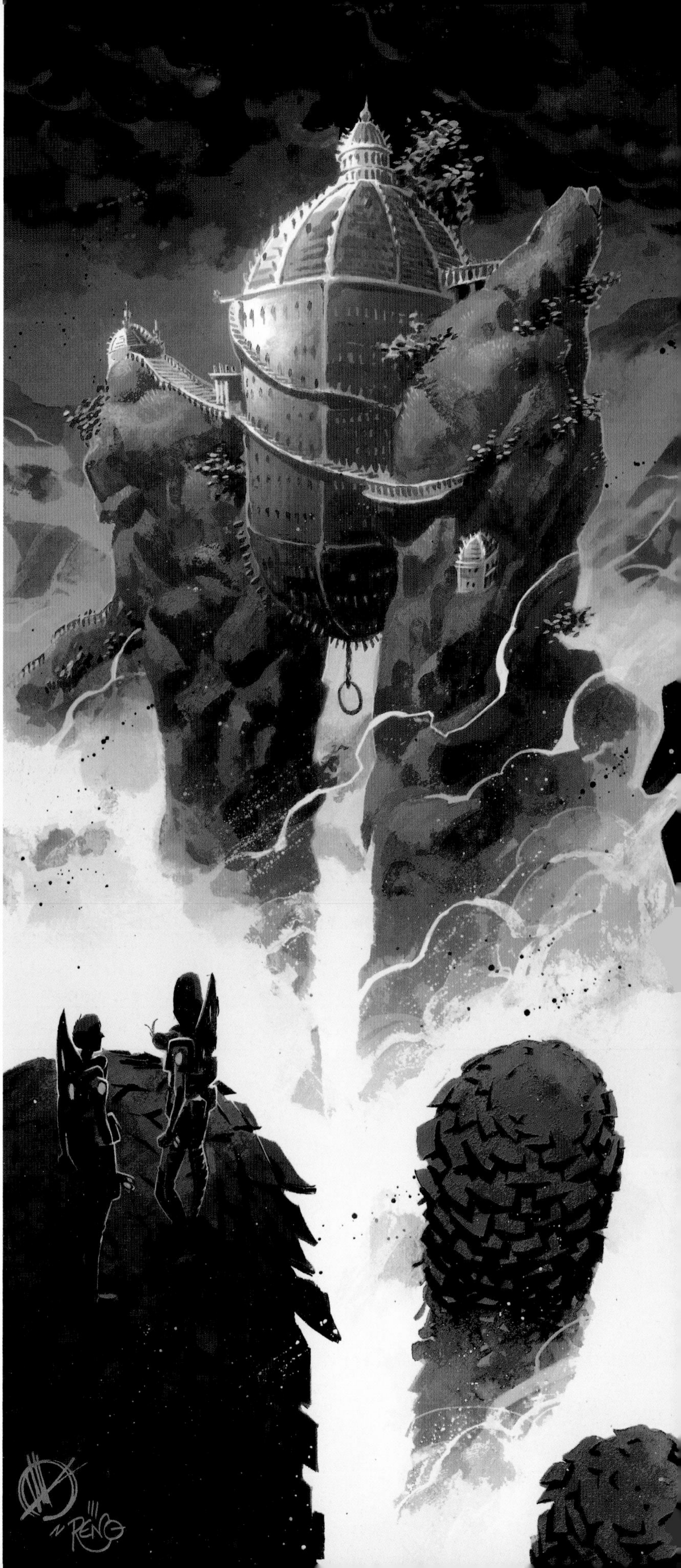

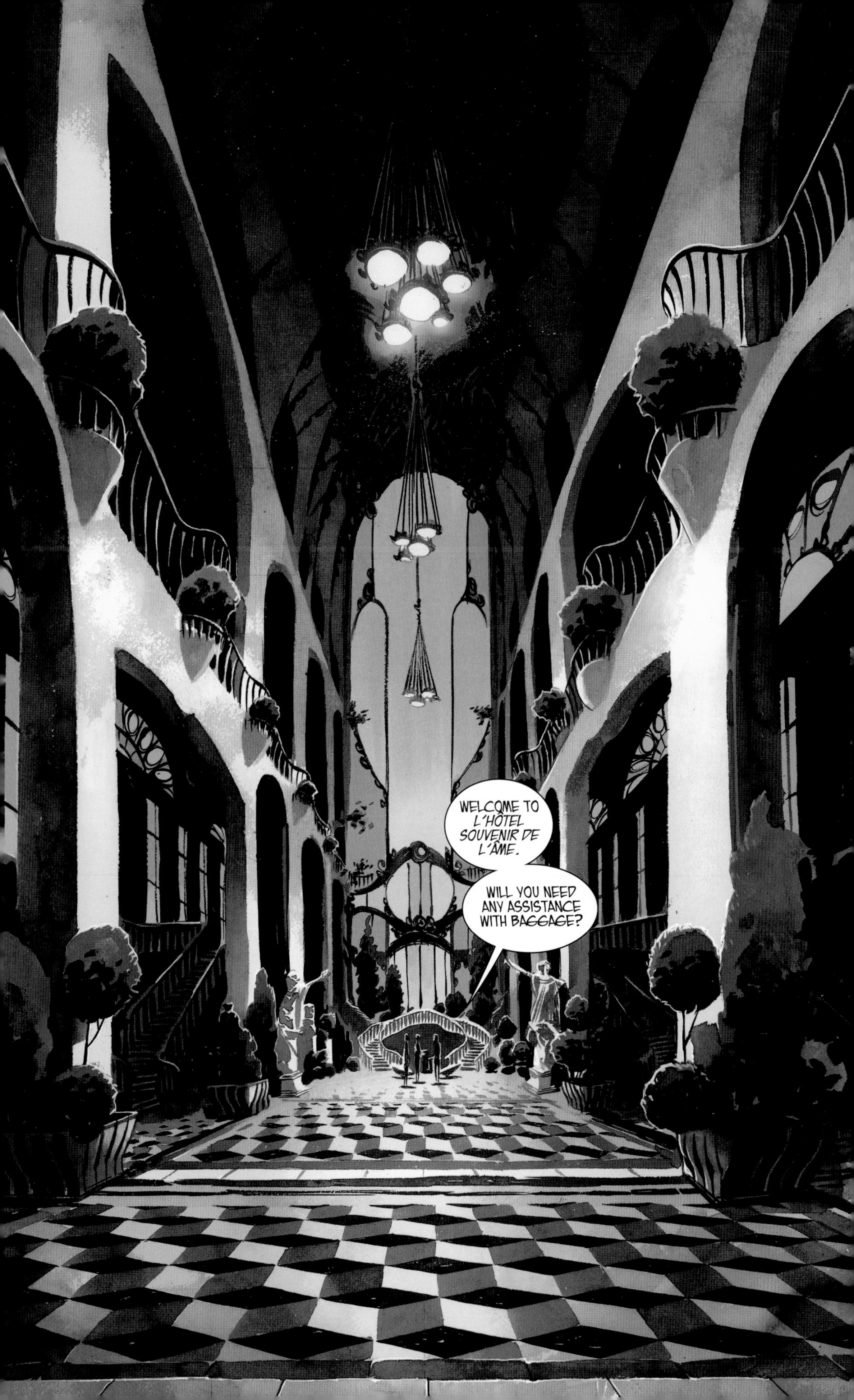
WELCOME TO L'HÔTEL SOUVENIR DE L'ÂME.
WILL YOU NEED ANY ASSISTANCE WITH BAGGAGE?

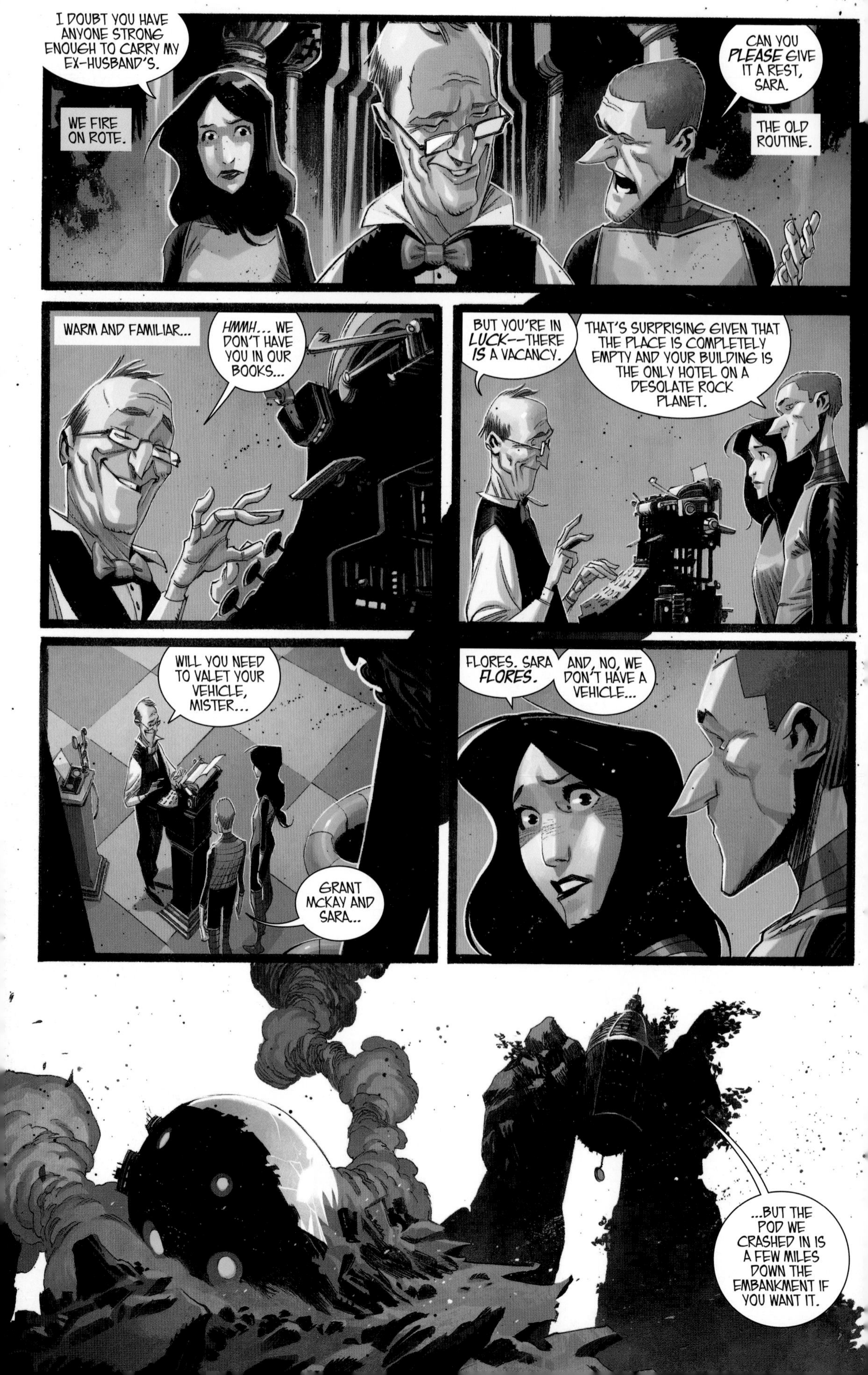
I DOUBT YOU HAVE ANYONE STRONG ENOUGH TO CARRY MY EX-HUSBAND'S.
WE FIRE ON ROTE.
CAN YOU PLEASE GIVE IT A REST, SARA.
THE OLD ROUTINE.
WARM AND FAMILIAR...
HMMH... WE DON'T HAVE YOU IN OUR BOOKS...
BUT YOU'RE IN LUCK--THERE IS A VACANCY.
THAT'S SURPRISING GIVEN THAT THE PLACE IS COMPLETELY EMPTY AND YOUR BUILDING IS THE ONLY HOTEL ON A DESOLATE ROCK PLANET.
WILL YOU NEED TO VALET YOUR VEHICLE, MISTER...
GRANT MCKAY AND SARA...
FLORES. SARA FLORES.
AND, NO, WE DON'T HAVE A VEHICLE...
...BUT THE POD WE CRASHED IN IS A FEW MILES DOWN THE EMBANKMENT IF YOU WANT IT.

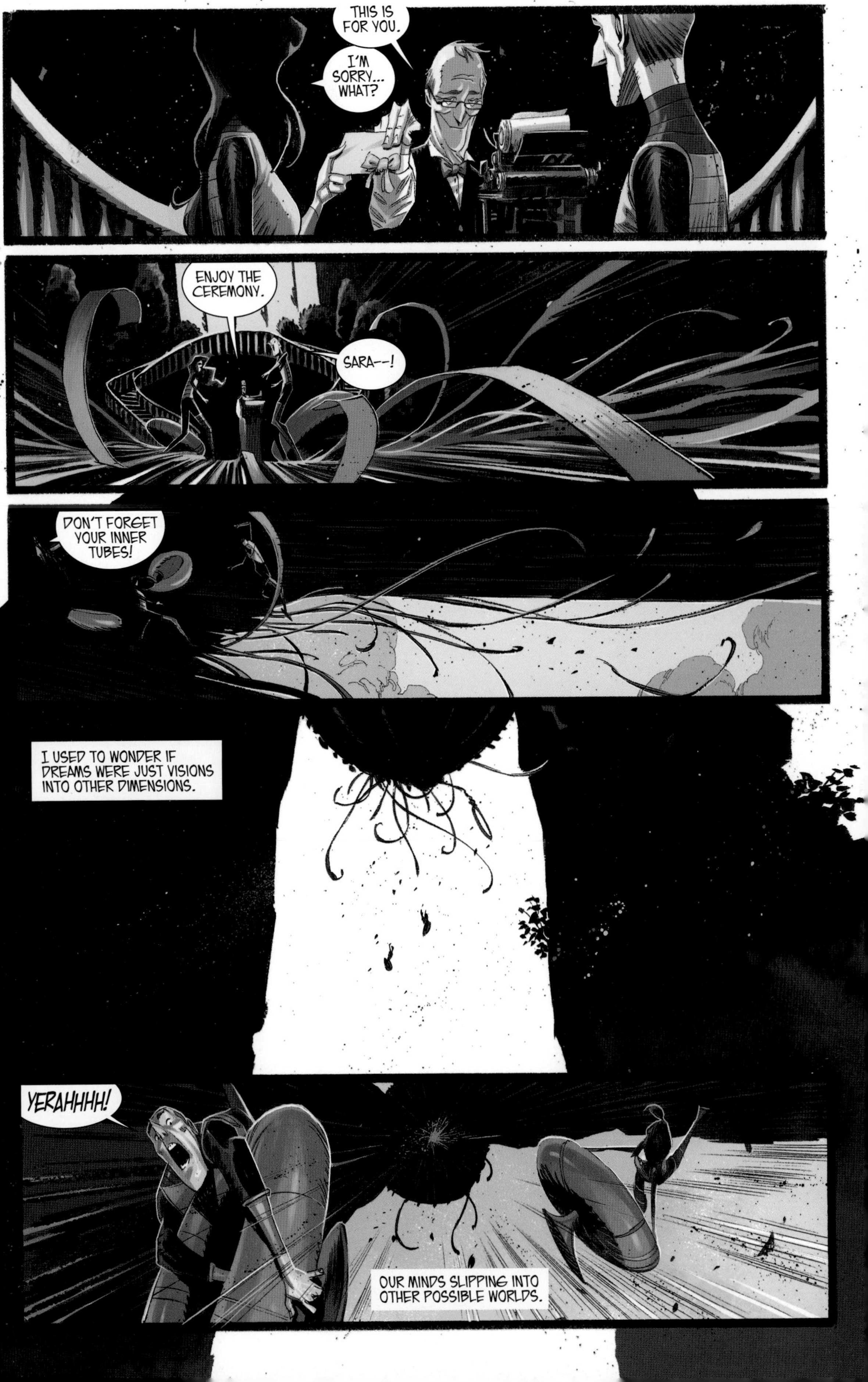
THIS IS FOR YOU.
I'M SORRY... WHAT?
ENJOY THE CEREMONY.
SARA--!
DON'T FORGET YOUR INNER TUBES!
I USED TO WONDER IF DREAMS WERE JUST VISIONS INTO OTHER DIMENSIONS.
YERAHHHH!
OUR MINDS SLIPPING INTO OTHER POSSIBLE WORLDS.

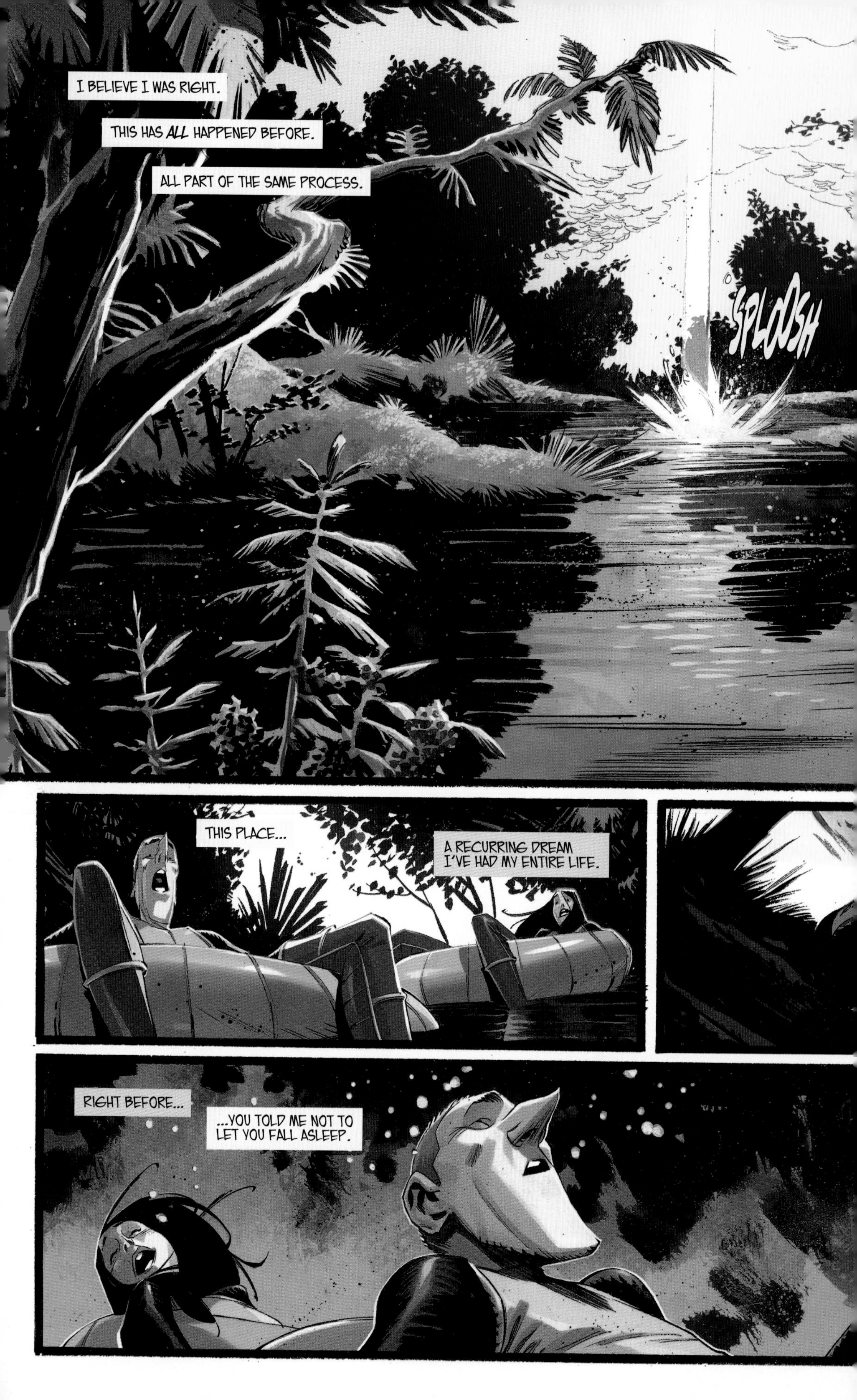
I BELIEVE I WAS RIGHT.
THIS HAS ALL HAPPENED BEFORE.
ALL PART OF THE SAME PROCESS.
SPLOOSH
THIS PLACE...
A RECURRING DREAM I'VE HAD MY ENTIRE LIFE.
RIGHT BEFORE...
...YOU TOLD ME NOT TO LET YOU FALL ASLEEP.

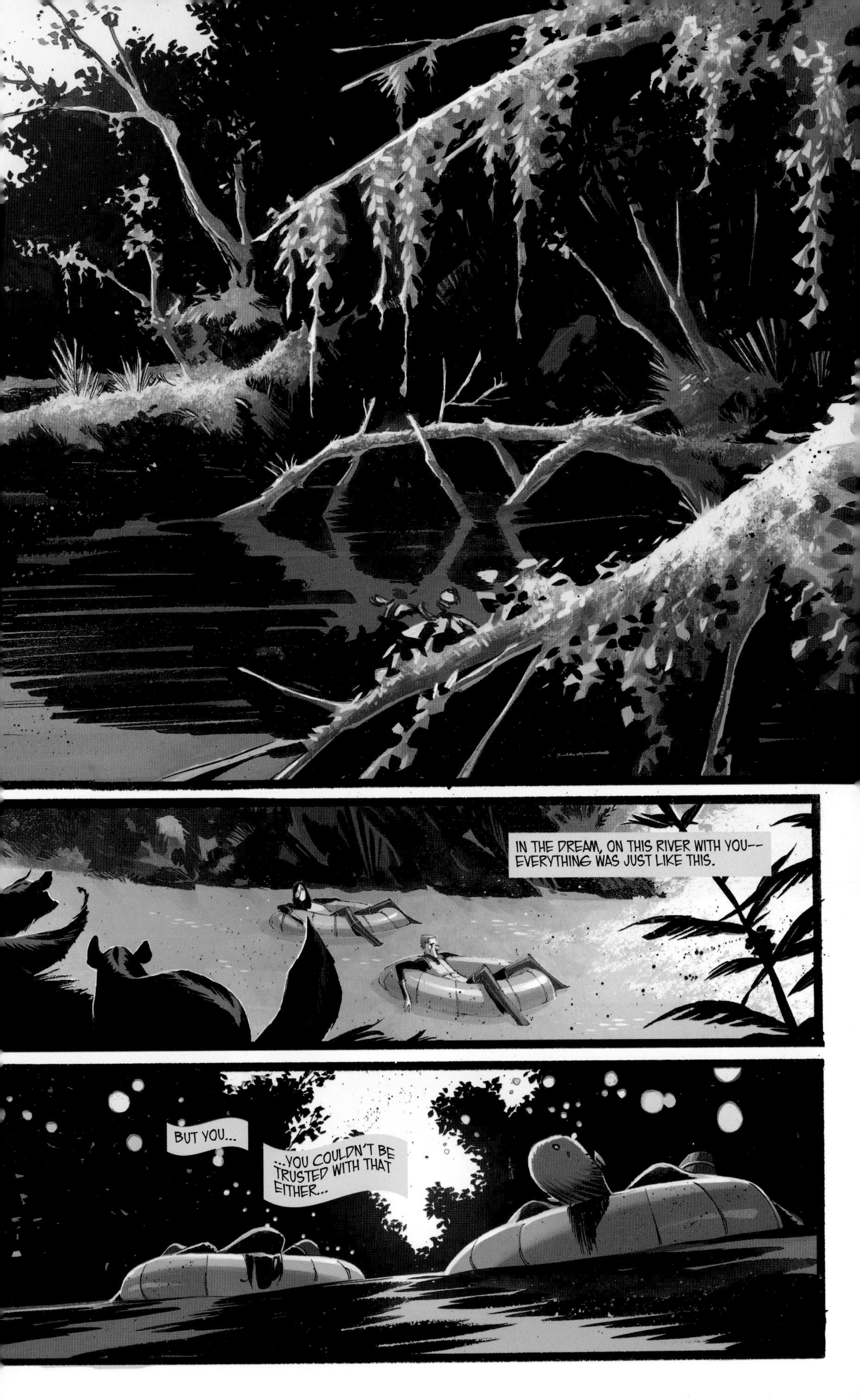
IN THE DREAM, ON THIS RIVER WITH YOU--
EVERYTHING WAS JUST LIKE THIS.
BUT YOU...
...YOU COULDN'T BE TRUSTED WITH THAT EITHER...

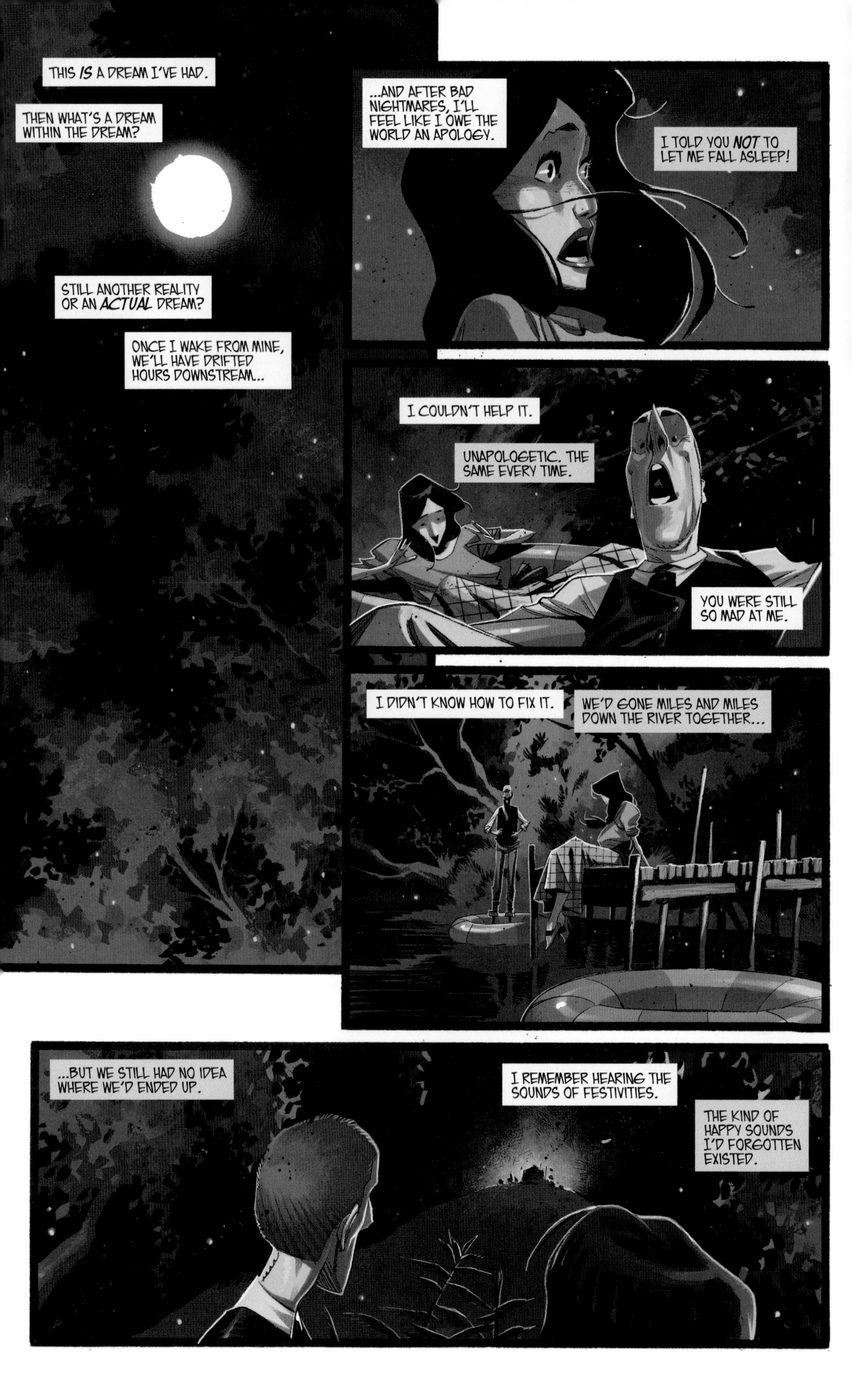
THIS *IS* A DREAM I'VE HAD.
THEN WHAT'S A DREAM WITHIN THE DREAM?
STILL ANOTHER REALITY OR AN *ACTUAL* DREAM?
ONCE I WAKE FROM MINE, WE'LL HAVE DRIFTED HOURS DOWNSTREAM...
...AND AFTER BAD NIGHTMARES, I'LL FEEL LIKE I OWE THE WORLD AN APOLOGY.
I TOLD YOU *NOT* TO LET ME FALL ASLEEP!
I COULDN'T HELP IT.
UNAPOLOGETIC. THE SAME EVERY TIME.
YOU WERE STILL SO MAD AT ME.
I DIDN'T KNOW HOW TO FIX IT.
WE'D GONE MILES AND MILES DOWN THE RIVER TOGETHER...
...BUT WE STILL HAD NO IDEA WHERE WE'D ENDED UP.
I REMEMBER HEARING THE SOUNDS OF FESTIVITIES.
THE KIND OF HAPPY SOUNDS I'D FORGOTTEN EXISTED.

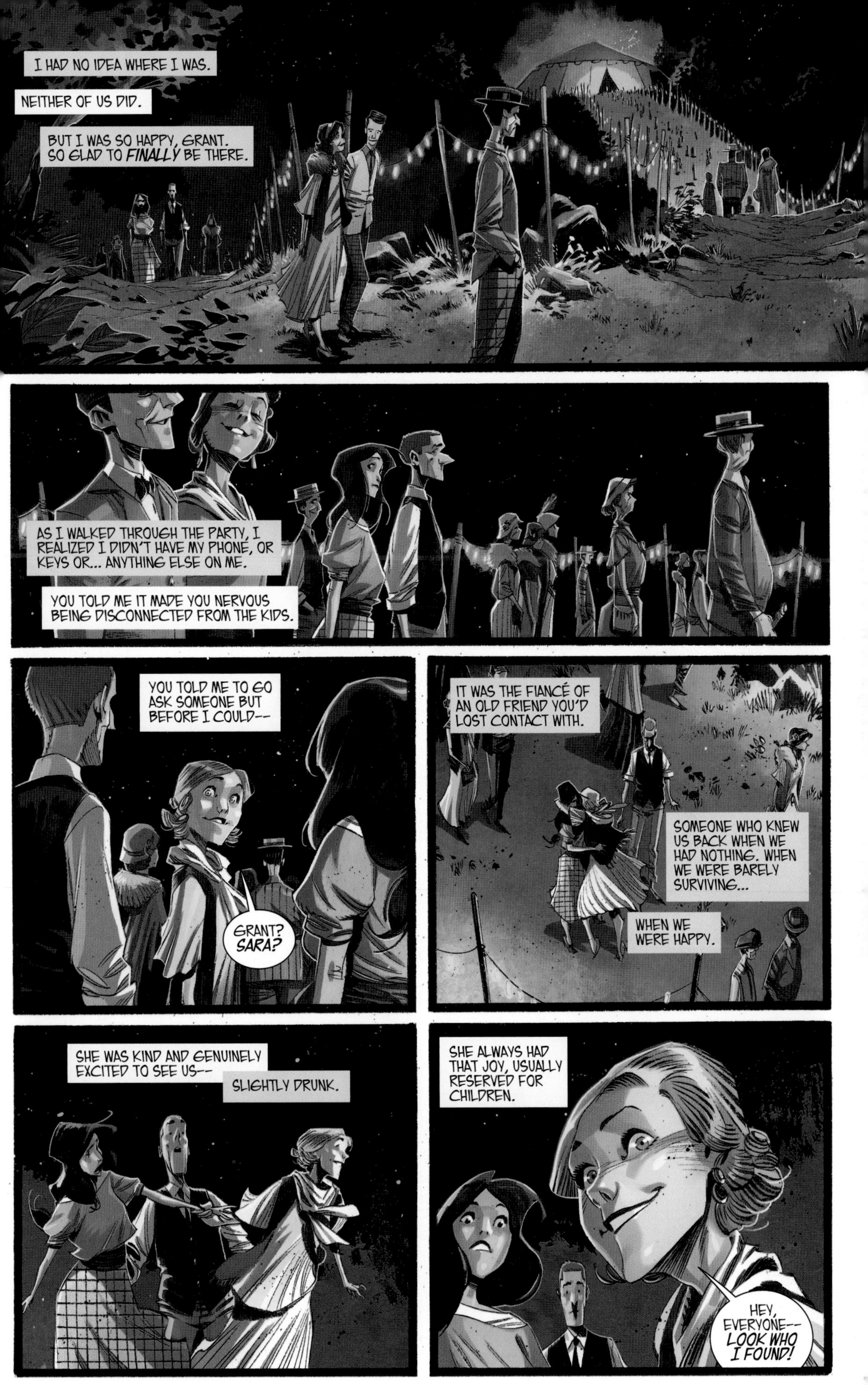

I HAD NO IDEA WHERE I WAS.
NEITHER OF US DID.
BUT I WAS SO HAPPY, GRANT. SO GLAD TO *FINALLY* BE THERE.
AS I WALKED THROUGH THE PARTY, I REALIZED I DIDN'T HAVE MY PHONE, OR KEYS OR... ANYTHING ELSE ON ME.
YOU TOLD ME IT MADE YOU NERVOUS BEING DISCONNECTED FROM THE KIDS.
YOU TOLD ME TO GO ASK SOMEONE BUT BEFORE I COULD--
GRANT? *SARA?*
IT WAS THE FIANCÉ OF AN OLD FRIEND YOU'D LOST CONTACT WITH.
SOMEONE WHO KNEW US BACK WHEN WE HAD NOTHING. WHEN WE WERE BARELY SURVIVING...
WHEN WE WERE HAPPY.
SHE WAS KIND AND GENUINELY EXCITED TO SEE US--
SLIGHTLY DRUNK.
SHE ALWAYS HAD THAT JOY, USUALLY RESERVED FOR CHILDREN.
HEY, EVERYONE-- *LOOK WHO I FOUND!*

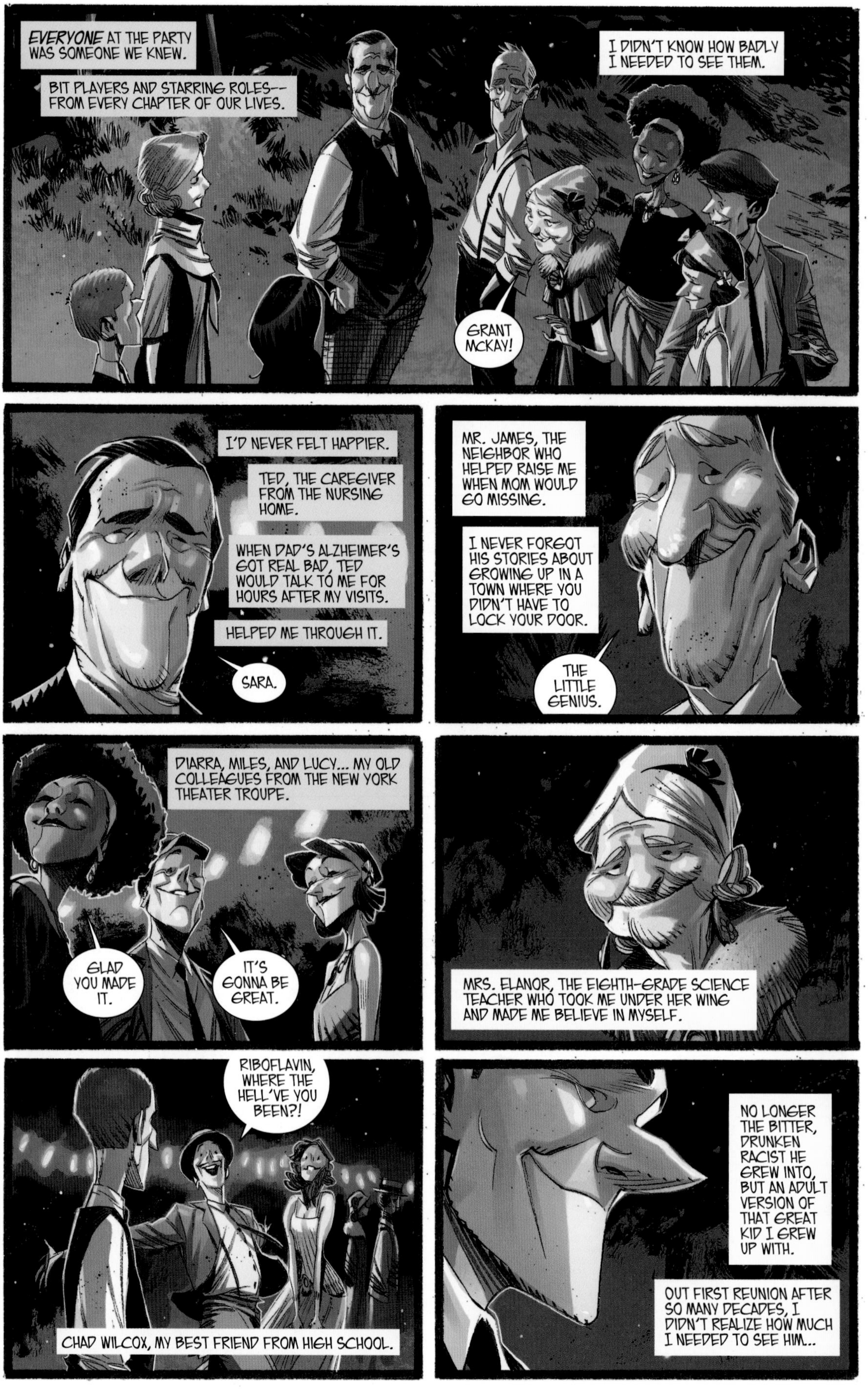
EVERYONE AT THE PARTY WAS SOMEONE WE KNEW.
BIT PLAYERS AND STARRING ROLES-- FROM EVERY CHAPTER OF OUR LIVES.
I DIDN'T KNOW HOW BADLY I NEEDED TO SEE THEM.
GRANT MCKAY!
I'D NEVER FELT HAPPIER.
TED, THE CAREGIVER FROM THE NURSING HOME.
WHEN DAD'S ALZHEIMER'S GOT REAL BAD, TED WOULD TALK TO ME FOR HOURS AFTER MY VISITS.
HELPED ME THROUGH IT.
SARA.
MR. JAMES, THE NEIGHBOR WHO HELPED RAISE ME WHEN MOM WOULD GO MISSING.
I NEVER FORGOT HIS STORIES ABOUT GROWING UP IN A TOWN WHERE YOU DIDN'T HAVE TO LOCK YOUR DOOR.
THE LITTLE GENIUS.
DIARRA, MILES, AND LUCY... MY OLD COLLEAGUES FROM THE NEW YORK THEATER TROUPE.
GLAD YOU MADE IT.
IT'S GONNA BE GREAT.
MRS. ELANOR, THE EIGHTH-GRADE SCIENCE TEACHER WHO TOOK ME UNDER HER WING AND MADE ME BELIEVE IN MYSELF.
RIBOFLAVIN, WHERE THE HELL'VE YOU BEEN?!
CHAD WILCOX, MY BEST FRIEND FROM HIGH SCHOOL.
NO LONGER THE BITTER, DRUNKEN RACIST HE GREW INTO, BUT AN ADULT VERSION OF THAT GREAT KID I GREW UP WITH.
OUT FIRST REUNION AFTER SO MANY DECADES, I DIDN'T REALIZE HOW MUCH I NEEDED TO SEE HIM...

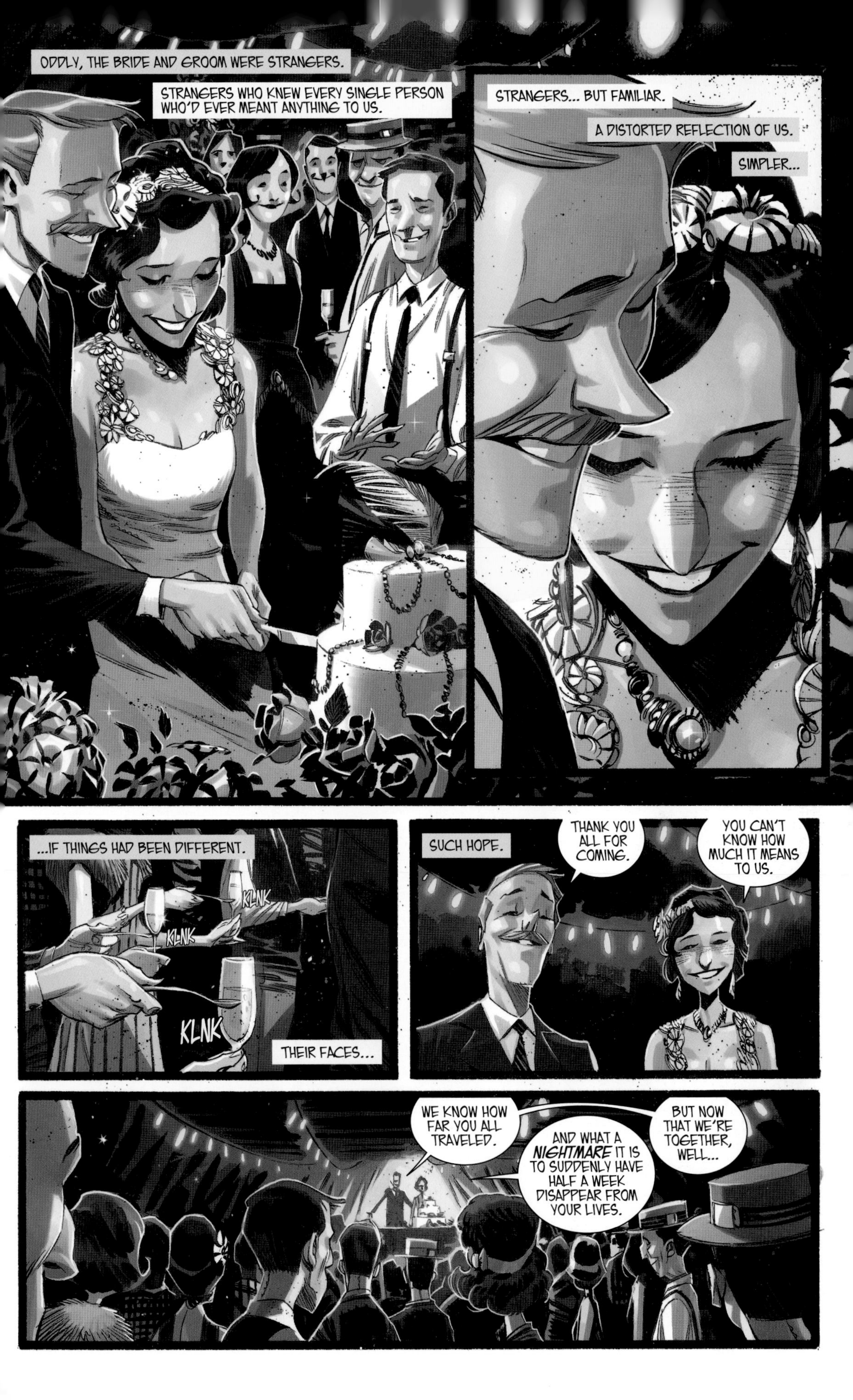

ODDLY, THE BRIDE AND GROOM WERE STRANGERS.
STRANGERS WHO KNEW EVERY SINGLE PERSON WHO'D EVER MEANT ANYTHING TO US.
STRANGERS... BUT FAMILIAR.
A DISTORTED REFLECTION OF US.
SIMPLER...
...IF THINGS HAD BEEN DIFFERENT.
KLNK
KLNK
KLNK
THEIR FACES...
SUCH HOPE.
THANK YOU ALL FOR COMING.
YOU CAN'T KNOW HOW MUCH IT MEANS TO US.
WE KNOW HOW FAR YOU ALL TRAVELED.
AND WHAT A NIGHTMARE IT IS TO SUDDENLY HAVE HALF A WEEK DISAPPEAR FROM YOUR LIVES.
BUT NOW THAT WE'RE TOGETHER, WELL...

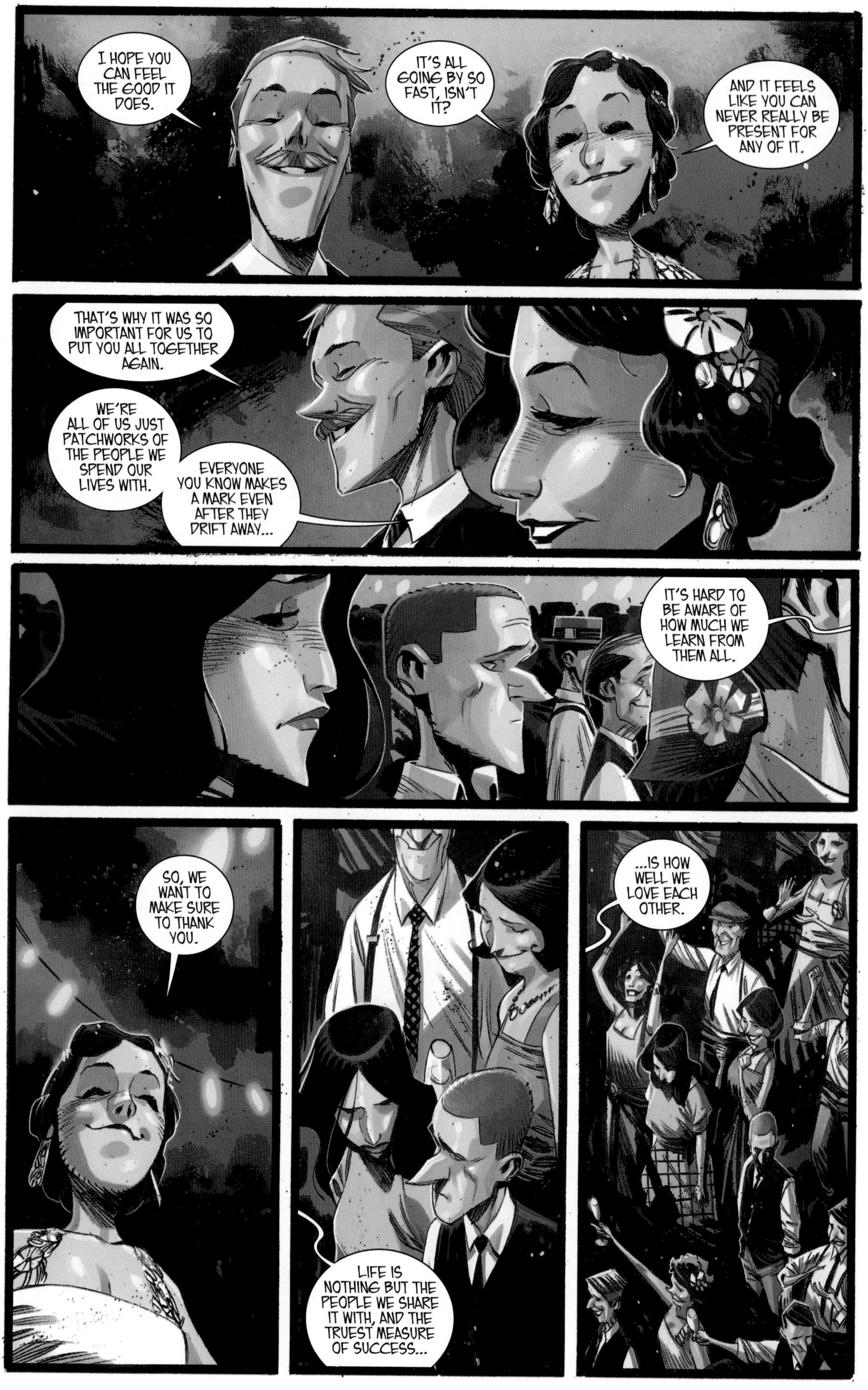
I HOPE YOU CAN FEEL THE GOOD IT DOES.
IT'S ALL GOING BY SO FAST, ISN'T IT?
AND IT FEELS LIKE YOU CAN NEVER REALLY BE PRESENT FOR ANY OF IT.
THAT'S WHY IT WAS SO IMPORTANT FOR US TO PUT YOU ALL TOGETHER AGAIN.
WE'RE ALL OF US JUST PATCHWORKS OF THE PEOPLE WE SPEND OUR LIVES WITH.
EVERYONE YOU KNOW MAKES A MARK EVEN AFTER THEY DRIFT AWAY...
IT'S HARD TO BE AWARE OF HOW MUCH WE LEARN FROM THEM ALL.
SO, WE WANT TO MAKE SURE TO THANK YOU.
LIFE IS NOTHING BUT THE PEOPLE WE SHARE IT WITH, AND THE TRUEST MEASURE OF SUCCESS...
...IS HOW WELL WE LOVE EACH OTHER.

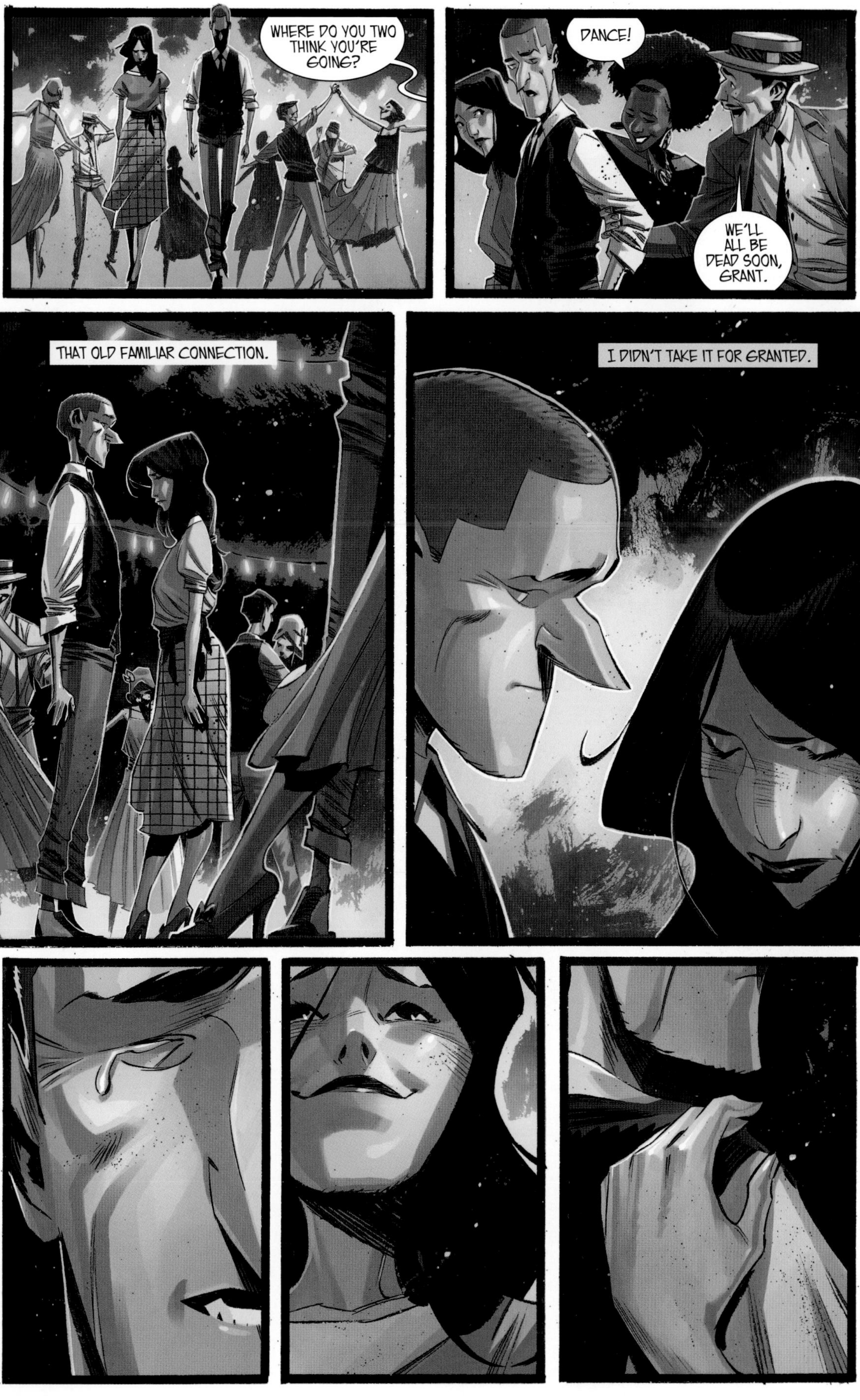
WHERE DO YOU TWO THINK YOU'RE GOING?
DANCE!
WE'LL ALL BE DEAD SOON, GRANT.
THAT OLD FAMILIAR CONNECTION.
I DIDN'T TAKE IT FOR GRANTED.

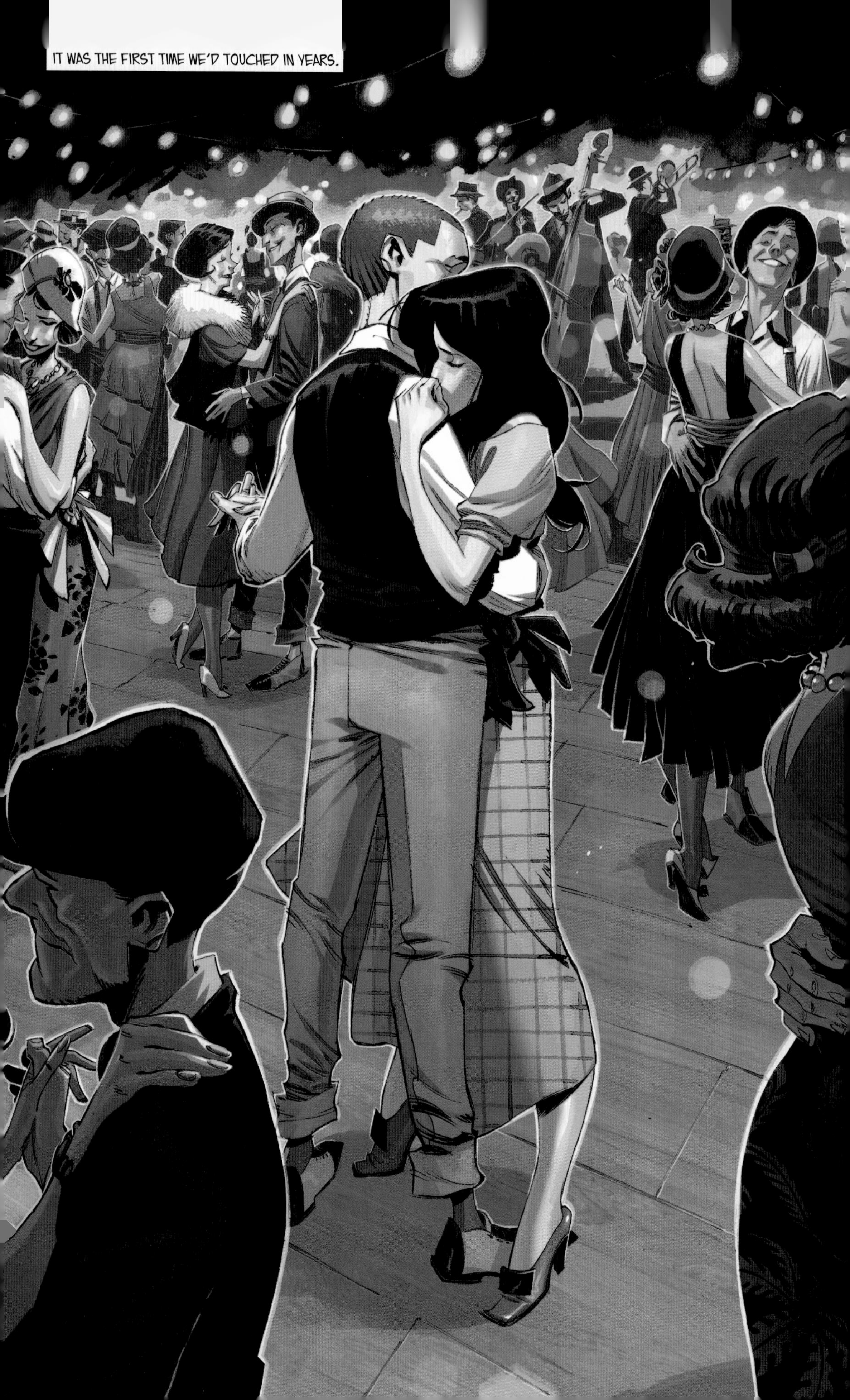
IT WAS THE FIRST TIME WE'D TOUCHED IN YEARS.

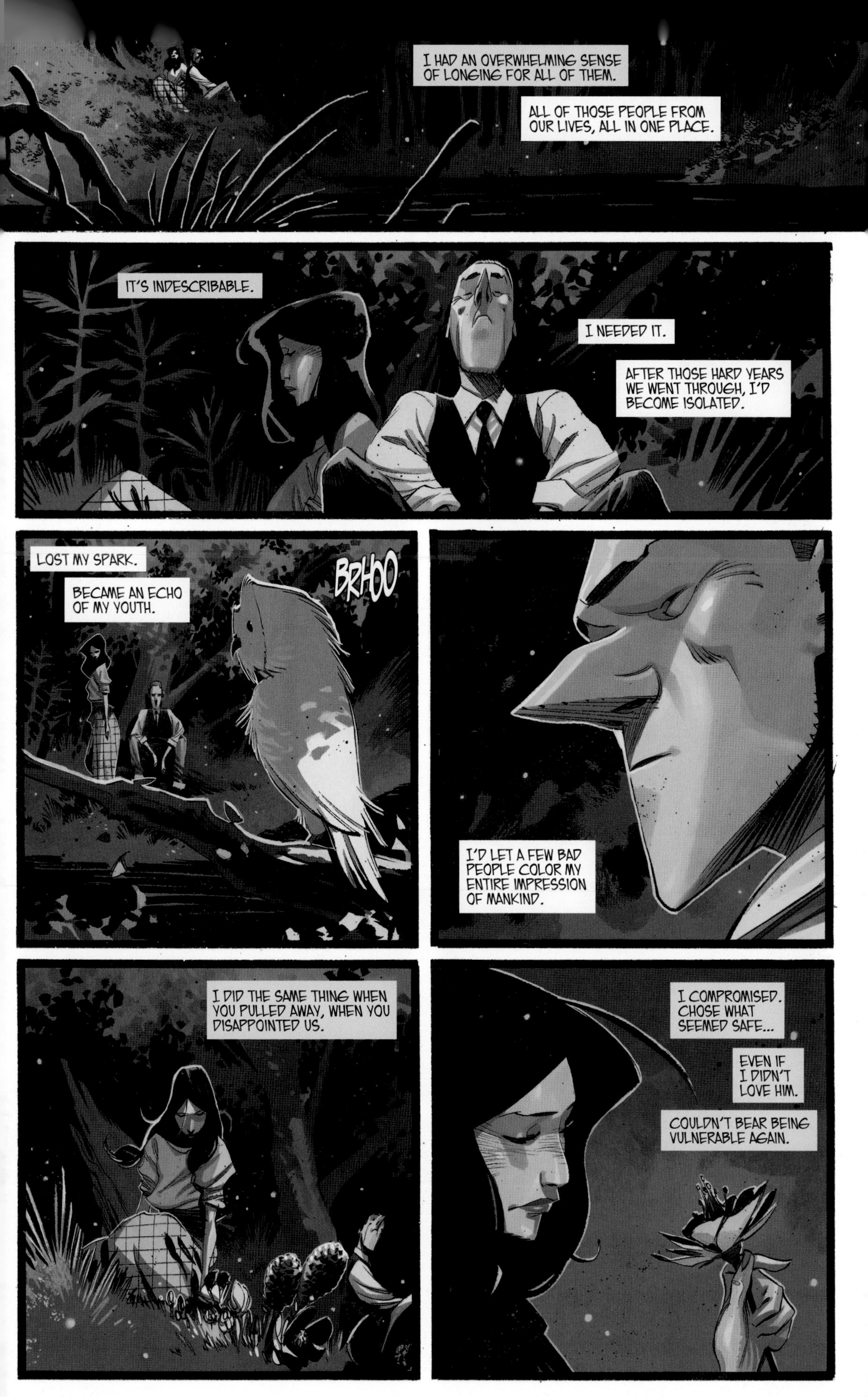
I HAD AN OVERWHELMING SENSE OF LONGING FOR ALL OF THEM.
ALL OF THOSE PEOPLE FROM OUR LIVES, ALL IN ONE PLACE.
IT'S INDESCRIBABLE.
I NEEDED IT.
AFTER THOSE HARD YEARS WE WENT THROUGH, I'D BECOME ISOLATED.
LOST MY SPARK.
BECAME AN ECHO OF MY YOUTH.
BRHOO
I'D LET A FEW BAD PEOPLE COLOR MY ENTIRE IMPRESSION OF MANKIND.
I DID THE SAME THING WHEN YOU PULLED AWAY, WHEN YOU DISAPPOINTED US.
I COMPROMISED. CHOSE WHAT SEEMED SAFE...
EVEN IF I DIDN'T LOVE HIM.
COULDN'T BEAR BEING VULNERABLE AGAIN.

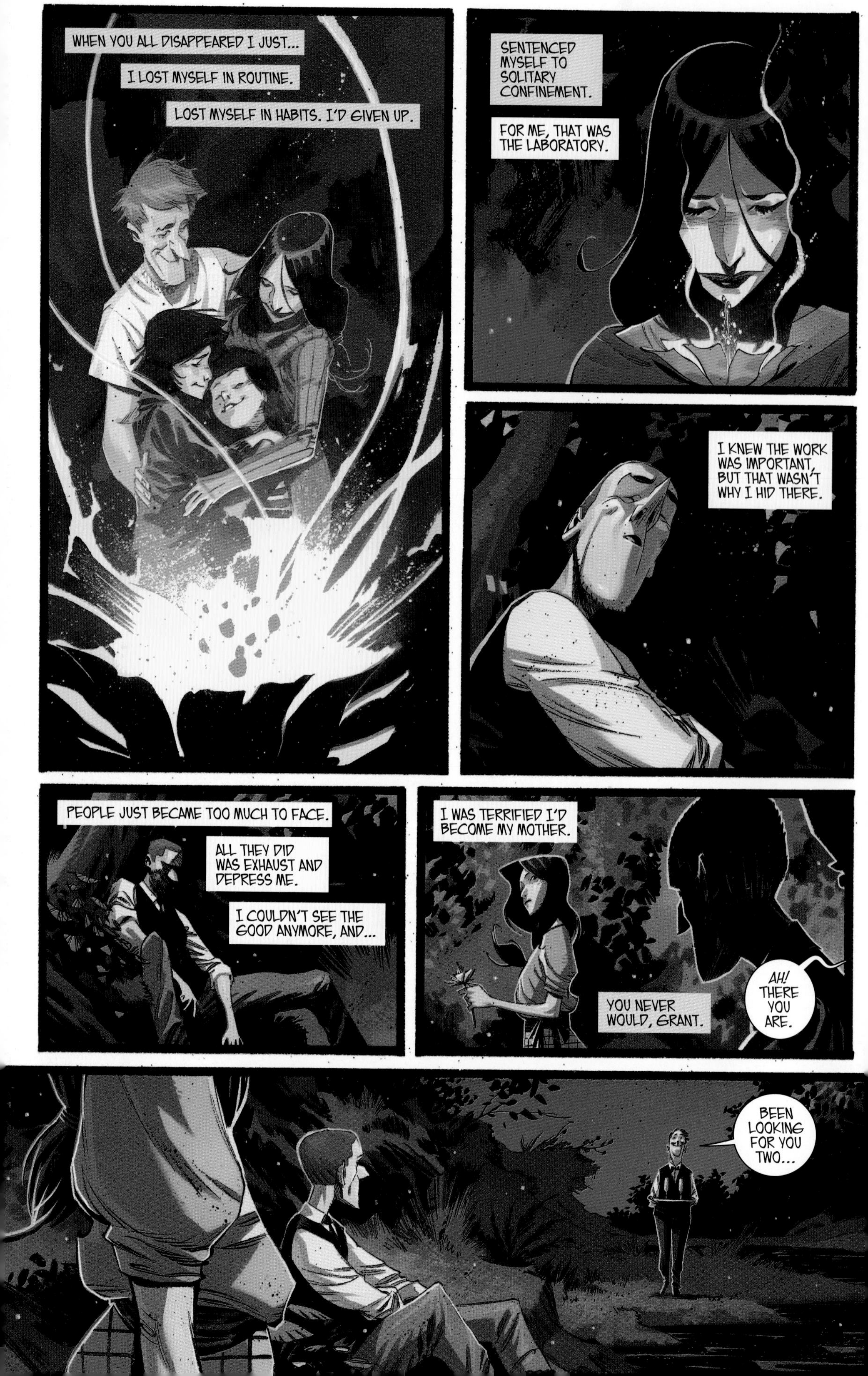
WHEN YOU ALL DISAPPEARED I JUST...
I LOST MYSELF IN ROUTINE.
LOST MYSELF IN HABITS. I'D GIVEN UP.
SENTENCED MYSELF TO SOLITARY CONFINEMENT.
FOR ME, THAT WAS THE LABORATORY.
I KNEW THE WORK WAS IMPORTANT, BUT THAT WASN'T WHY I HID THERE.
PEOPLE JUST BECAME TOO MUCH TO FACE.
ALL THEY DID WAS EXHAUST AND DEPRESS ME.
I COULDN'T SEE THE GOOD ANYMORE, AND...
I WAS TERRIFIED I'D BECOME MY MOTHER.
YOU NEVER WOULD, GRANT.
AH! THERE YOU ARE.
BEEN LOOKING FOR YOU TWO...

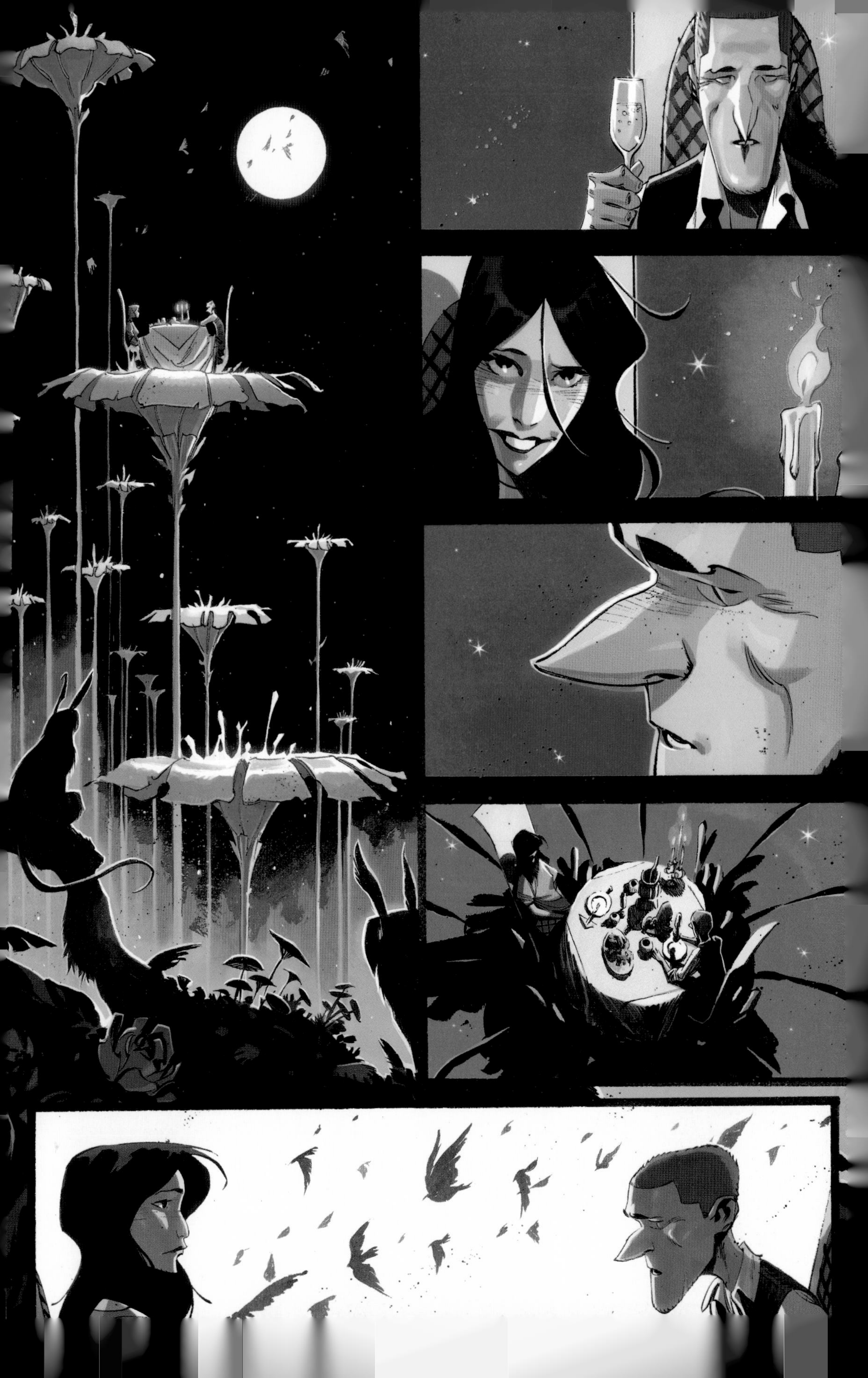

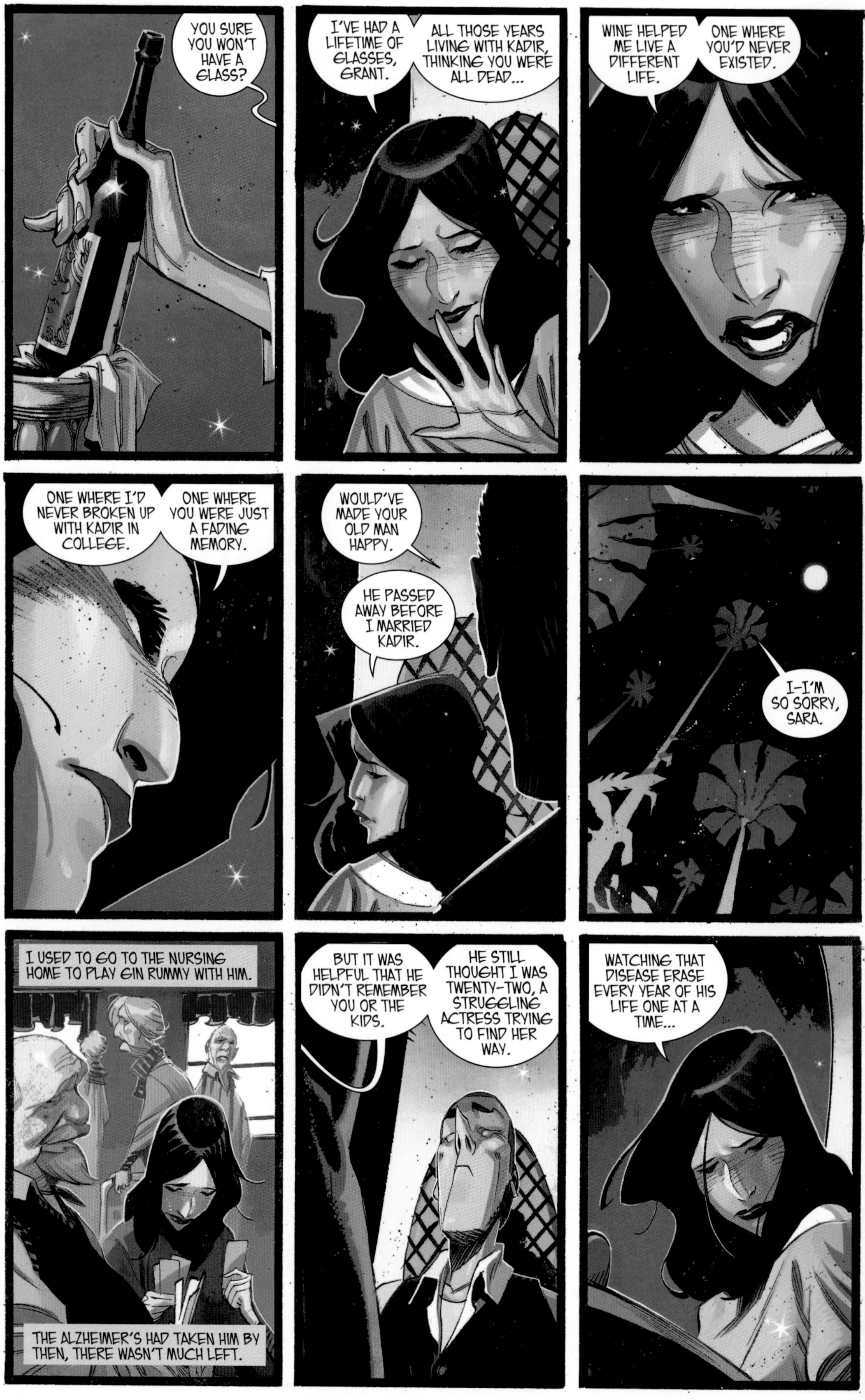
YOU SURE YOU WON'T HAVE A GLASS?
I'VE HAD A LIFETIME OF GLASSES, GRANT.
ALL THOSE YEARS LIVING WITH KADIR, THINKING YOU WERE ALL DEAD...
WINE HELPED ME LIVE A DIFFERENT LIFE.
ONE WHERE YOU'D NEVER EXISTED.
ONE WHERE I'D NEVER BROKEN UP WITH KADIR IN COLLEGE.
ONE WHERE YOU WERE JUST A FADING MEMORY.
WOULD'VE MADE YOUR OLD MAN HAPPY.
HE PASSED AWAY BEFORE I MARRIED KADIR.
I-I'M SO SORRY, SARA.
I USED TO GO TO THE NURSING HOME TO PLAY GIN RUMMY WITH HIM.
THE ALZHEIMER'S HAD TAKEN HIM BY THEN, THERE WASN'T MUCH LEFT.
BUT IT WAS HELPFUL THAT HE DIDN'T REMEMBER YOU OR THE KIDS.
HE STILL THOUGHT I WAS TWENTY-TWO, A STRUGGLING ACTRESS TRYING TO FIND HER WAY.
WATCHING THAT DISEASE ERASE EVERY YEAR OF HIS LIFE ONE AT A TIME...

IT MADE ME AFRAID THERE'S NO POINT TO *ANY* OF IT.

IT CAN ALL JUST DISAPPEAR.

EVERY MEMORY, EVERY LOVE, EVERY SINGLE MOMENT OF IT...

IT'S ALL JUST ONE CHEMICAL MISFIRE AWAY FROM BEING ERASED.

I CAN'T IMAGINE HOW IT WAS FOR YOU...

I'M SORRY I WASN'T THERE.

IT'S HARD TO CHANGE AN EMOTION, YOU KNOW?

ALL THOSE YEARS THINKING YOU HAD DONE THESE TERRIBLE THINGS, ONLY TO FIND OUT KADIR WAS LYING TO ME...

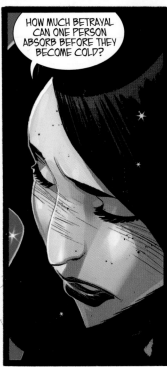

HOW MUCH BETRAYAL CAN ONE PERSON ABSORB BEFORE THEY BECOME COLD?

OH--
WOW!

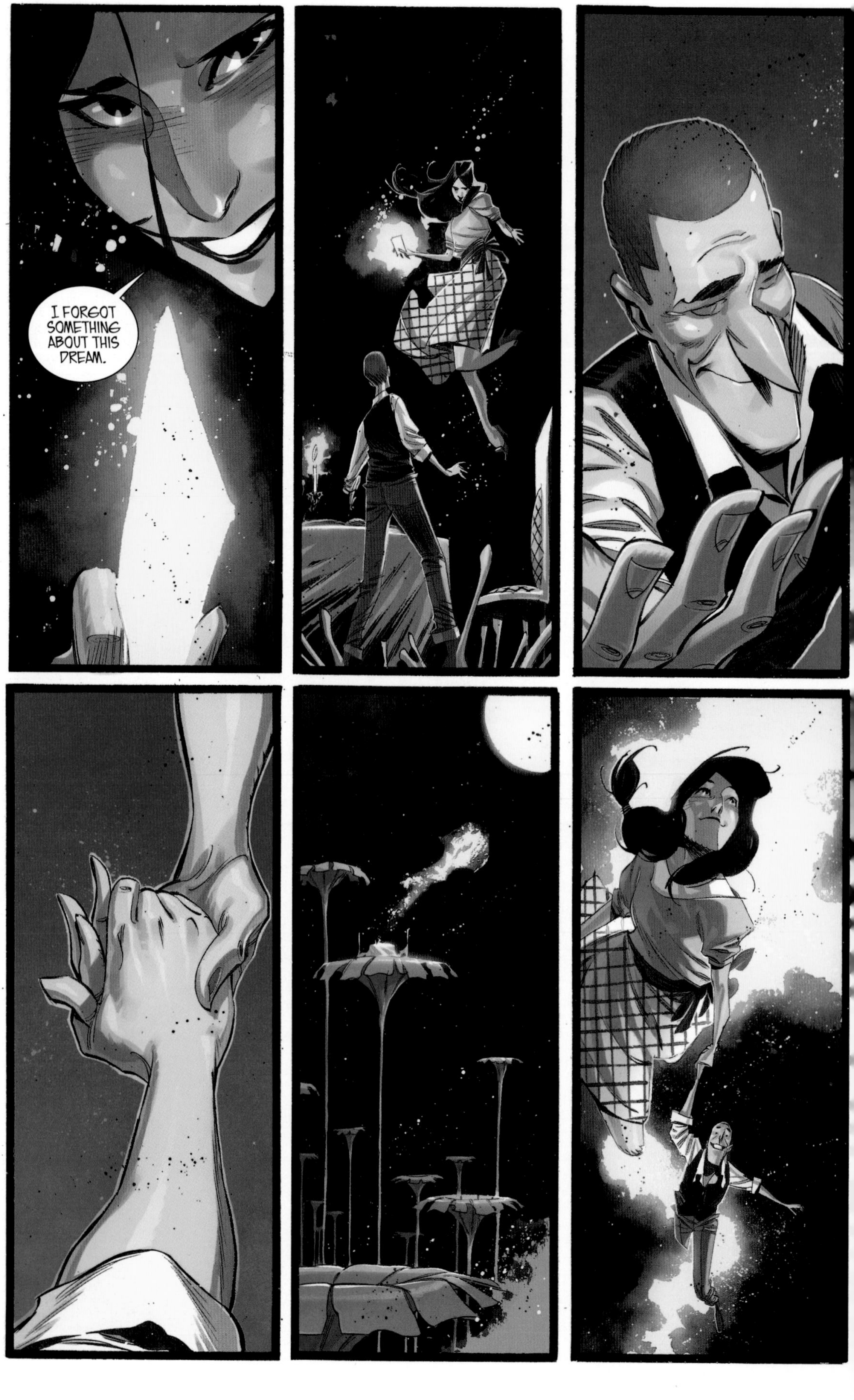
I FORGOT SOMETHING ABOUT THIS DREAM.

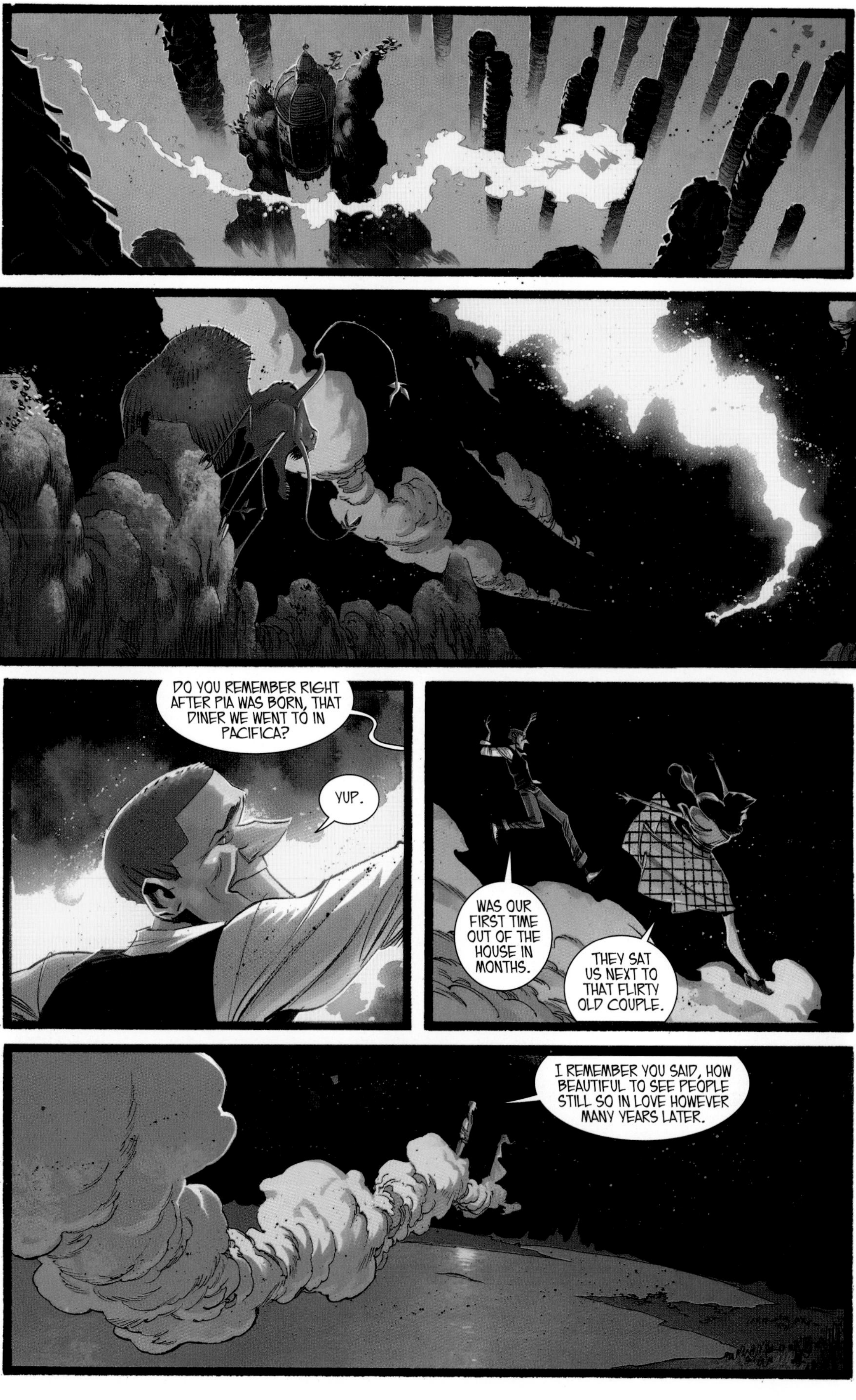
DO YOU REMEMBER RIGHT AFTER PIA WAS BORN, THAT DINER WE WENT TO IN PACIFICA?
YUP.
WAS OUR FIRST TIME OUT OF THE HOUSE IN MONTHS.
THEY SAT US NEXT TO THAT FLIRTY OLD COUPLE.
I REMEMBER YOU SAID, HOW BEAUTIFUL TO SEE PEOPLE STILL SO IN LOVE HOWEVER MANY YEARS LATER.

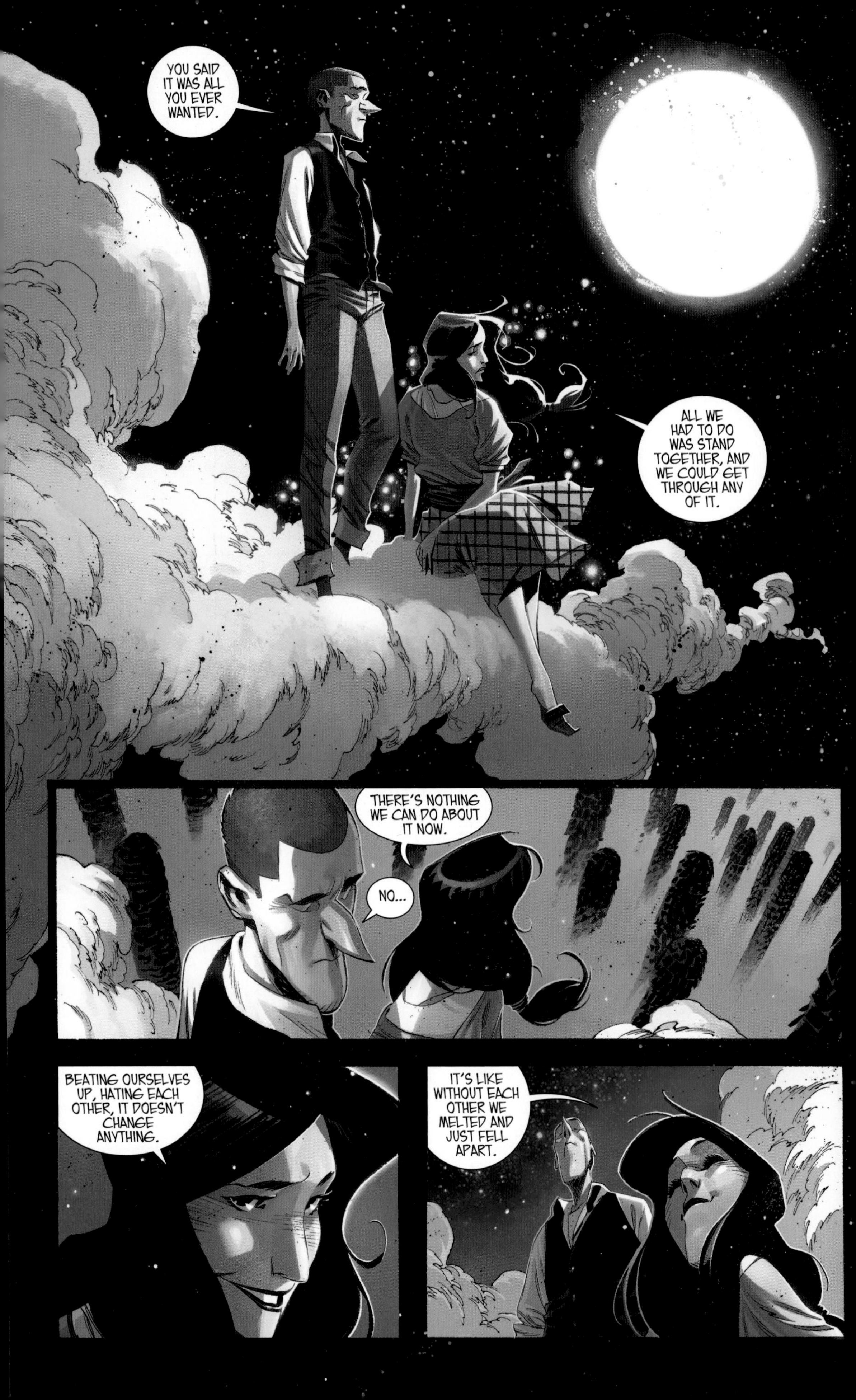
YOU SAID IT WAS ALL YOU EVER WANTED.
ALL WE HAD TO DO WAS STAND TOGETHER, AND WE COULD GET THROUGH ANY OF IT.
THERE'S NOTHING WE CAN DO ABOUT IT NOW.
NO...
BEATING OURSELVES UP, HATING EACH OTHER, IT DOESN'T CHANGE ANYTHING.
IT'S LIKE WITHOUT EACH OTHER WE MELTED AND JUST FELL APART.

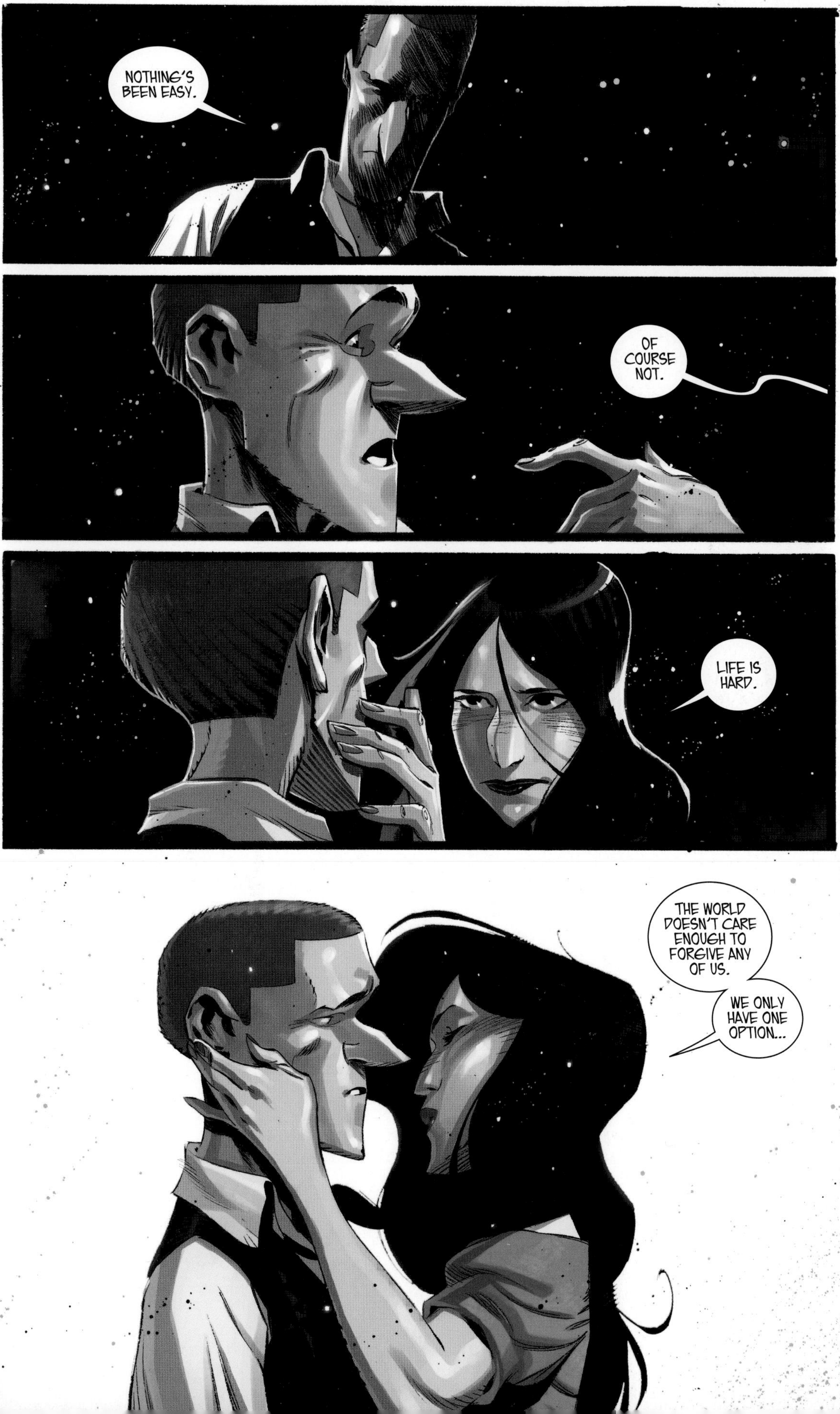
NOTHING'S BEEN EASY.
OF COURSE NOT.
LIFE IS HARD.
THE WORLD DOESN'T CARE ENOUGH TO FORGIVE ANY OF US.
WE ONLY HAVE ONE OPTION...

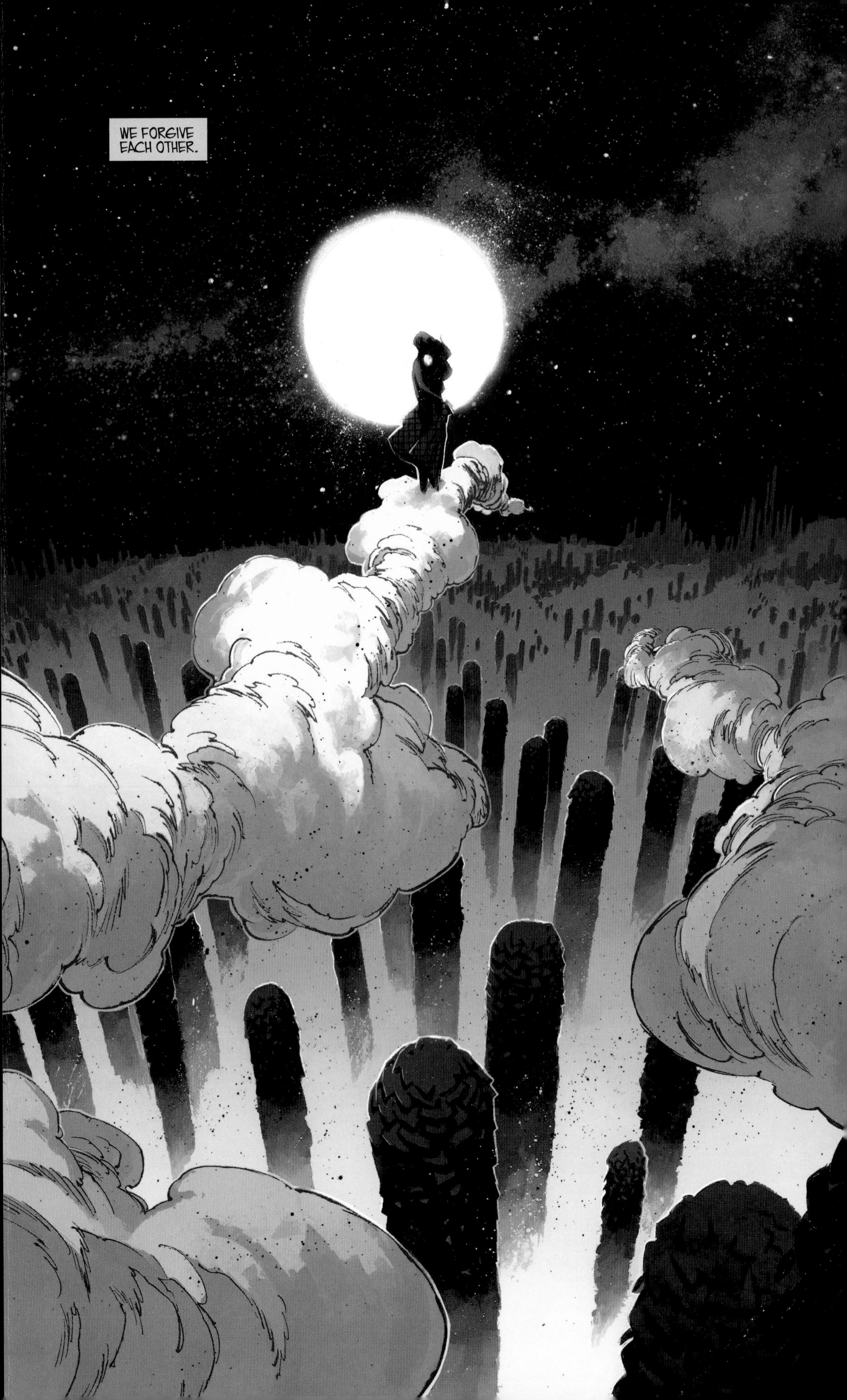
WE FORGIVE EACH OTHER.

37

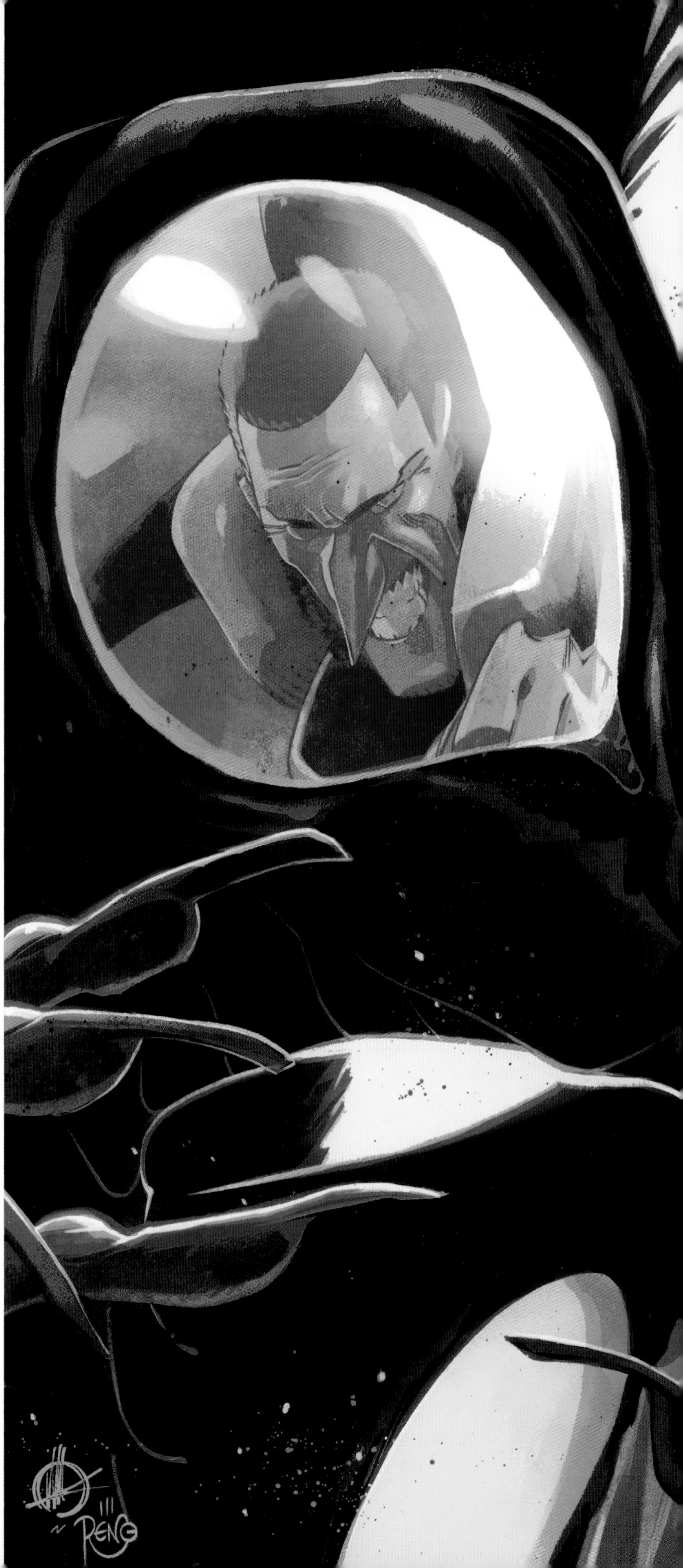

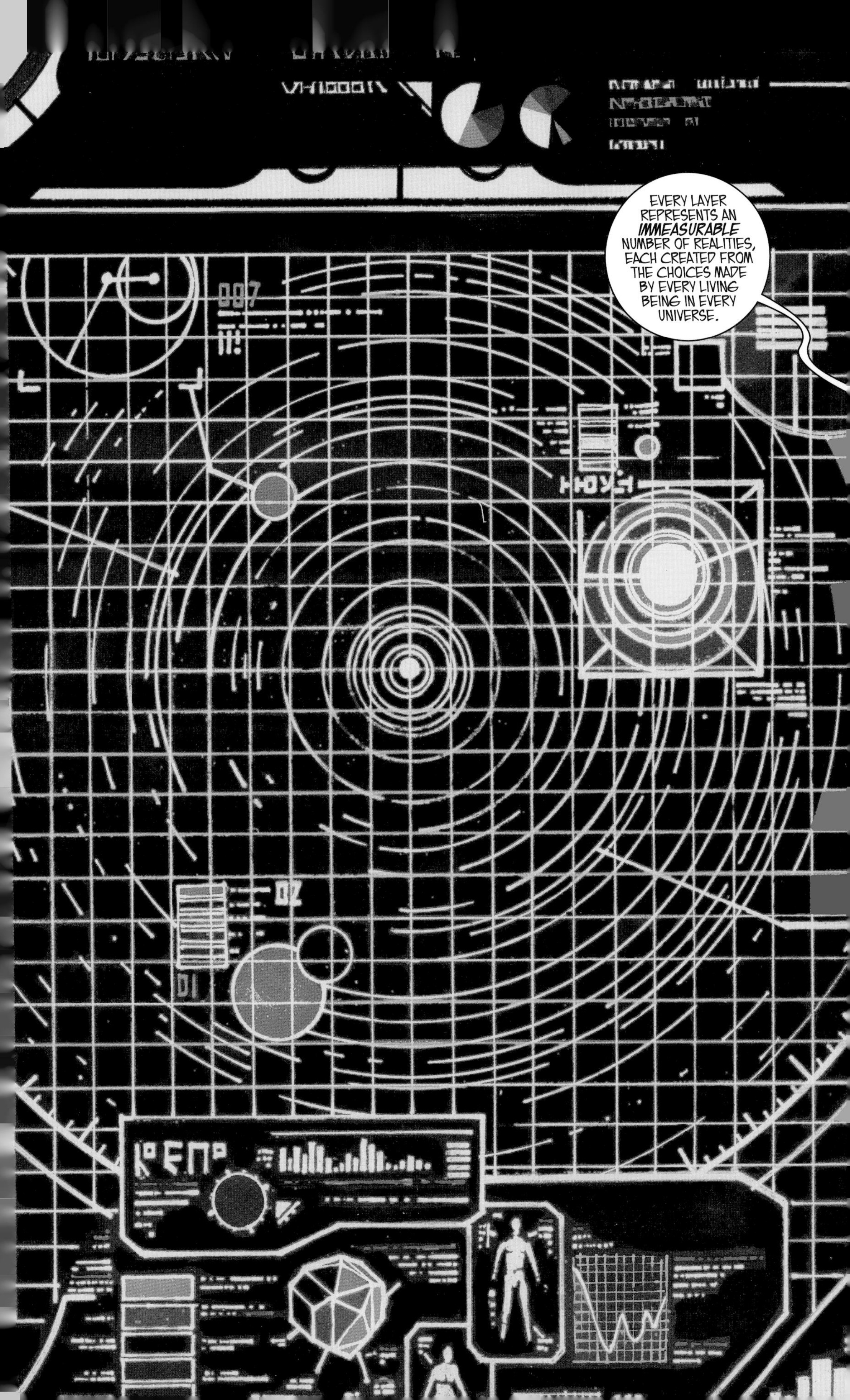
EVERY LAYER REPRESENTS AN IMMEASURABLE NUMBER OF REALITIES, EACH CREATED FROM THE CHOICES MADE BY EVERY LIVING BEING IN EVERY UNIVERSE.

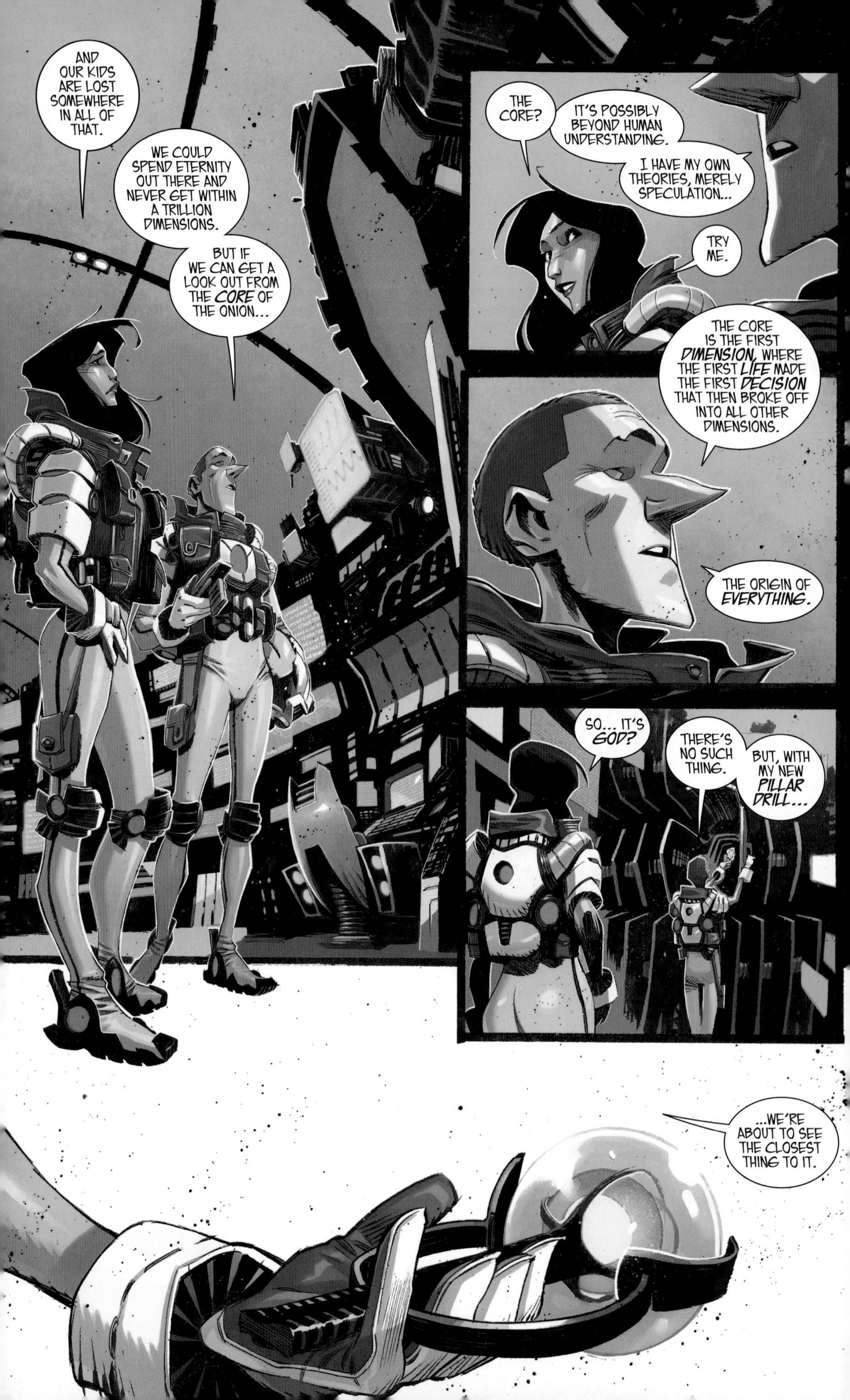
AND OUR KIDS ARE LOST SOMEWHERE IN ALL OF THAT.
WE COULD SPEND ETERNITY OUT THERE AND NEVER GET WITHIN A TRILLION DIMENSIONS.
BUT IF WE CAN GET A LOOK OUT FROM THE *CORE* OF THE ONION...
THE CORE?
IT'S POSSIBLY BEYOND HUMAN UNDERSTANDING.
I HAVE MY OWN THEORIES, MERELY SPECULATION...
TRY ME.
THE CORE IS THE FIRST *DIMENSION*, WHERE THE FIRST *LIFE* MADE THE FIRST *DECISION* THAT THEN BROKE OFF INTO ALL OTHER DIMENSIONS.
THE ORIGIN OF *EVERYTHING.*
SO... IT'S *GOD?*
THERE'S NO SUCH THING.
BUT, WITH MY NEW *PILLAR DRILL*...
...WE'RE ABOUT TO SEE THE CLOSEST THING TO IT.

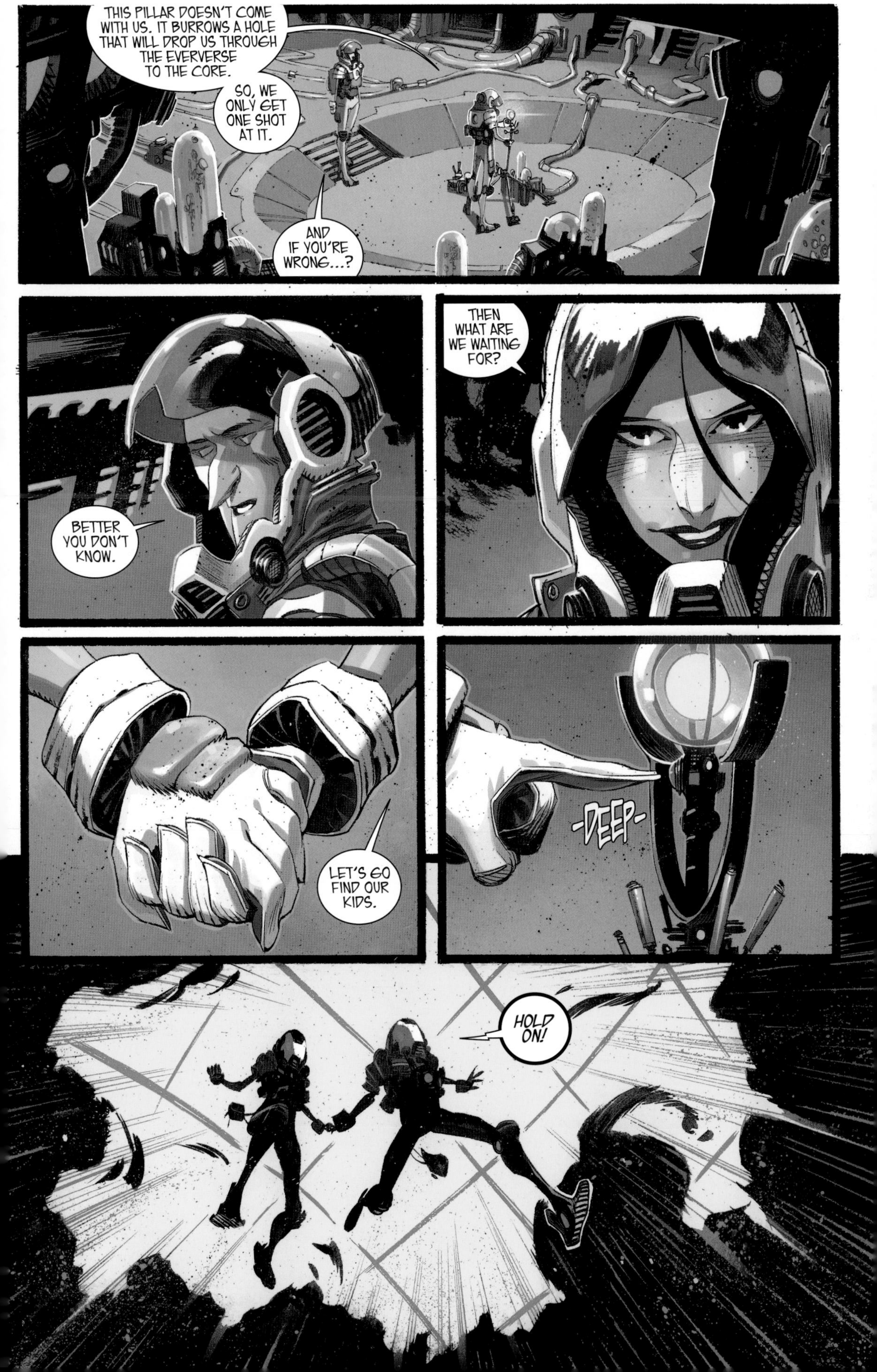
THIS PILLAR DOESN'T COME WITH US. IT BURROWS A HOLE THAT WILL DROP US THROUGH THE EVERVERSE TO THE CORE.
SO, WE ONLY GET ONE SHOT AT IT.
AND IF YOU'RE WRONG...?
BETTER YOU DON'T KNOW.
THEN WHAT ARE WE WAITING FOR?
LET'S GO FIND OUR KIDS.
-DEEP-
HOLD ON!

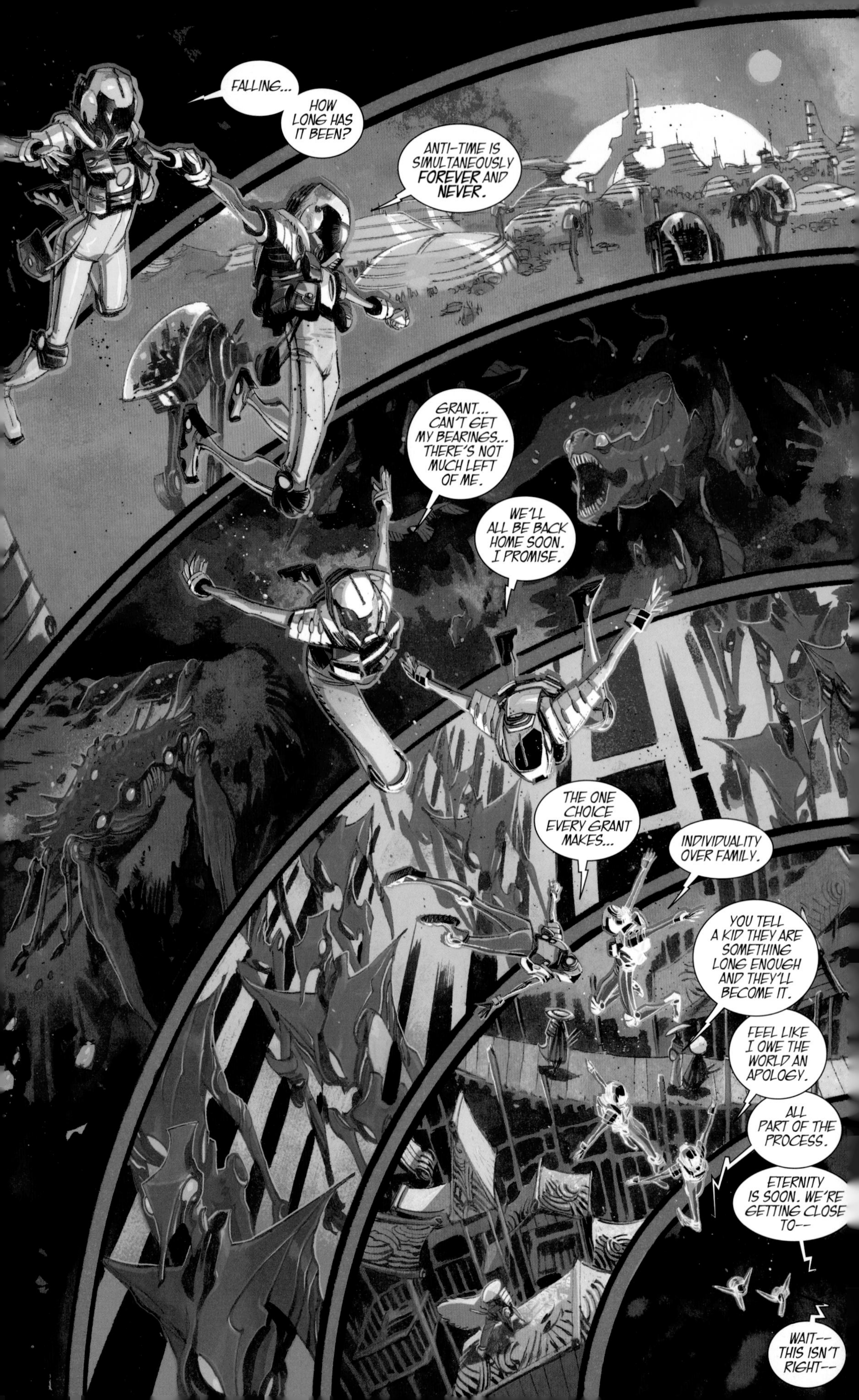
FALLING...
HOW LONG HAS IT BEEN?
ANTI-TIME IS SIMULTANEOUSLY FOREVER AND NEVER.
GRANT... CAN'T GET MY BEARINGS... THERE'S NOT MUCH LEFT OF ME.
WE'LL ALL BE BACK HOME SOON. I PROMISE.
THE ONE CHOICE EVERY GRANT MAKES...
INDIVIDUALITY OVER FAMILY.
YOU TELL A KID THEY ARE SOMETHING LONG ENOUGH AND THEY'LL BECOME IT.
FEEL LIKE I OWE THE WORLD AN APOLOGY.
ALL PART OF THE PROCESS.
ETERNITY IS SOON. WE'RE GETTING CLOSE TO--
WAIT-- THIS ISN'T RIGHT--

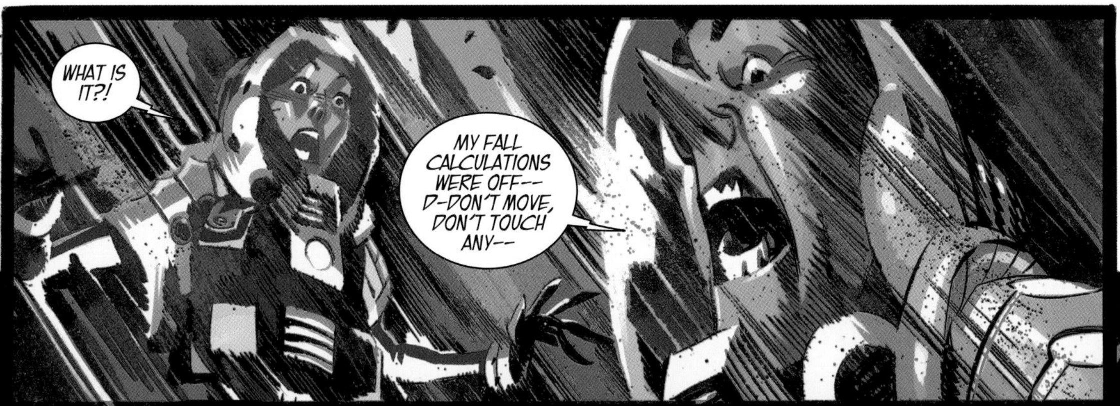
WHAT IS IT?!
MY FALL CALCULATIONS WERE OFF-- D-DON'T MOVE, DON'T TOUCH ANY--

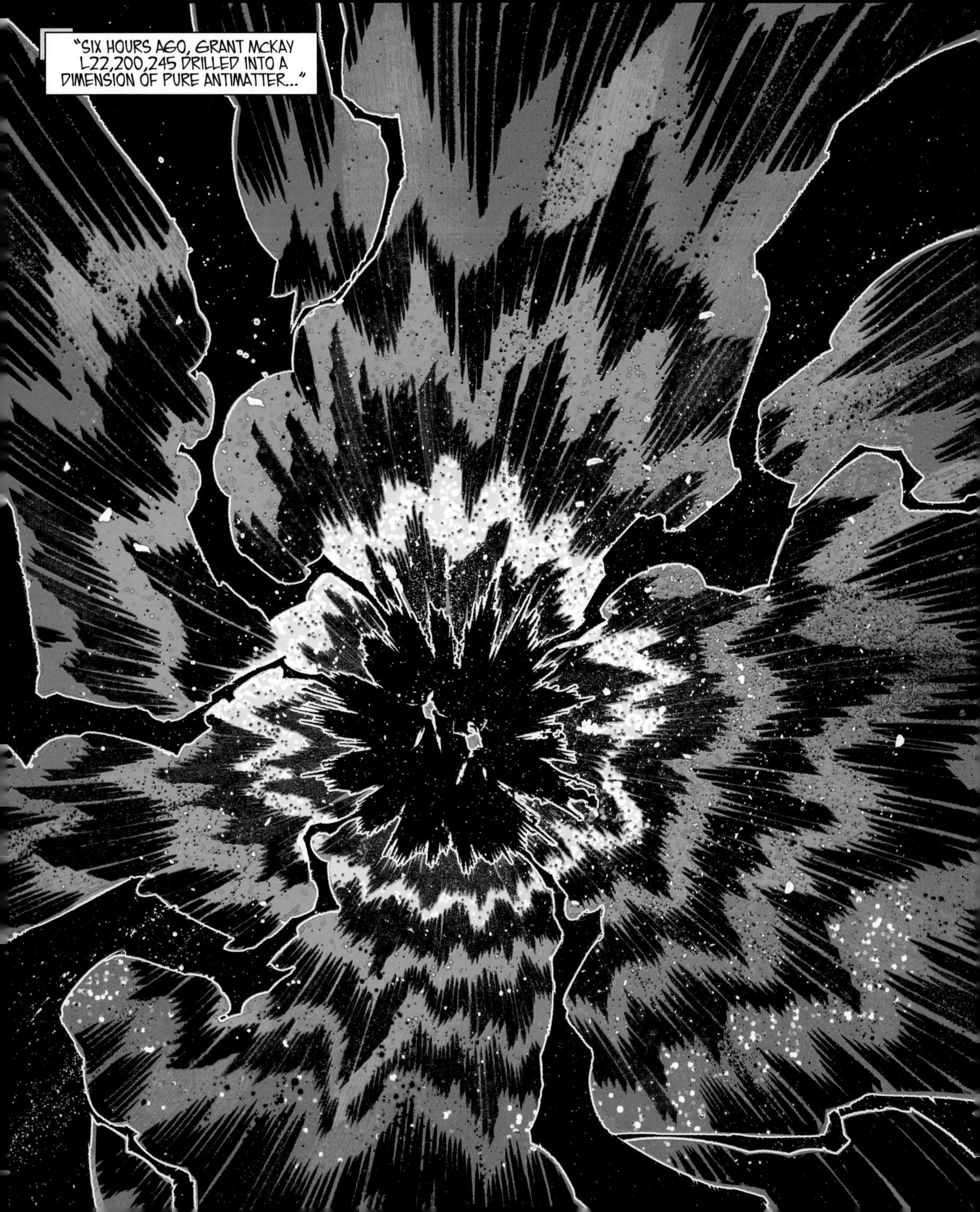
"SIX HOURS AGO, GRANT MCKAY L22,200,245 DRILLED INTO A DIMENSION OF PURE ANTIMATTER..."

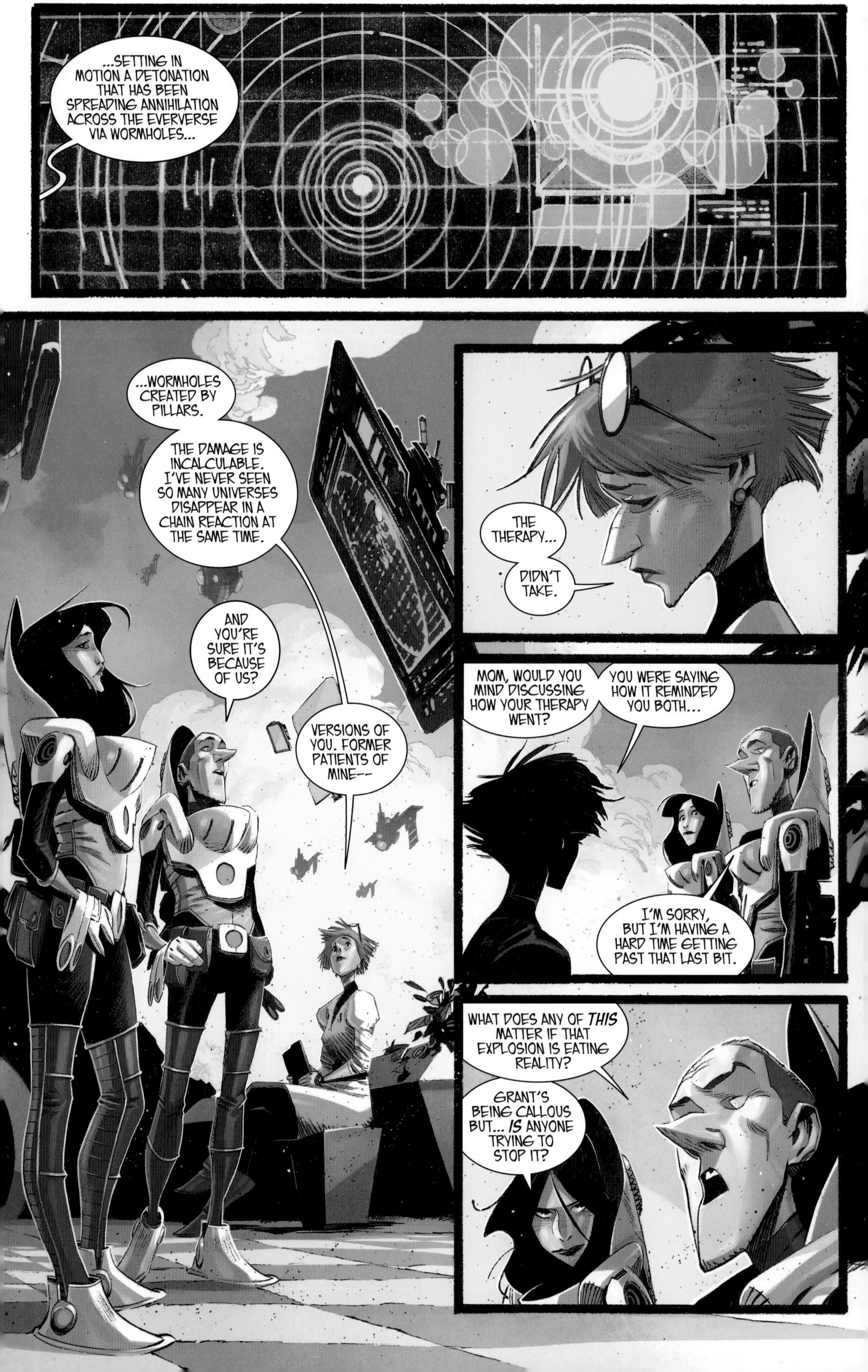
...SETTING IN MOTION A DETONATION THAT HAS BEEN SPREADING ANNIHILATION ACROSS THE EVERVERSE VIA WORMHOLES...
...WORMHOLES CREATED BY PILLARS.
THE DAMAGE IS INCALCULABLE. I'VE NEVER SEEN SO MANY UNIVERSES DISAPPEAR IN A CHAIN REACTION AT THE SAME TIME.
AND YOU'RE SURE IT'S BECAUSE OF US?
VERSIONS OF YOU. FORMER PATIENTS OF MINE--
THE THERAPY...
DIDN'T TAKE.
MOM, WOULD YOU MIND DISCUSSING HOW YOUR THERAPY WENT?
YOU WERE SAYING HOW IT REMINDED YOU BOTH...
I'M SORRY, BUT I'M HAVING A HARD TIME GETTING PAST THAT LAST BIT.
WHAT DOES ANY OF *THIS* MATTER IF THAT EXPLOSION IS EATING REALITY?
GRANT'S BEING CALLOUS BUT... *IS* ANYONE TRYING TO STOP IT?

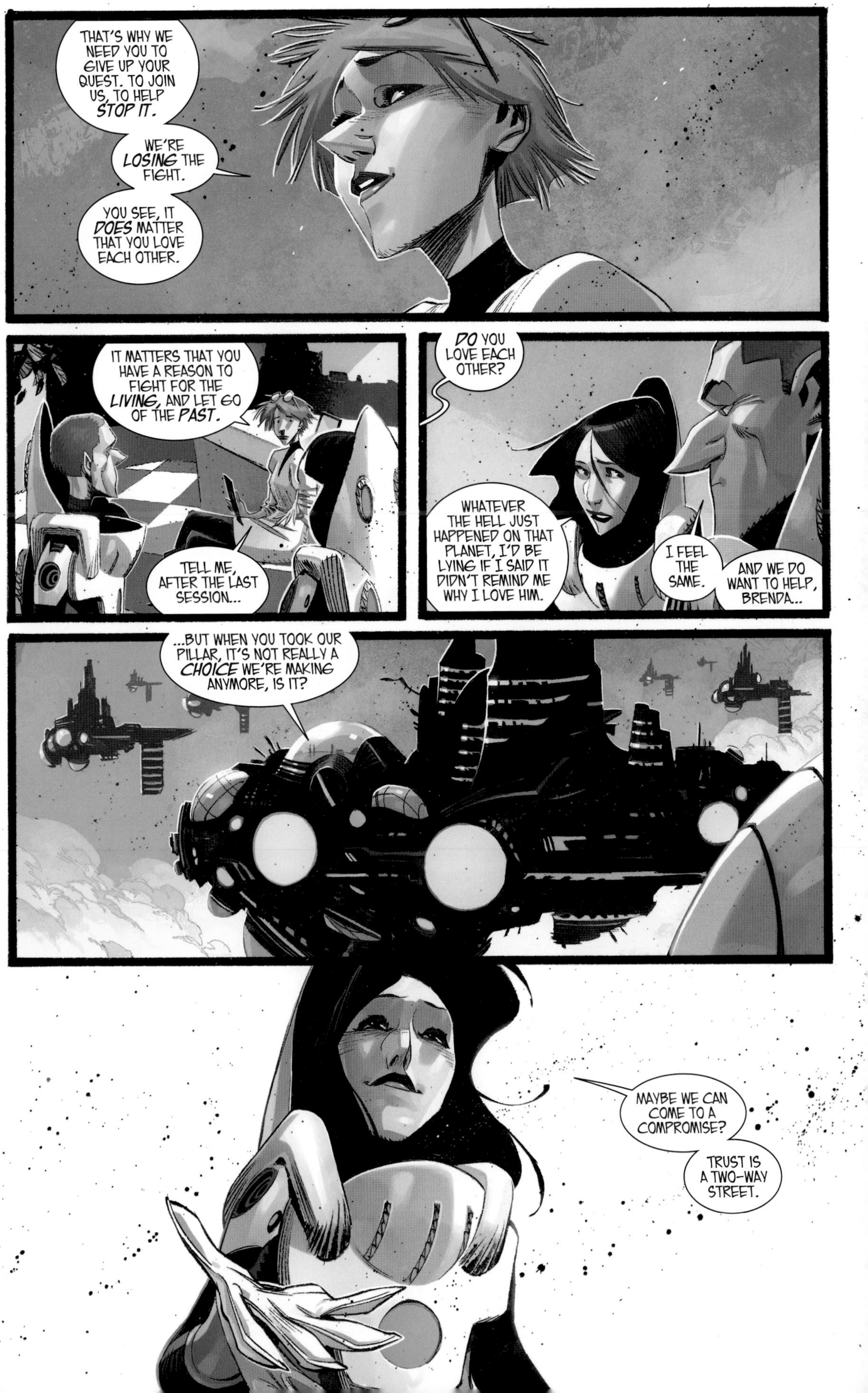
THAT'S WHY WE NEED YOU TO GIVE UP YOUR QUEST. TO JOIN US, TO HELP STOP IT.
WE'RE LOSING THE FIGHT.
YOU SEE, IT DOES MATTER THAT YOU LOVE EACH OTHER.
IT MATTERS THAT YOU HAVE A REASON TO FIGHT FOR THE LIVING, AND LET GO OF THE PAST.
TELL ME, AFTER THE LAST SESSION...
DO YOU LOVE EACH OTHER?
WHATEVER THE HELL JUST HAPPENED ON THAT PLANET, I'D BE LYING IF I SAID IT DIDN'T REMIND ME WHY I LOVE HIM.
I FEEL THE SAME.
AND WE DO WANT TO HELP, BRENDA...
...BUT WHEN YOU TOOK OUR PILLAR, IT'S NOT REALLY A CHOICE WE'RE MAKING ANYMORE, IS IT?
MAYBE WE CAN COME TO A COMPROMISE?
TRUST IS A TWO-WAY STREET.

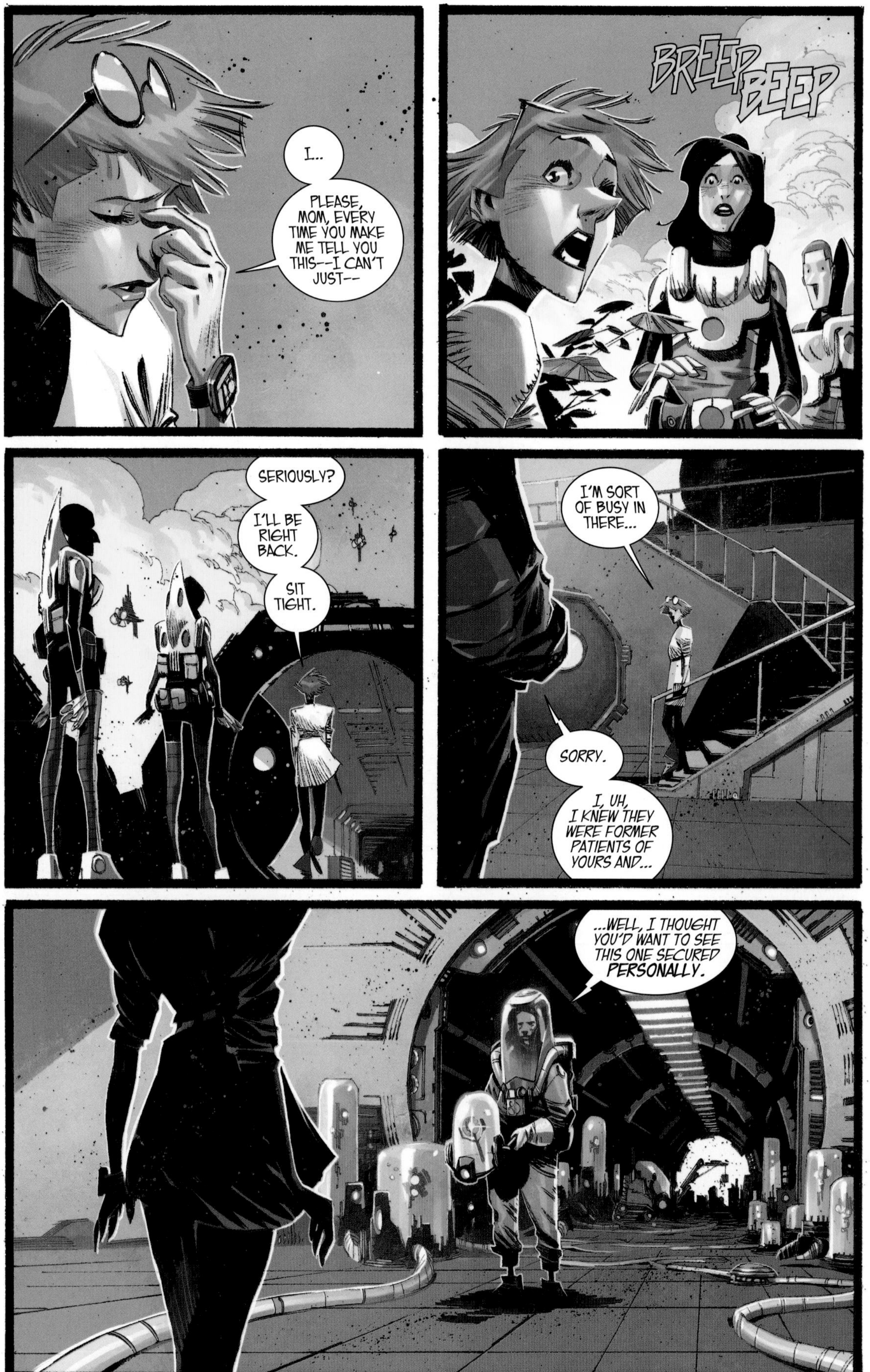
I...
PLEASE, MOM, EVERY TIME YOU MAKE ME TELL YOU THIS--I CAN'T JUST--
BREEP BEEP
SERIOUSLY?
I'LL BE RIGHT BACK.
SIT TIGHT.
I'M SORT OF BUSY IN THERE...
SORRY.
I, UH, I KNEW THEY WERE FORMER PATIENTS OF YOURS AND...
...WELL, I THOUGHT YOU'D WANT TO SEE THIS ONE SECURED **PERSONALLY**.

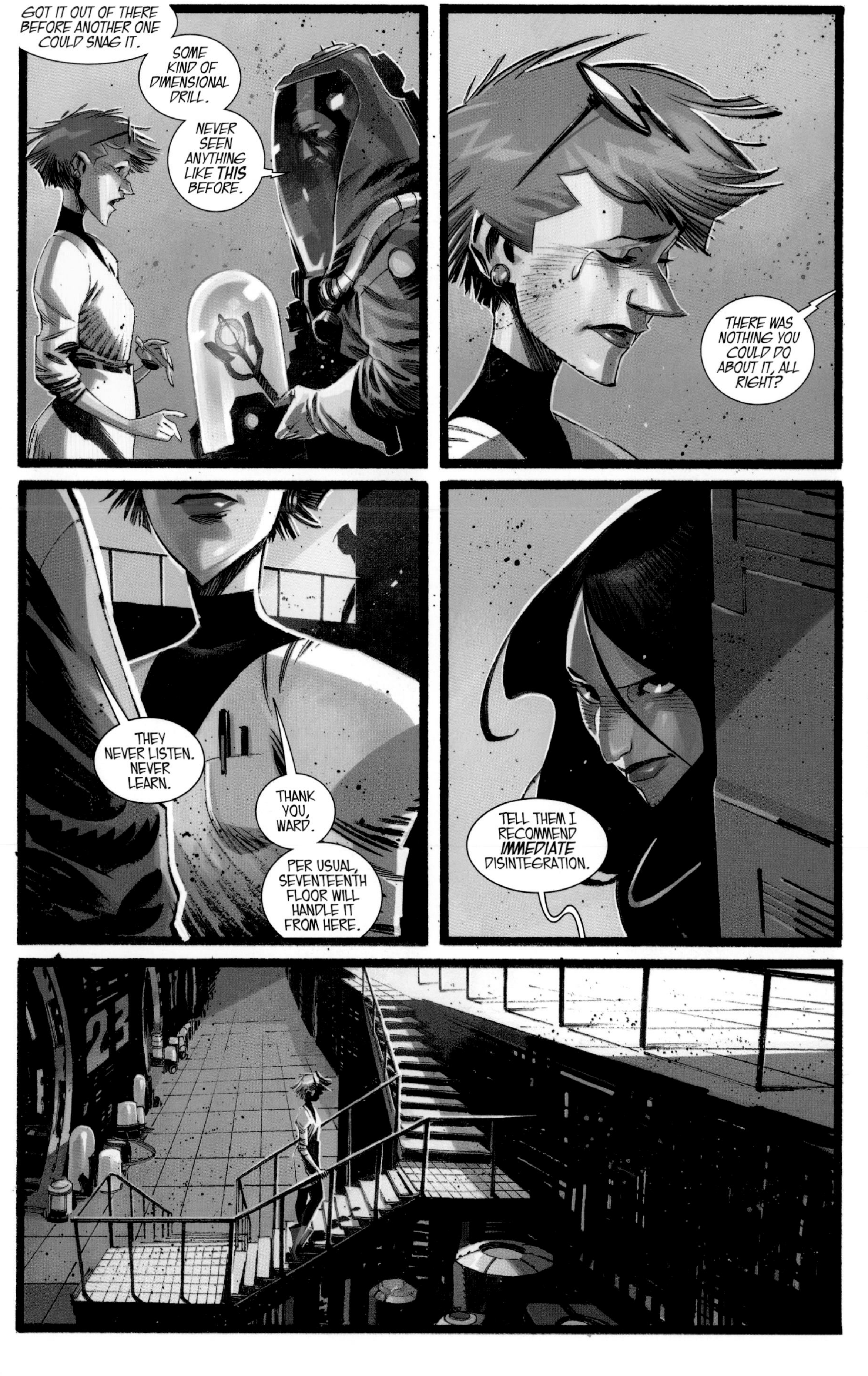
GOT IT OUT OF THERE BEFORE ANOTHER ONE COULD SNAG IT.
SOME KIND OF DIMENSIONAL DRILL.
NEVER SEEN ANYTHING LIKE THIS BEFORE.
THERE WAS NOTHING YOU COULD DO ABOUT IT, ALL RIGHT?
THEY NEVER LISTEN. NEVER LEARN.
THANK YOU, WARD.
PER USUAL, SEVENTEENTH FLOOR WILL HANDLE IT FROM HERE.
TELL THEM I RECOMMEND IMMEDIATE DISINTEGRATION.
23

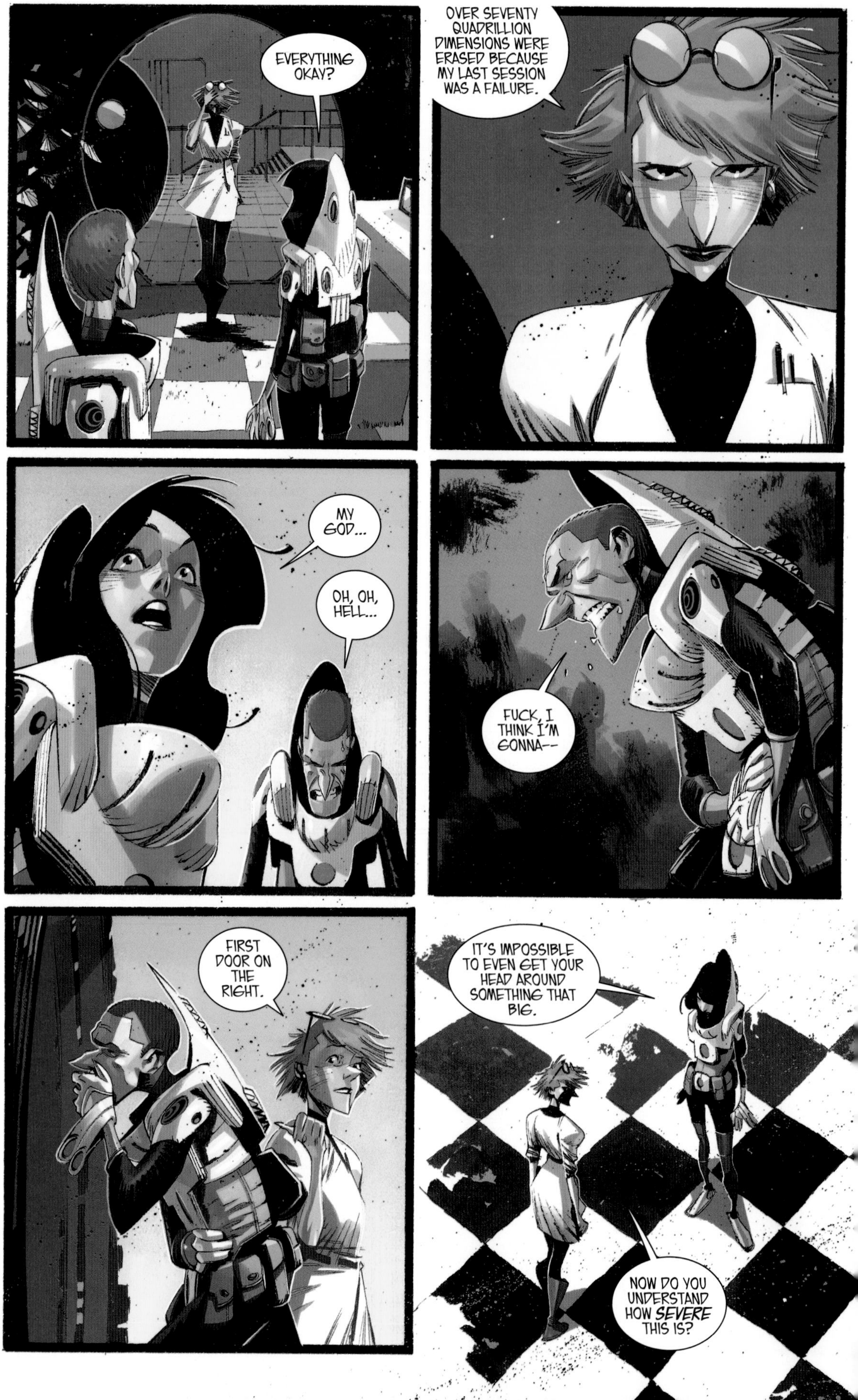
EVERYTHING OKAY?
OVER SEVENTY QUADRILLION DIMENSIONS WERE ERASED BECAUSE MY LAST SESSION WAS A FAILURE.
MY GOD...
OH, OH, HELL...
FUCK, I THINK I'M GONNA--
FIRST DOOR ON THE RIGHT.
IT'S IMPOSSIBLE TO EVEN GET YOUR HEAD AROUND SOMETHING THAT BIG.
NOW DO YOU UNDERSTAND HOW *SEVERE* THIS IS?

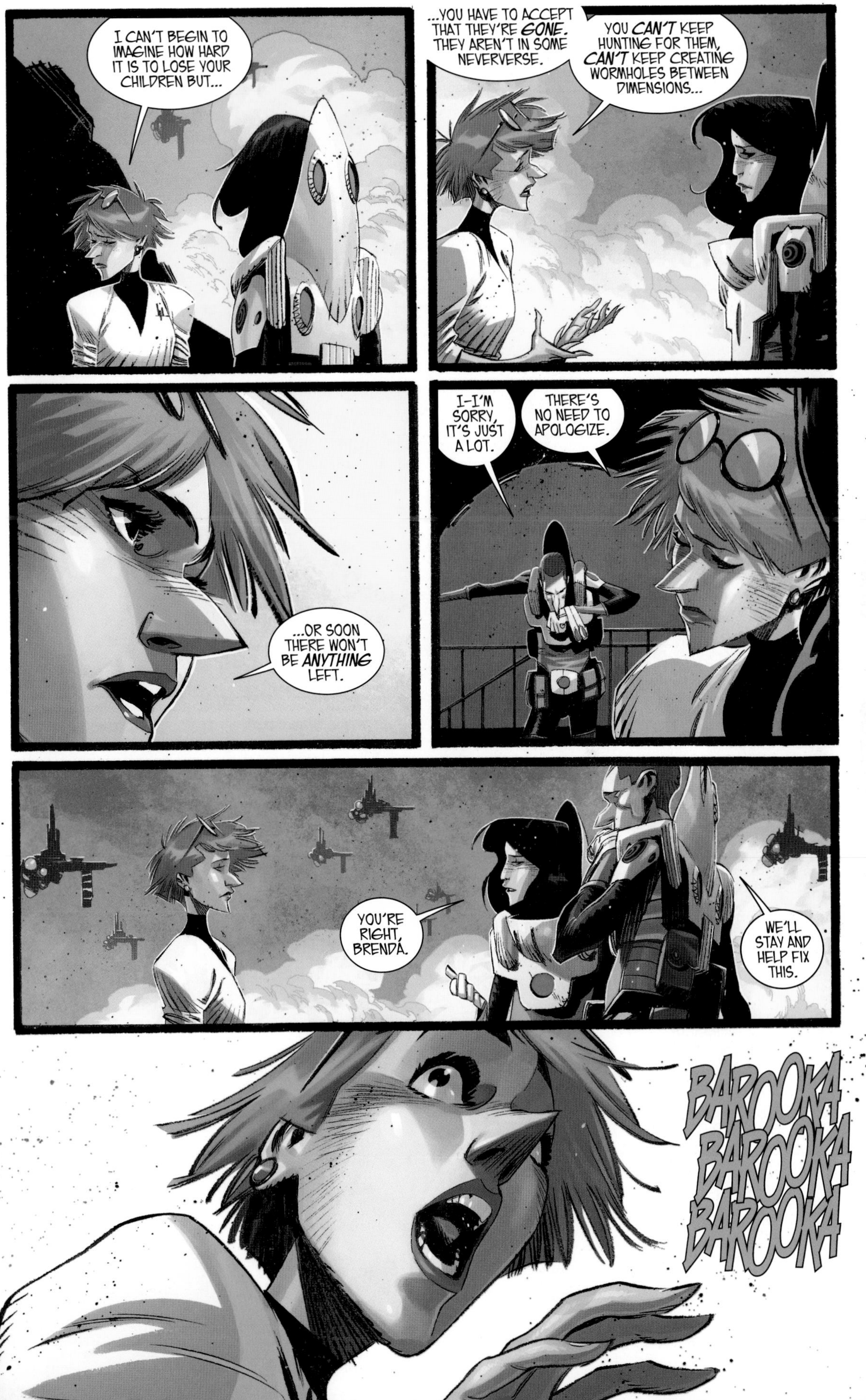
I CAN'T BEGIN TO IMAGINE HOW HARD IT IS TO LOSE YOUR CHILDREN BUT...
...YOU HAVE TO ACCEPT THAT THEY'RE GONE. THEY AREN'T IN SOME NEVERVERSE.
YOU CAN'T KEEP HUNTING FOR THEM, CAN'T KEEP CREATING WORMHOLES BETWEEN DIMENSIONS...
...OR SOON THERE WON'T BE ANYTHING LEFT.
I-I'M SORRY, IT'S JUST A LOT.
THERE'S NO NEED TO APOLOGIZE.
YOU'RE RIGHT, BRENDA.
WE'LL STAY AND HELP FIX THIS.
BAROOKA
BAROOKA
BAROOKA

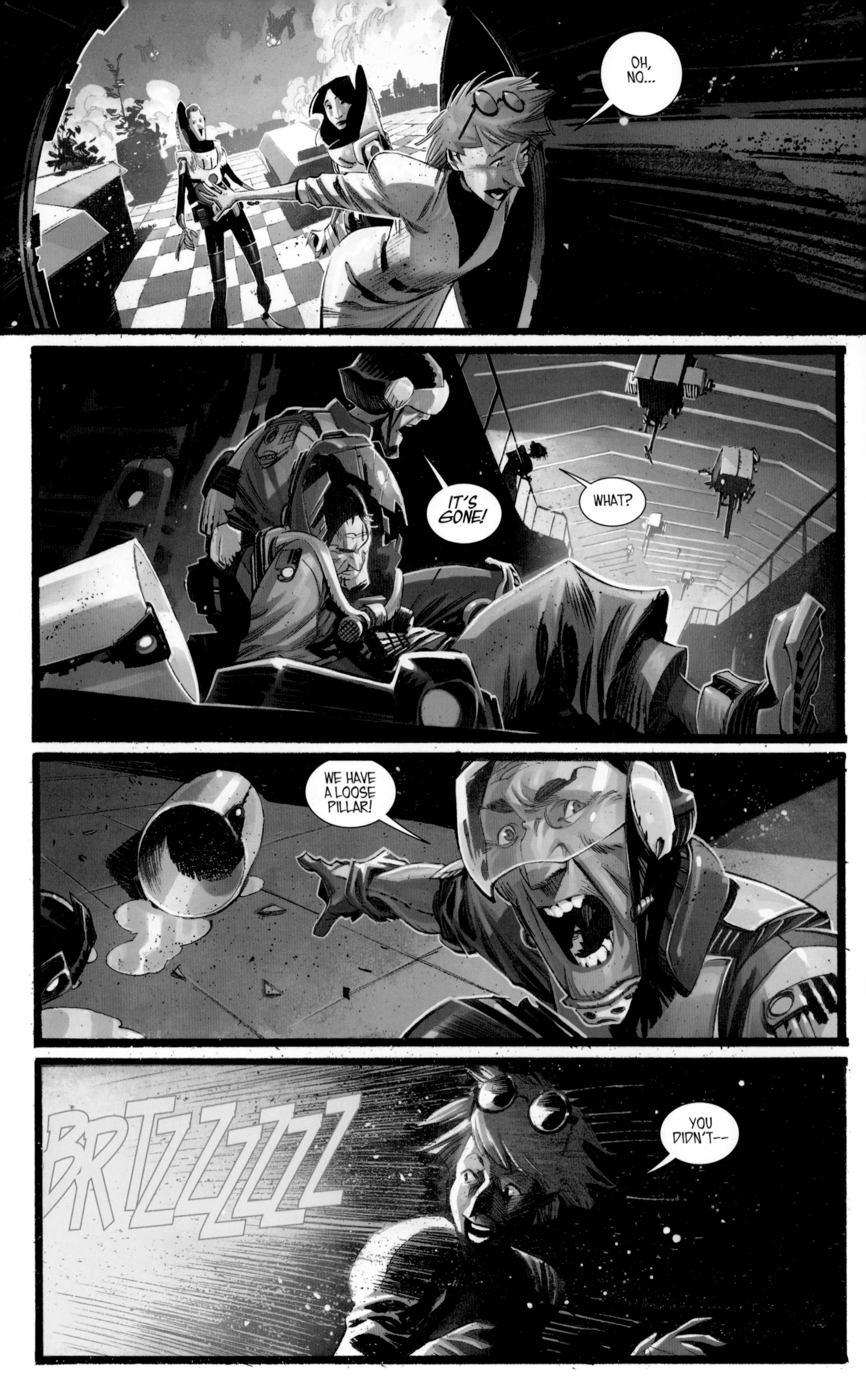
OH, NO...
IT'S GONE!
WHAT?
WE HAVE A LOOSE PILLAR!
BRTZZZZZ
YOU DIDN'T--

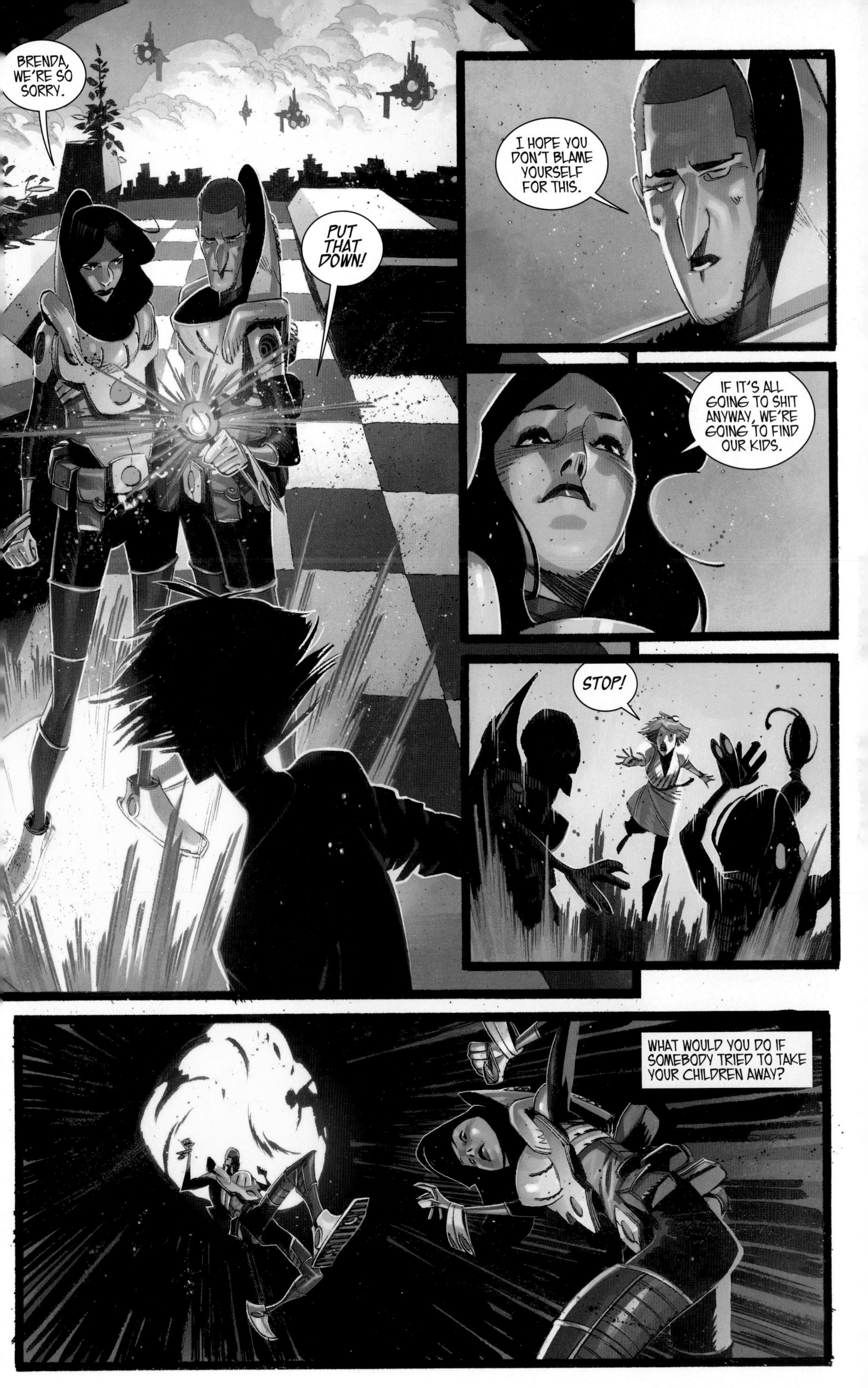
BRENDA, WE'RE SO SORRY.
PUT THAT DOWN!
I HOPE YOU DON'T BLAME YOURSELF FOR THIS.
IF IT'S ALL GOING TO SHIT ANYWAY, WE'RE GOING TO FIND OUR KIDS.
STOP!
WHAT WOULD YOU DO IF SOMEBODY TRIED TO TAKE YOUR CHILDREN AWAY?

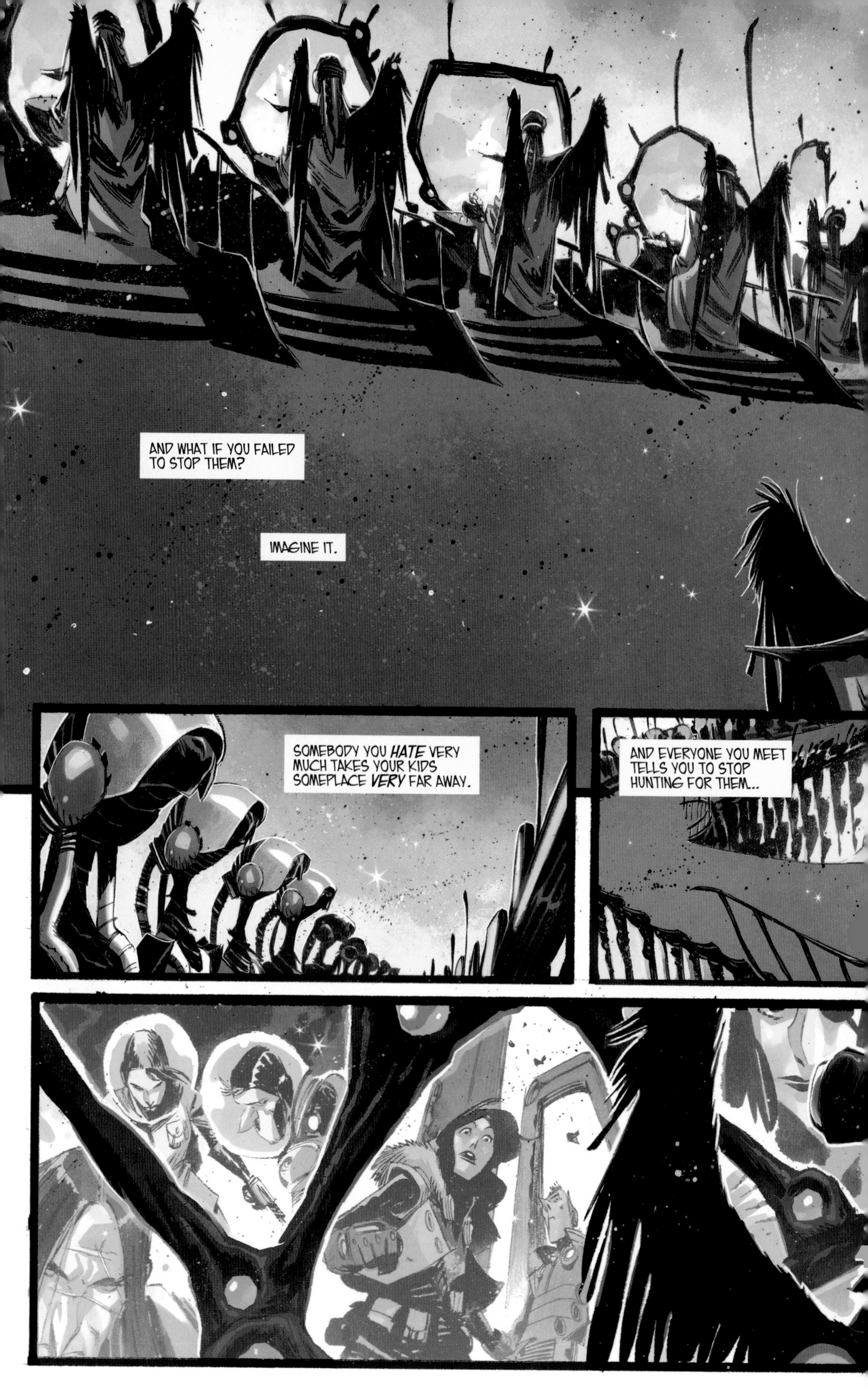
AND WHAT IF YOU FAILED TO STOP THEM?
IMAGINE IT.
SOMEBODY YOU HATE VERY MUCH TAKES YOUR KIDS SOMEPLACE VERY FAR AWAY.
AND EVERYONE YOU MEET TELLS YOU TO STOP HUNTING FOR THEM...

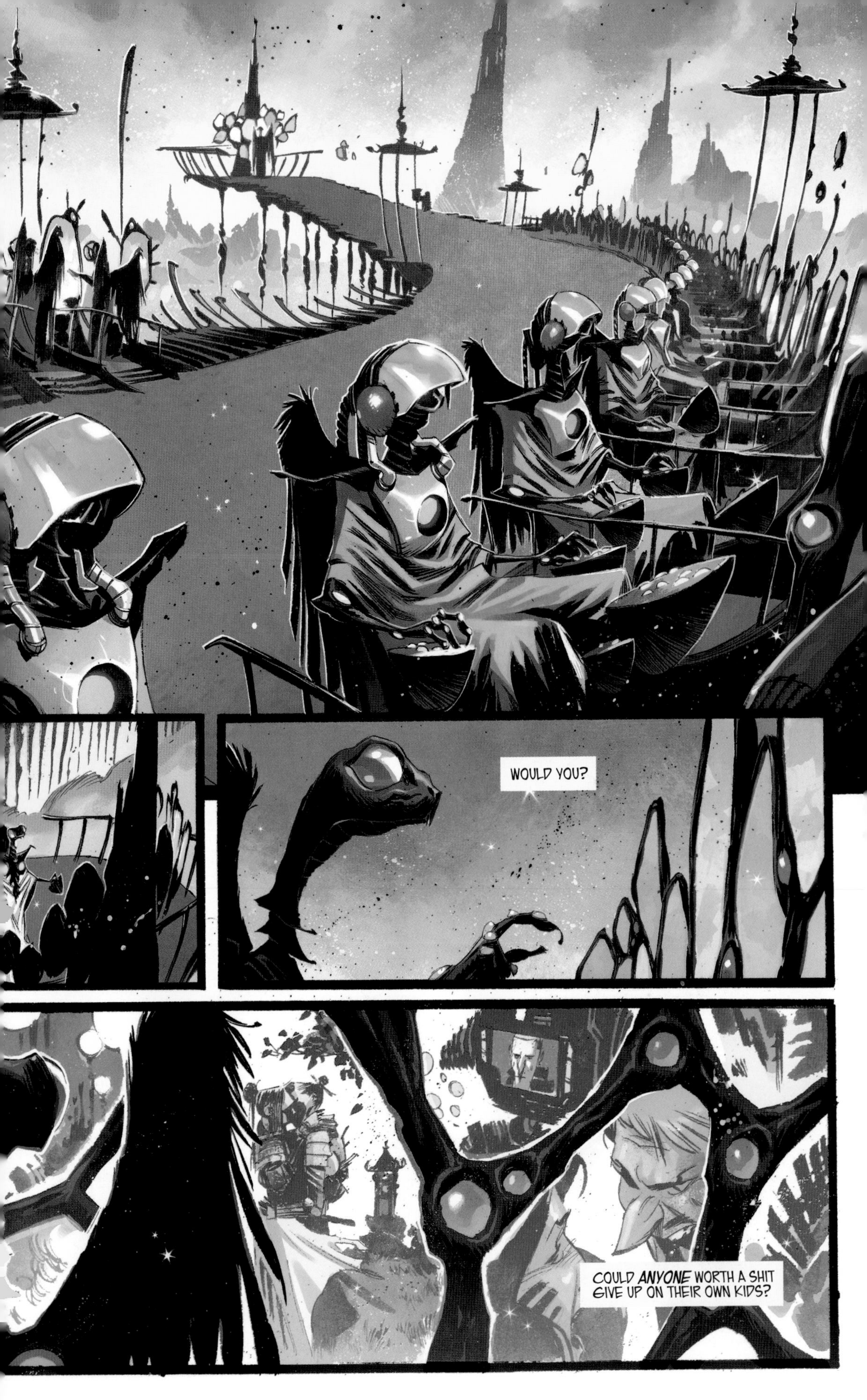
WOULD YOU?
COULD ANYONE WORTH A SHIT GIVE UP ON THEIR OWN KIDS?

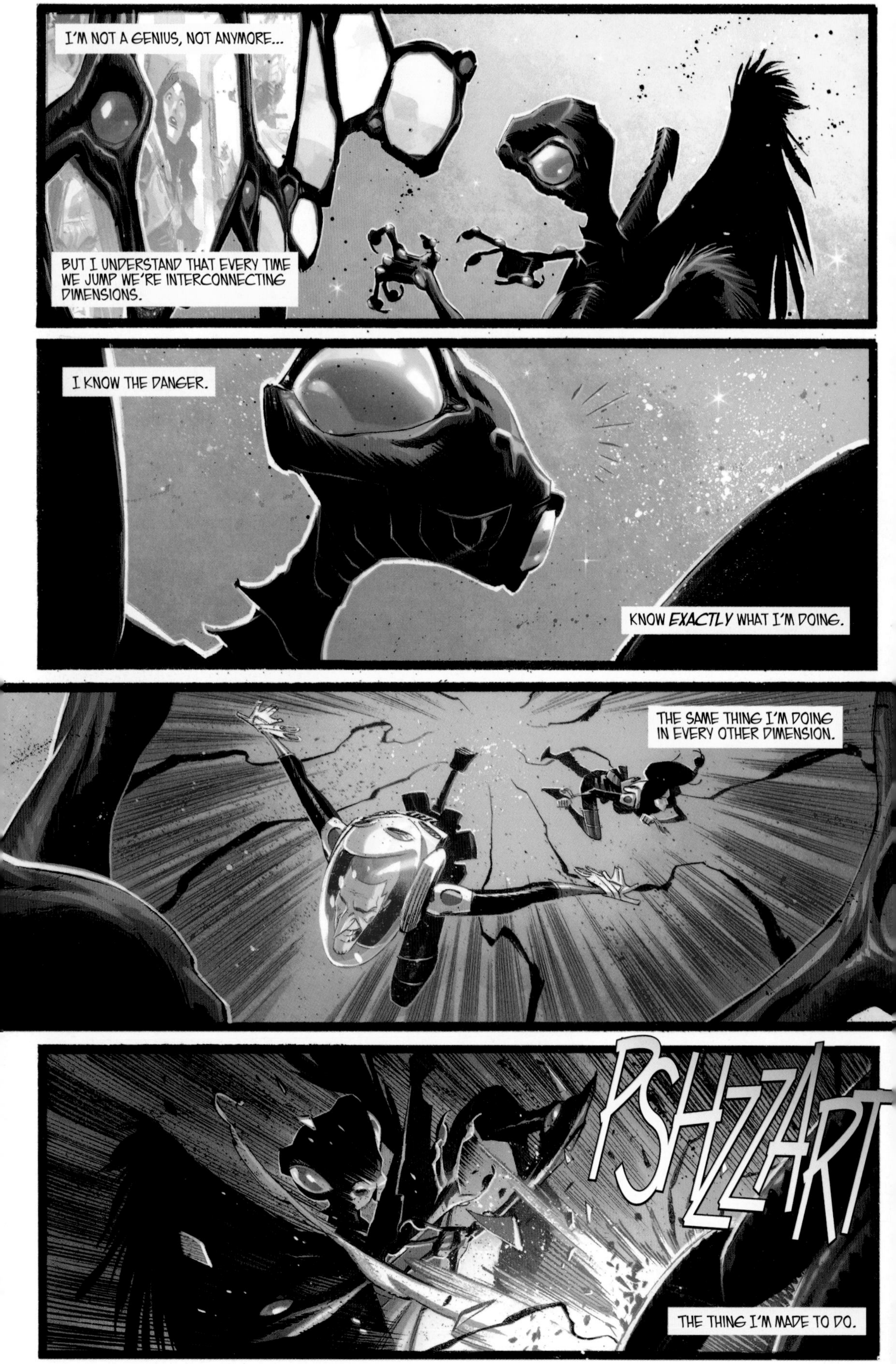
I'M NOT A GENIUS, NOT ANYMORE...
BUT I UNDERSTAND THAT EVERY TIME WE JUMP WE'RE INTERCONNECTING DIMENSIONS.
I KNOW THE DANGER.
KNOW EXACTLY WHAT I'M DOING.
THE SAME THING I'M DOING IN EVERY OTHER DIMENSION.
PSHZZART
THE THING I'M MADE TO DO.

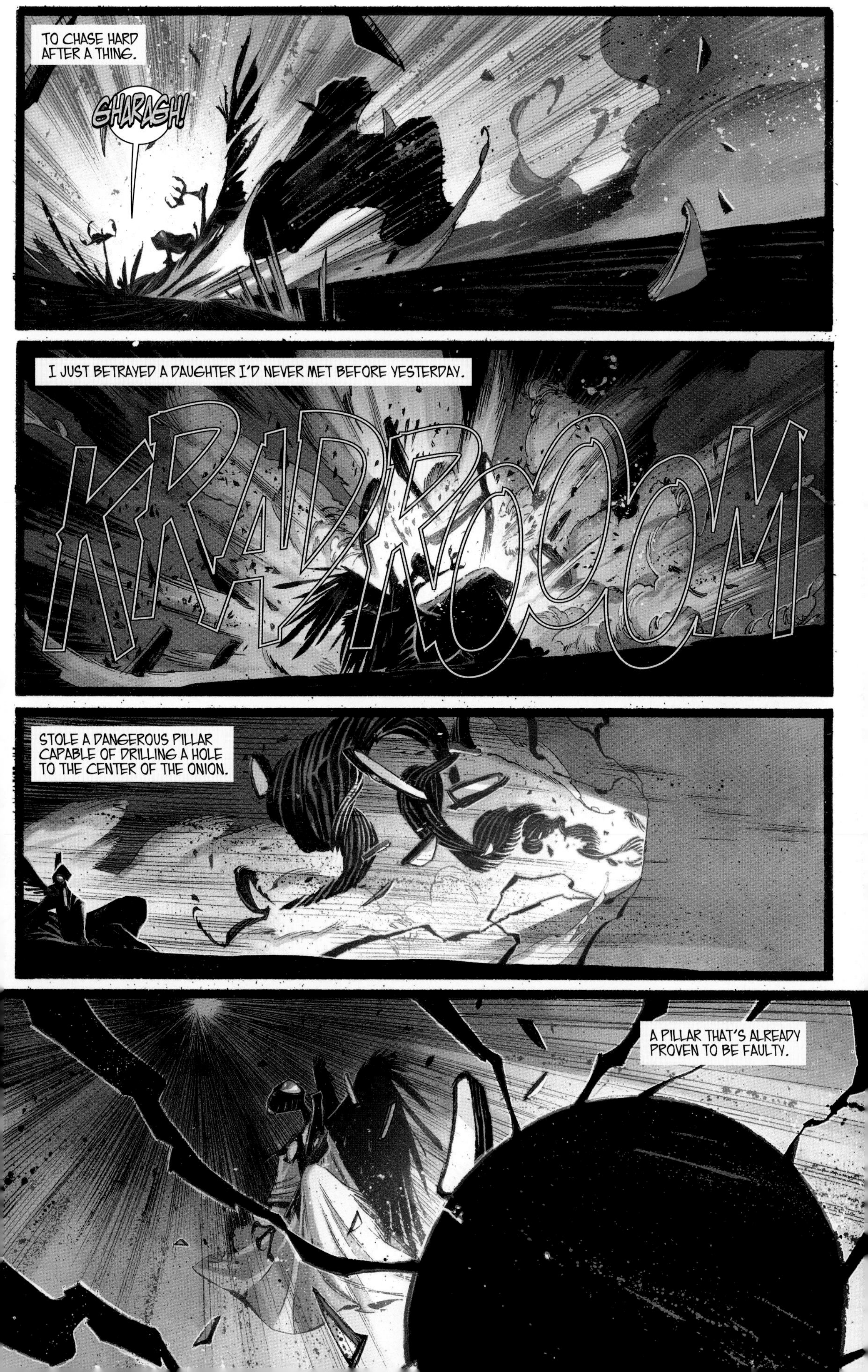

TO CHASE HARD AFTER A THING.
GHARASH!
I JUST BETRAYED A DAUGHTER I'D NEVER MET BEFORE YESTERDAY.
KRADROOOM
STOLE A DANGEROUS PILLAR CAPABLE OF DRILLING A HOLE TO THE CENTER OF THE ONION.
A PILLAR THAT'S ALREADY PROVEN TO BE FAULTY.

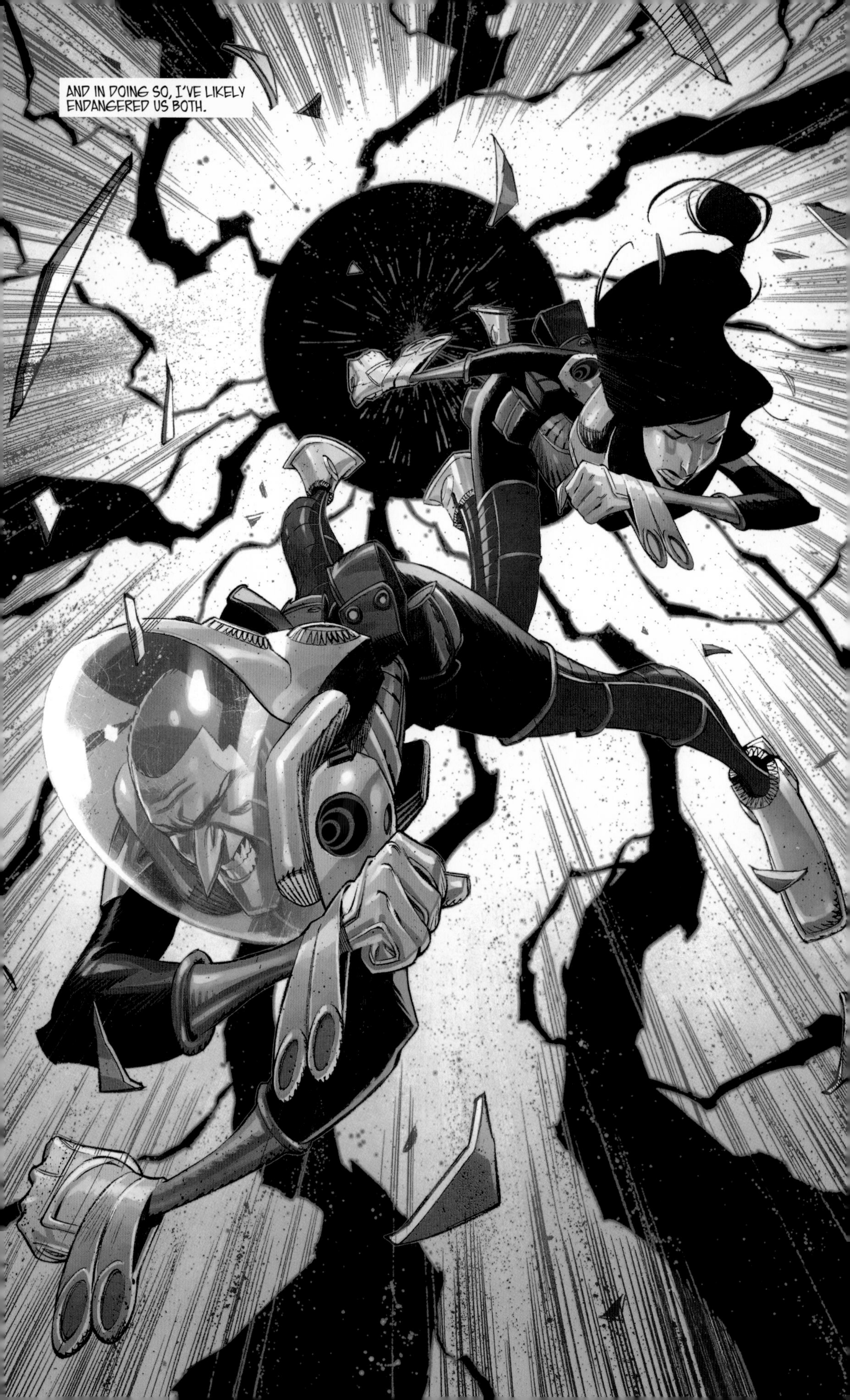
AND IN DOING SO, I'VE LIKELY ENDANGERED US BOTH.

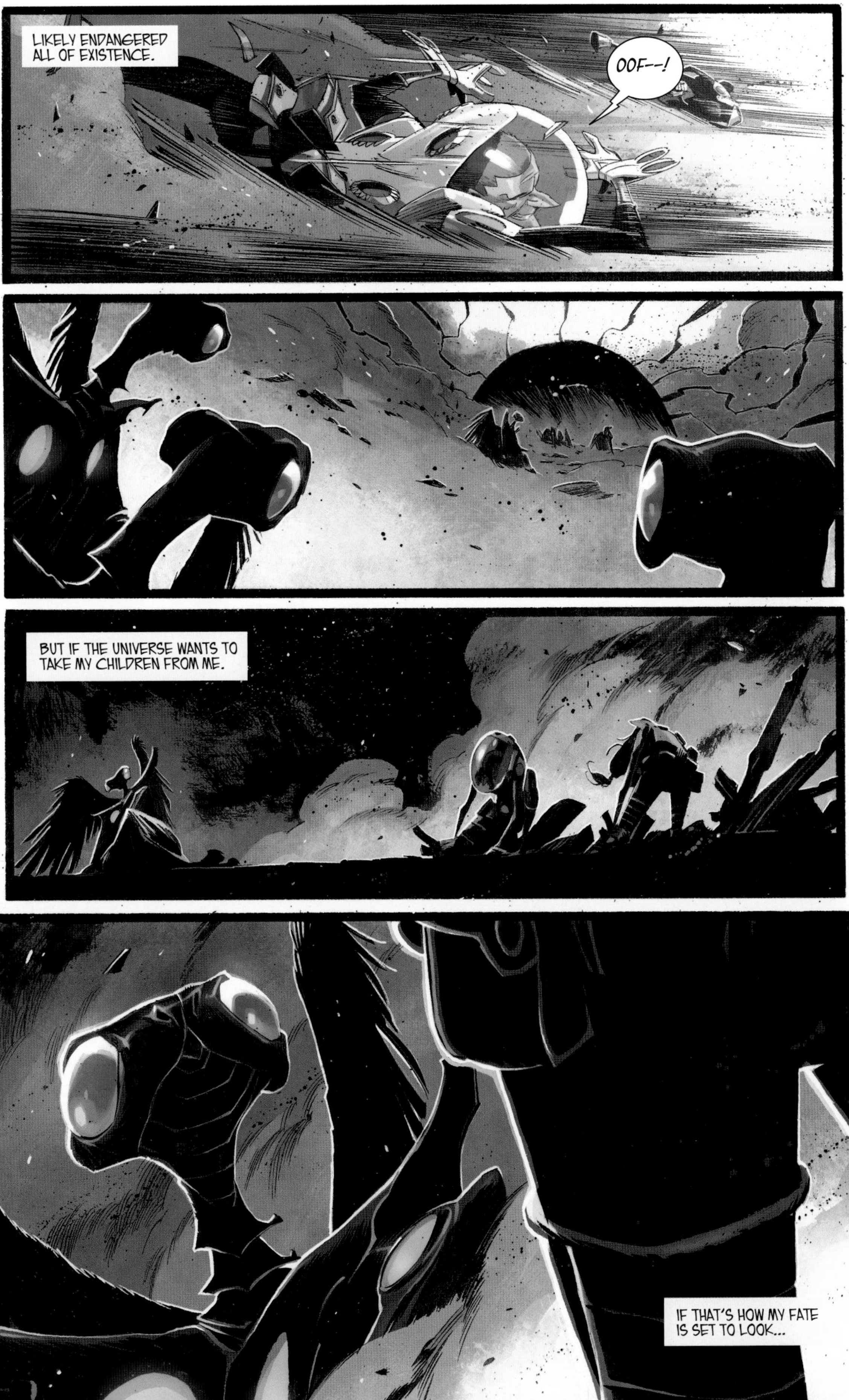
LIKELY ENDANGERED ALL OF EXISTENCE.
OOF--!
BUT IF THE UNIVERSE WANTS TO TAKE MY CHILDREN FROM ME.
IF THAT'S HOW MY FATE IS SET TO LOOK...

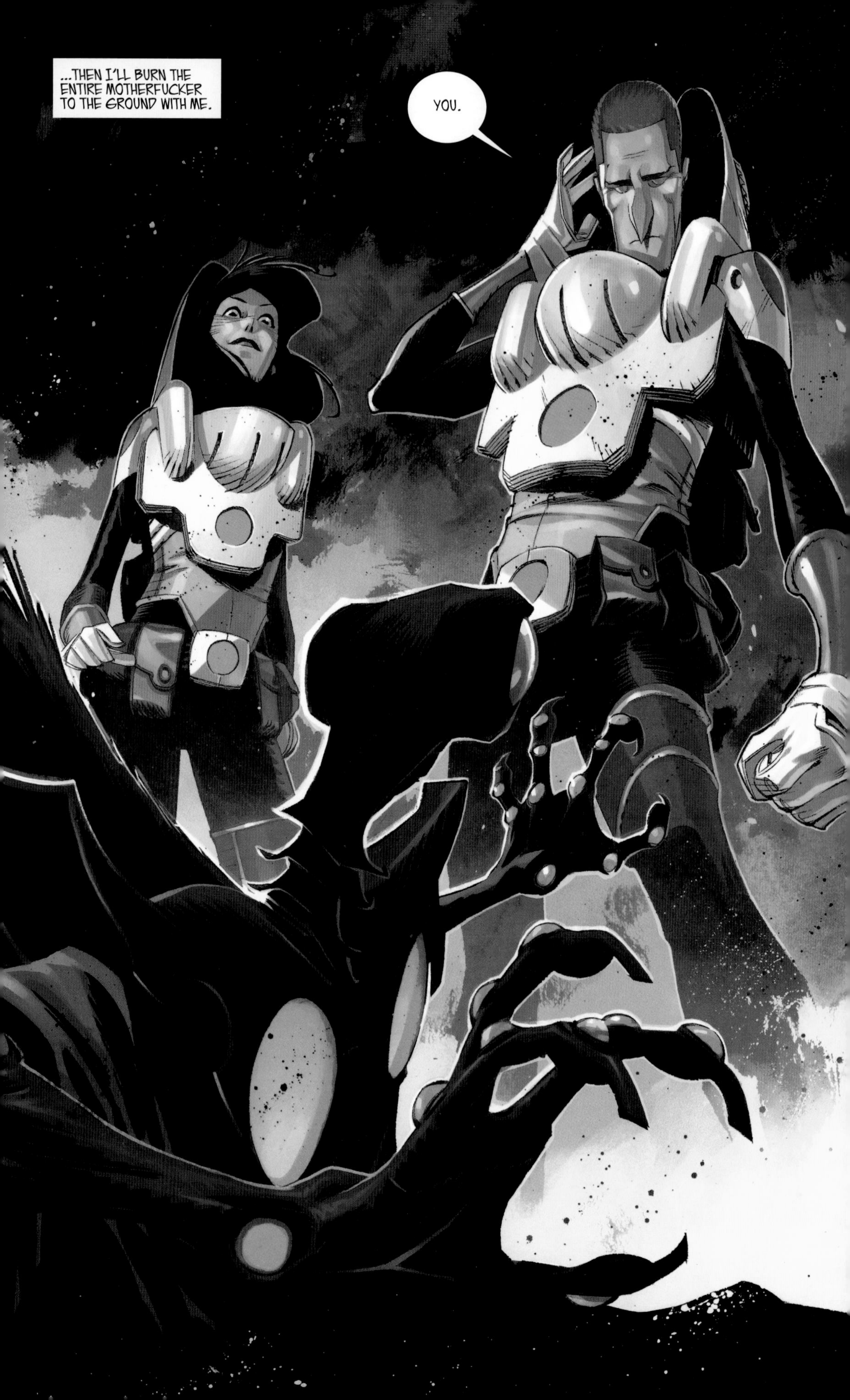
...THEN I'LL BURN THE ENTIRE MOTHERFUCKER TO THE GROUND WITH ME.
YOU.

38

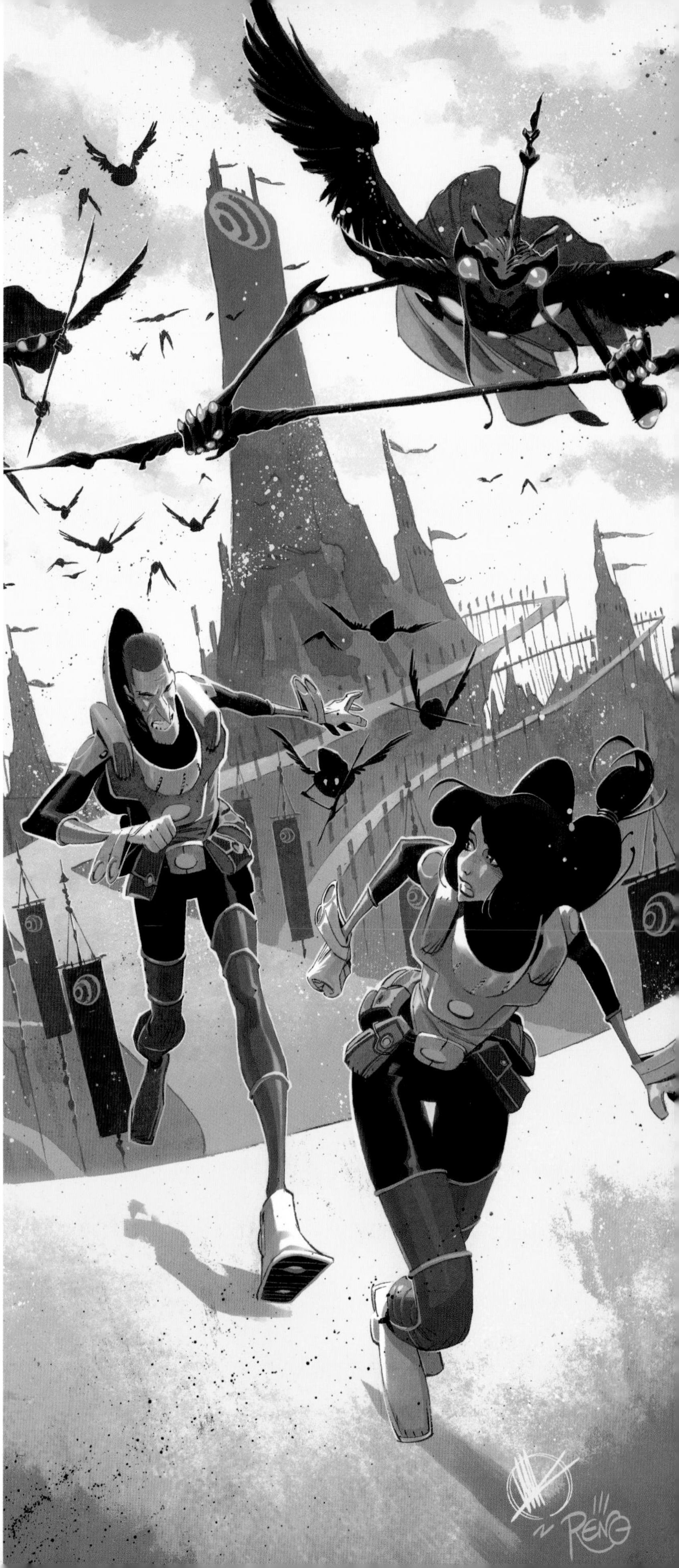

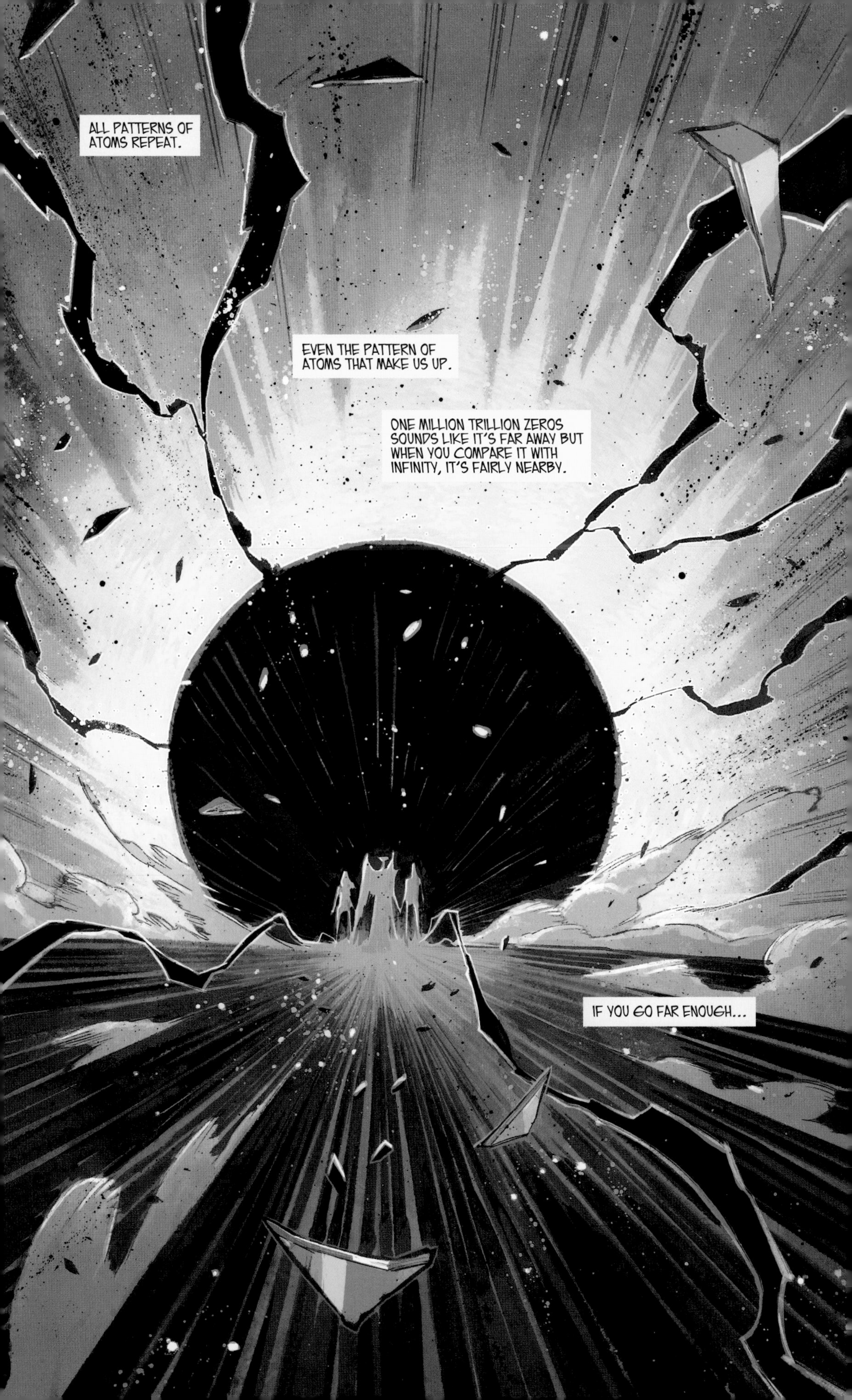
ALL PATTERNS OF ATOMS REPEAT.
EVEN THE PATTERN OF ATOMS THAT MAKE US UP.
ONE MILLION TRILLION ZEROS SOUNDS LIKE IT'S FAR AWAY BUT WHEN YOU COMPARE IT WITH INFINITY, IT'S FAIRLY NEARBY.
IF YOU GO FAR ENOUGH...

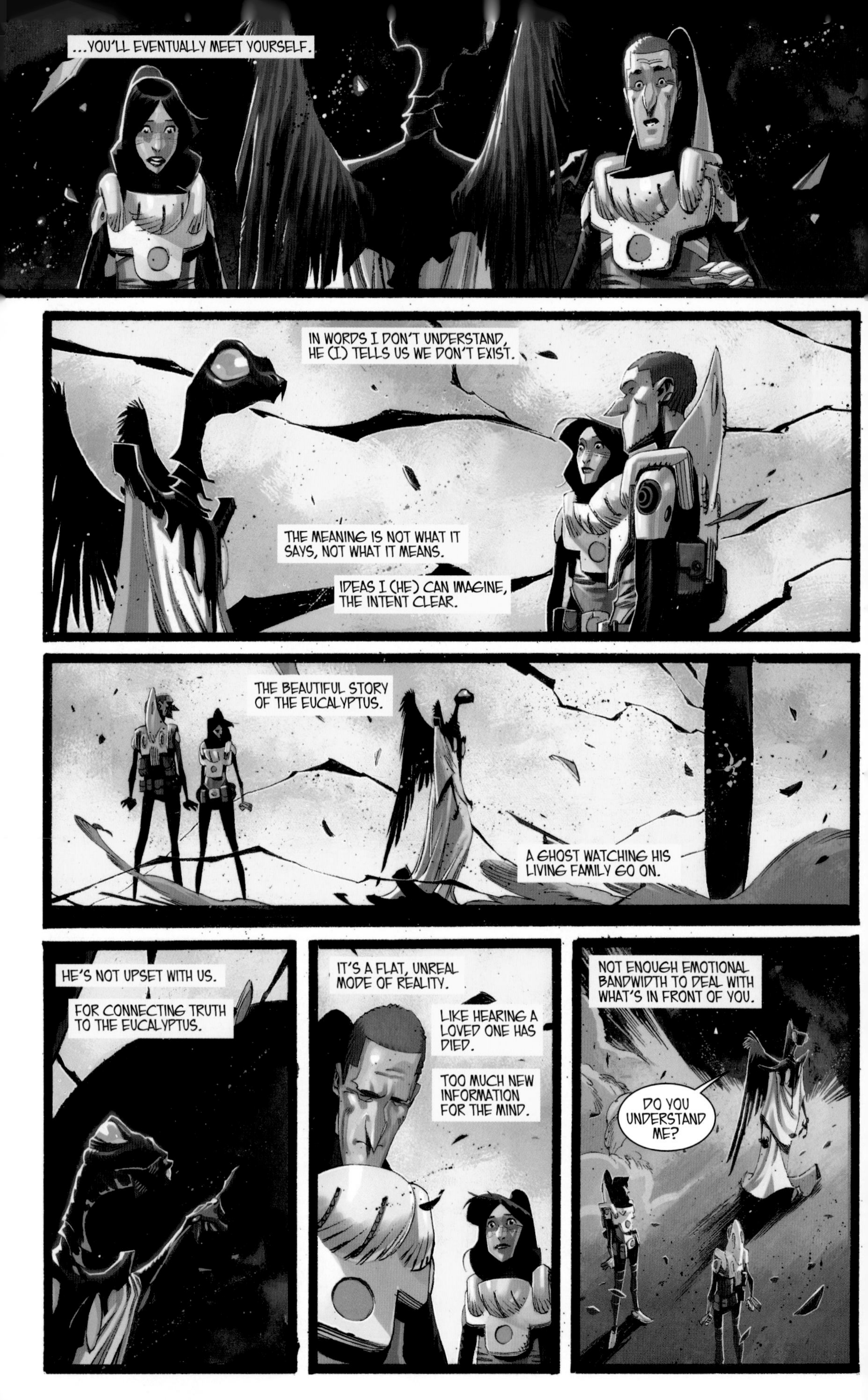

...YOU'LL EVENTUALLY MEET YOURSELF.
IN WORDS I DON'T UNDERSTAND, HE (I) TELLS US WE DON'T EXIST.
THE MEANING IS NOT WHAT IT SAYS, NOT WHAT IT MEANS.
IDEAS I (HE) CAN IMAGINE, THE INTENT CLEAR.
THE BEAUTIFUL STORY OF THE EUCALYPTUS.
A GHOST WATCHING HIS LIVING FAMILY GO ON.
HE'S NOT UPSET WITH US.
FOR CONNECTING TRUTH TO THE EUCALYPTUS.
IT'S A FLAT, UNREAL MODE OF REALITY.
LIKE HEARING A LOVED ONE HAS DIED.
TOO MUCH NEW INFORMATION FOR THE MIND.
NOT ENOUGH EMOTIONAL BANDWIDTH TO DEAL WITH WHAT'S IN FRONT OF YOU.
DO YOU UNDERSTAND ME?

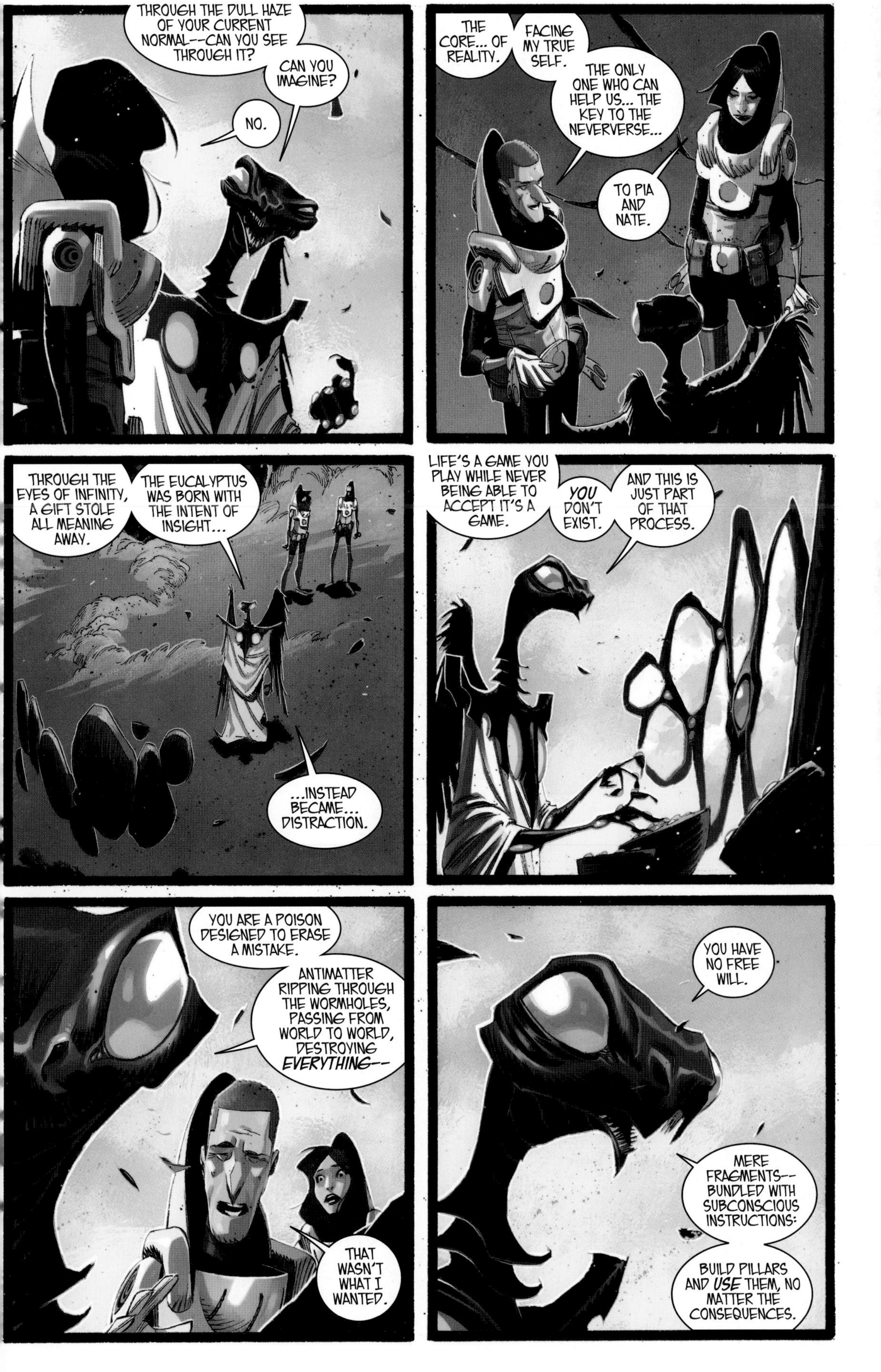
THROUGH THE DULL HAZE OF YOUR CURRENT NORMAL--CAN YOU SEE THROUGH IT?
CAN YOU IMAGINE?
NO.
THE CORE... OF REALITY.
FACING MY TRUE SELF.
THE ONLY ONE WHO CAN HELP US... THE KEY TO THE NEVERVERSE...
TO PIA AND NATE.
THROUGH THE EYES OF INFINITY, A GIFT STOLE ALL MEANING AWAY.
THE EUCALYPTUS WAS BORN WITH THE INTENT OF INSIGHT...
...INSTEAD BECAME... DISTRACTION.
LIFE'S A GAME YOU PLAY WHILE NEVER BEING ABLE TO ACCEPT IT'S A GAME.
YOU DON'T EXIST.
AND THIS IS JUST PART OF THAT PROCESS.
YOU ARE A POISON DESIGNED TO ERASE A MISTAKE.
ANTIMATTER RIPPING THROUGH THE WORMHOLES, PASSING FROM WORLD TO WORLD, DESTROYING *EVERYTHING*--
THAT WASN'T WHAT I WANTED.
YOU HAVE NO FREE WILL.
MERE FRAGMENTS--BUNDLED WITH SUBCONSCIOUS INSTRUCTIONS:
BUILD PILLARS AND *USE* THEM, NO MATTER THE CONSEQUENCES.

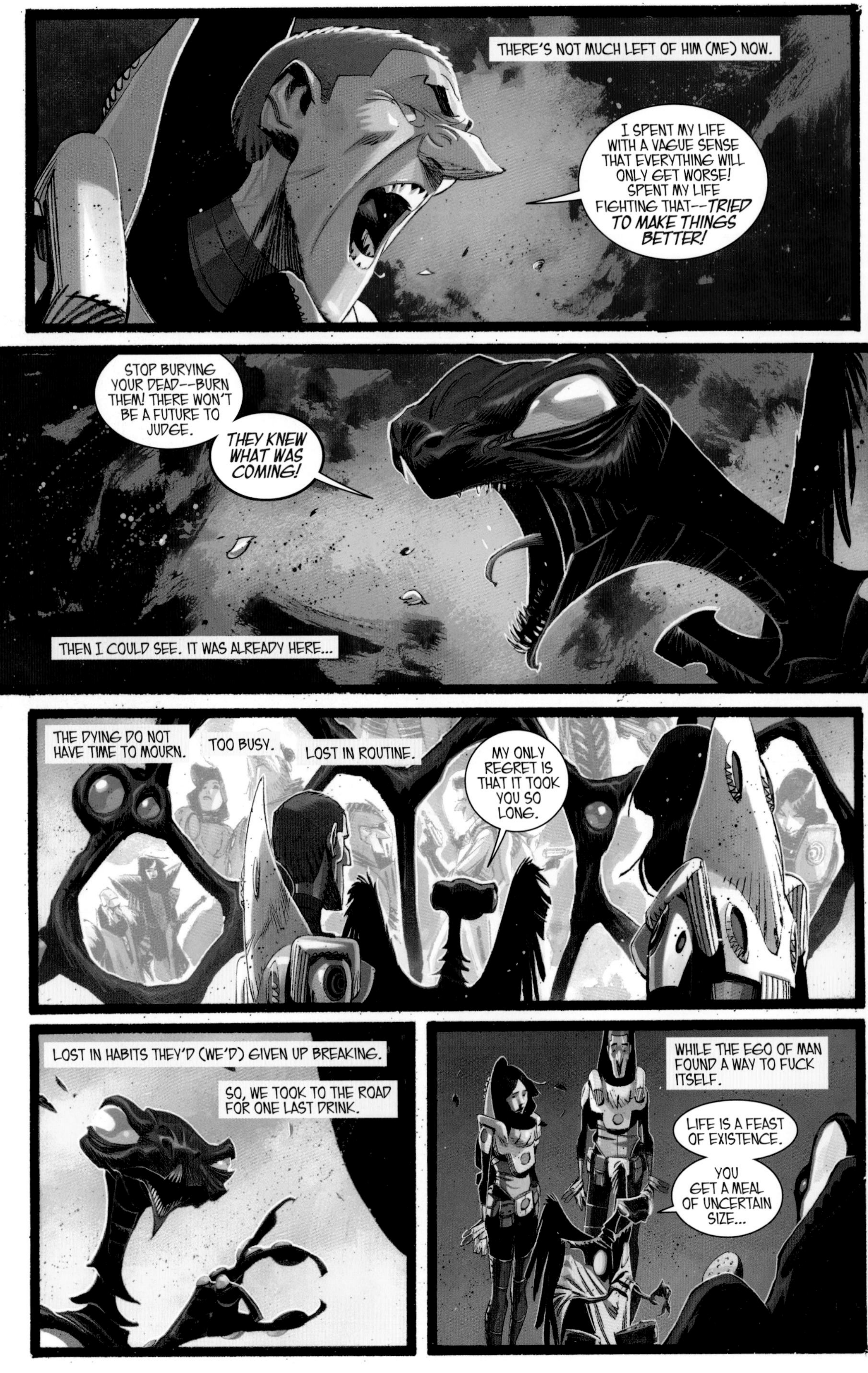
THERE'S NOT MUCH LEFT OF HIM (ME) NOW.
I SPENT MY LIFE WITH A VAGUE SENSE THAT EVERYTHING WILL ONLY GET WORSE! SPENT MY LIFE FIGHTING THAT--TRIED TO MAKE THINGS BETTER!
STOP BURYING YOUR DEAD--BURN THEM! THERE WON'T BE A FUTURE TO JUDGE.
THEY KNEW WHAT WAS COMING!
THEN I COULD SEE. IT WAS ALREADY HERE...
THE DYING DO NOT HAVE TIME TO MOURN.
TOO BUSY.
LOST IN ROUTINE.
MY ONLY REGRET IS THAT IT TOOK YOU SO LONG.
LOST IN HABITS THEY'D (WE'D) GIVEN UP BREAKING.
SO, WE TOOK TO THE ROAD FOR ONE LAST DRINK.
WHILE THE EGO OF MAN FOUND A WAY TO FUCK ITSELF.
LIFE IS A FEAST OF EXISTENCE.
YOU GET A MEAL OF UNCERTAIN SIZE...

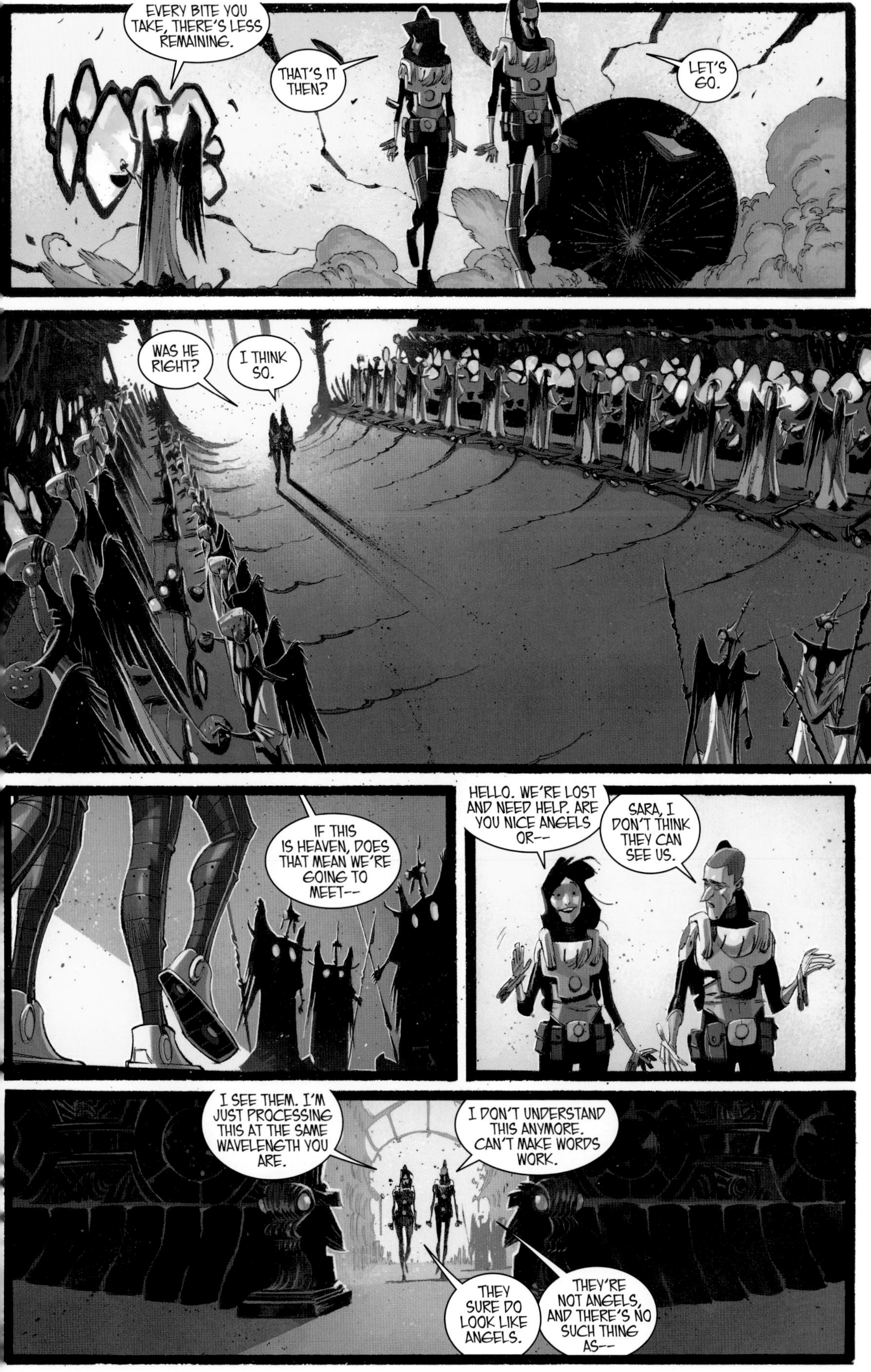
EVERY BITE YOU TAKE, THERE'S LESS REMAINING.
THAT'S IT THEN?
LET'S GO.
WAS HE RIGHT?
I THINK SO.
IF THIS IS HEAVEN, DOES THAT MEAN WE'RE GOING TO MEET--
HELLO. WE'RE LOST AND NEED HELP. ARE YOU NICE ANGELS OR--
SARA, I DON'T THINK THEY CAN SEE US.
I SEE THEM. I'M JUST PROCESSING THIS AT THE SAME WAVELENGTH YOU ARE.
I DON'T UNDERSTAND THIS ANYMORE. CAN'T MAKE WORDS WORK.
THEY SURE DO LOOK LIKE ANGELS.
THEY'RE NOT ANGELS, AND THERE'S NO SUCH THING AS--

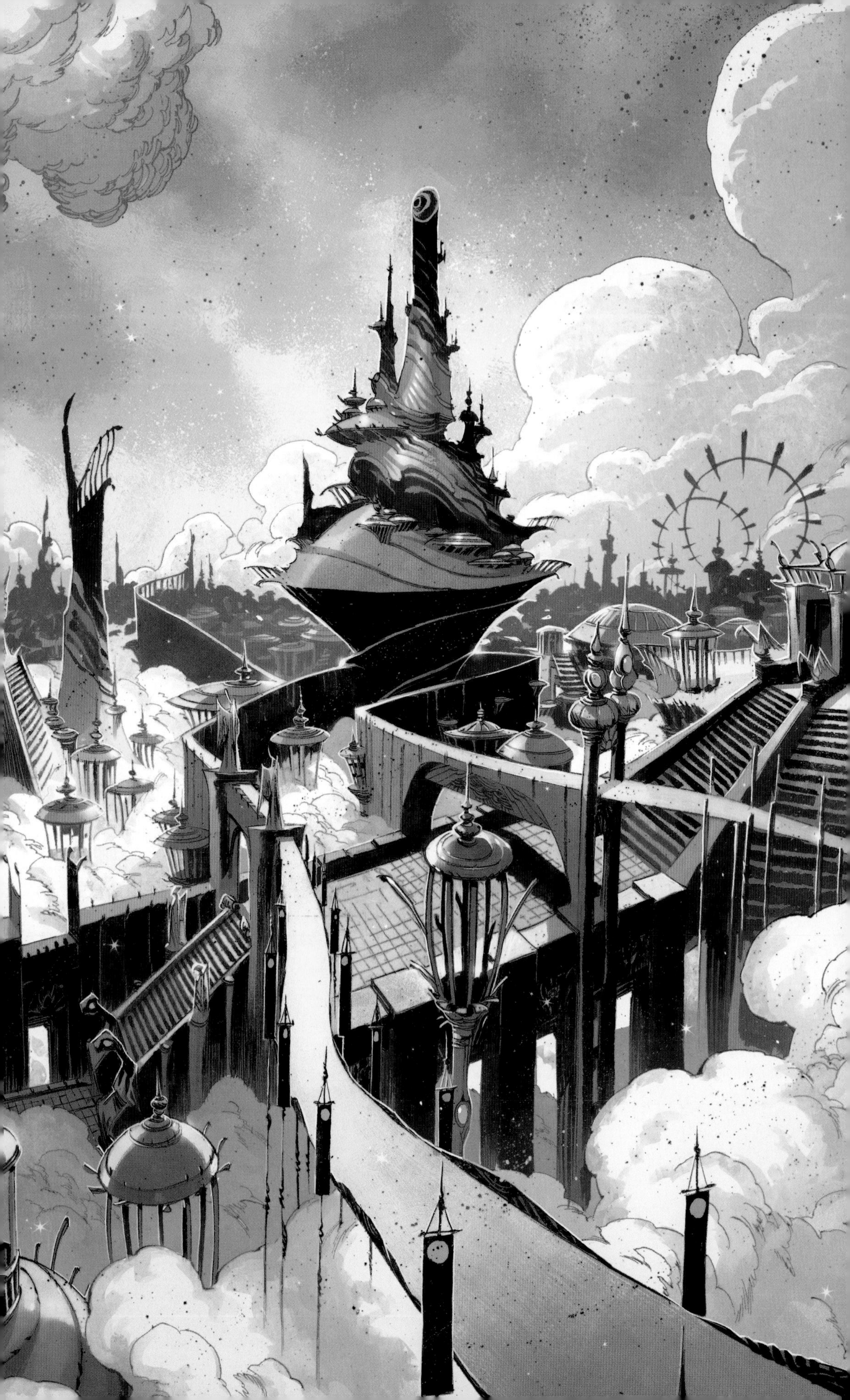

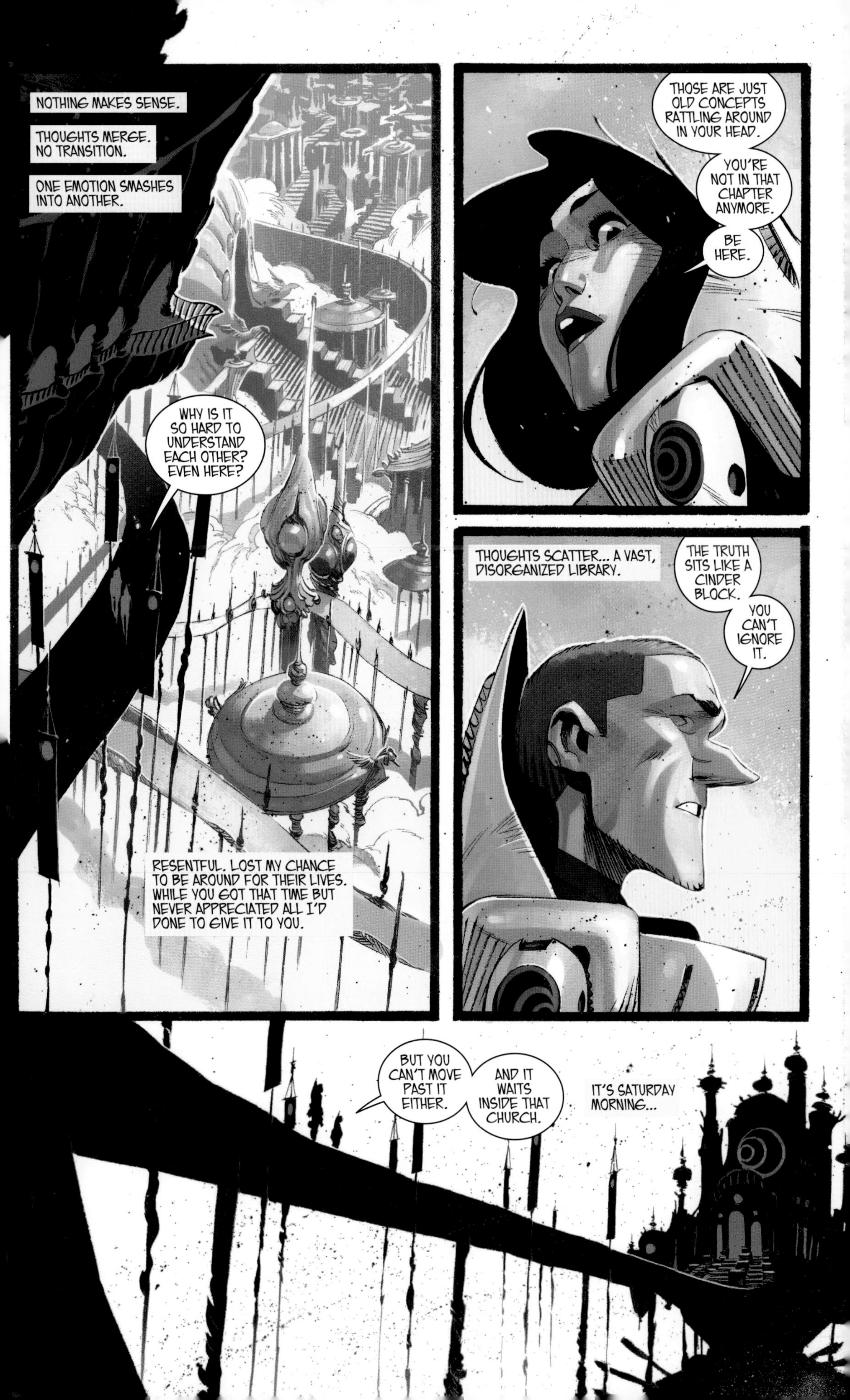
NOTHING MAKES SENSE.
THOUGHTS MERGE. NO TRANSITION.
ONE EMOTION SMASHES INTO ANOTHER.
WHY IS IT SO HARD TO UNDERSTAND EACH OTHER? EVEN HERE?
RESENTFUL. LOST MY CHANCE TO BE AROUND FOR THEIR LIVES. WHILE YOU GOT THAT TIME BUT NEVER APPRECIATED ALL I'D DONE TO GIVE IT TO YOU.
THOSE ARE JUST OLD CONCEPTS RATTLING AROUND IN YOUR HEAD.
YOU'RE NOT IN THAT CHAPTER ANYMORE.
BE HERE.
THOUGHTS SCATTER... A VAST, DISORGANIZED LIBRARY.
THE TRUTH SITS LIKE A CINDER BLOCK.
YOU CAN'T IGNORE IT.
BUT YOU CAN'T MOVE PAST IT EITHER.
AND IT WAITS INSIDE THAT CHURCH.
IT'S SATURDAY MORNING...

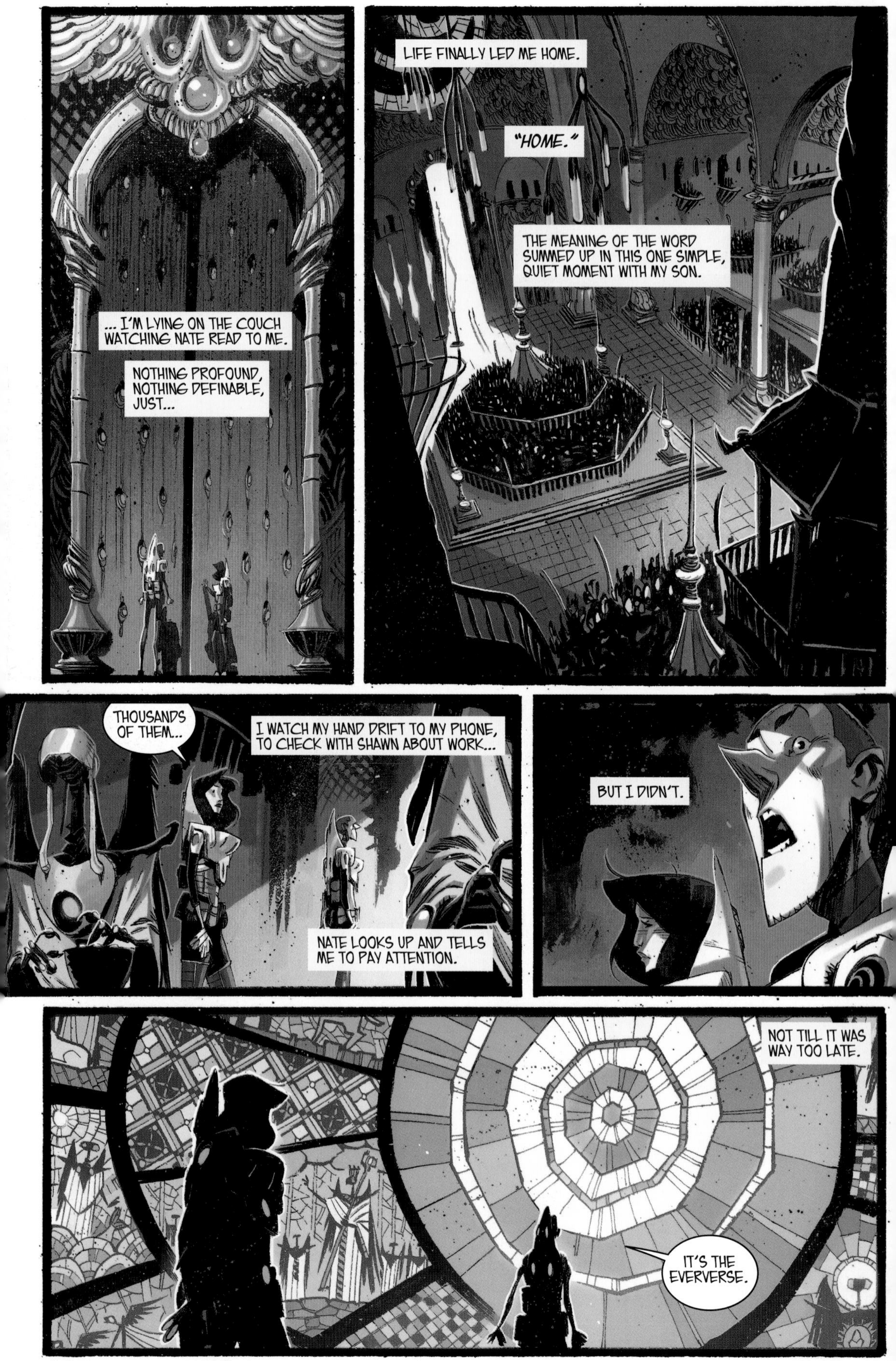
... I'M LYING ON THE COUCH WATCHING NATE READ TO ME.
NOTHING PROFOUND, NOTHING DEFINABLE, JUST...
LIFE FINALLY LED ME HOME.
"HOME."
THE MEANING OF THE WORD SUMMED UP IN THIS ONE SIMPLE, QUIET MOMENT WITH MY SON.
THOUSANDS OF THEM...
I WATCH MY HAND DRIFT TO MY PHONE, TO CHECK WITH SHAWN ABOUT WORK...
NATE LOOKS UP AND TELLS ME TO PAY ATTENTION.
BUT I DIDN'T.
NOT TILL IT WAS WAY TOO LATE.
IT'S THE EVERVERSE.

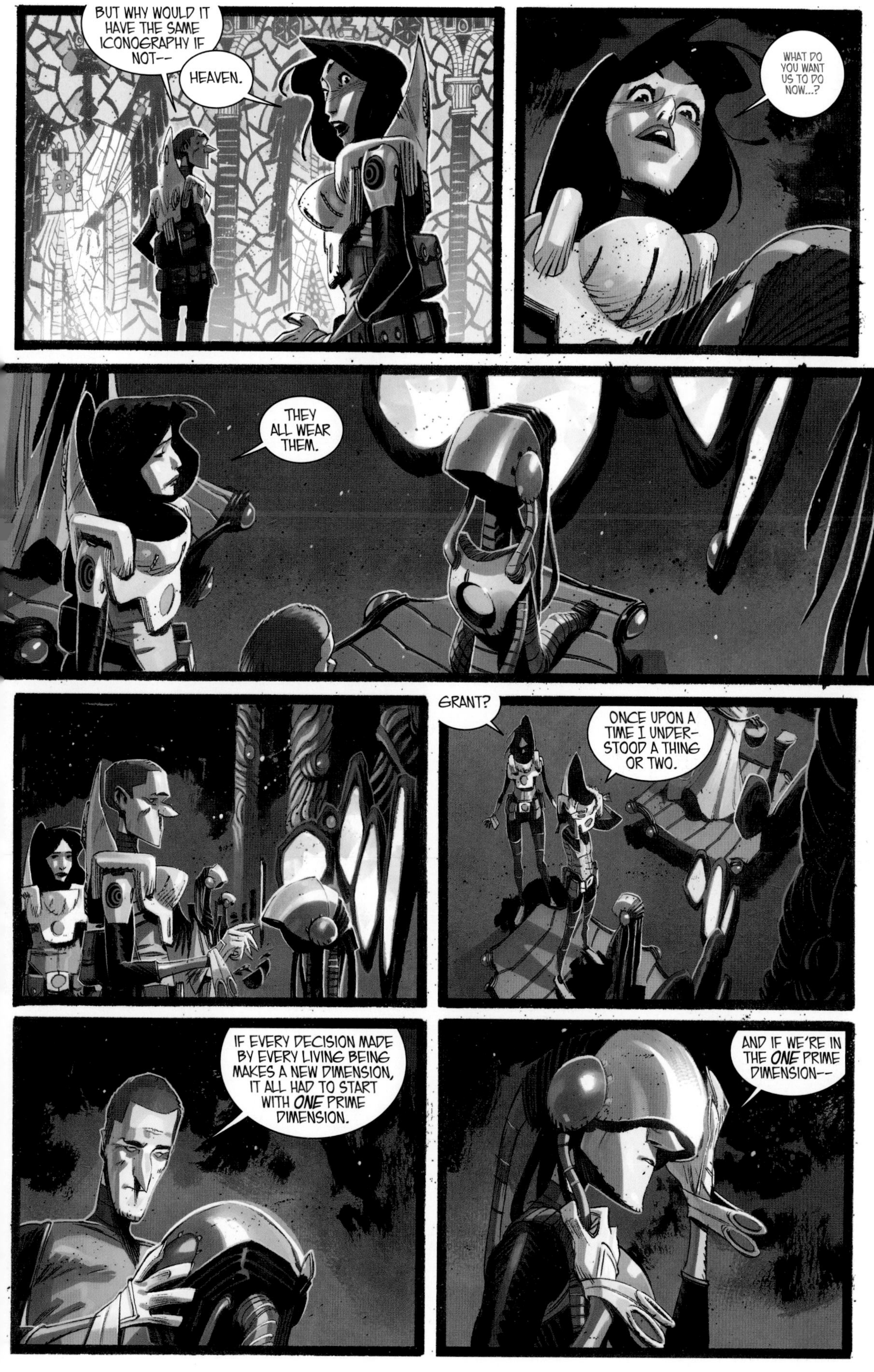
BUT WHY WOULD IT HAVE THE SAME ICONOGRAPHY IF NOT--
HEAVEN.
WHAT DO YOU WANT US TO DO NOW...?
THEY ALL WEAR THEM.
GRANT?
ONCE UPON A TIME I UNDER-STOOD A THING OR TWO.
IF EVERY DECISION MADE BY EVERY LIVING BEING MAKES A NEW DIMENSION, IT ALL HAD TO START WITH ONE PRIME DIMENSION.
AND IF WE'RE IN THE ONE PRIME DIMENSION--

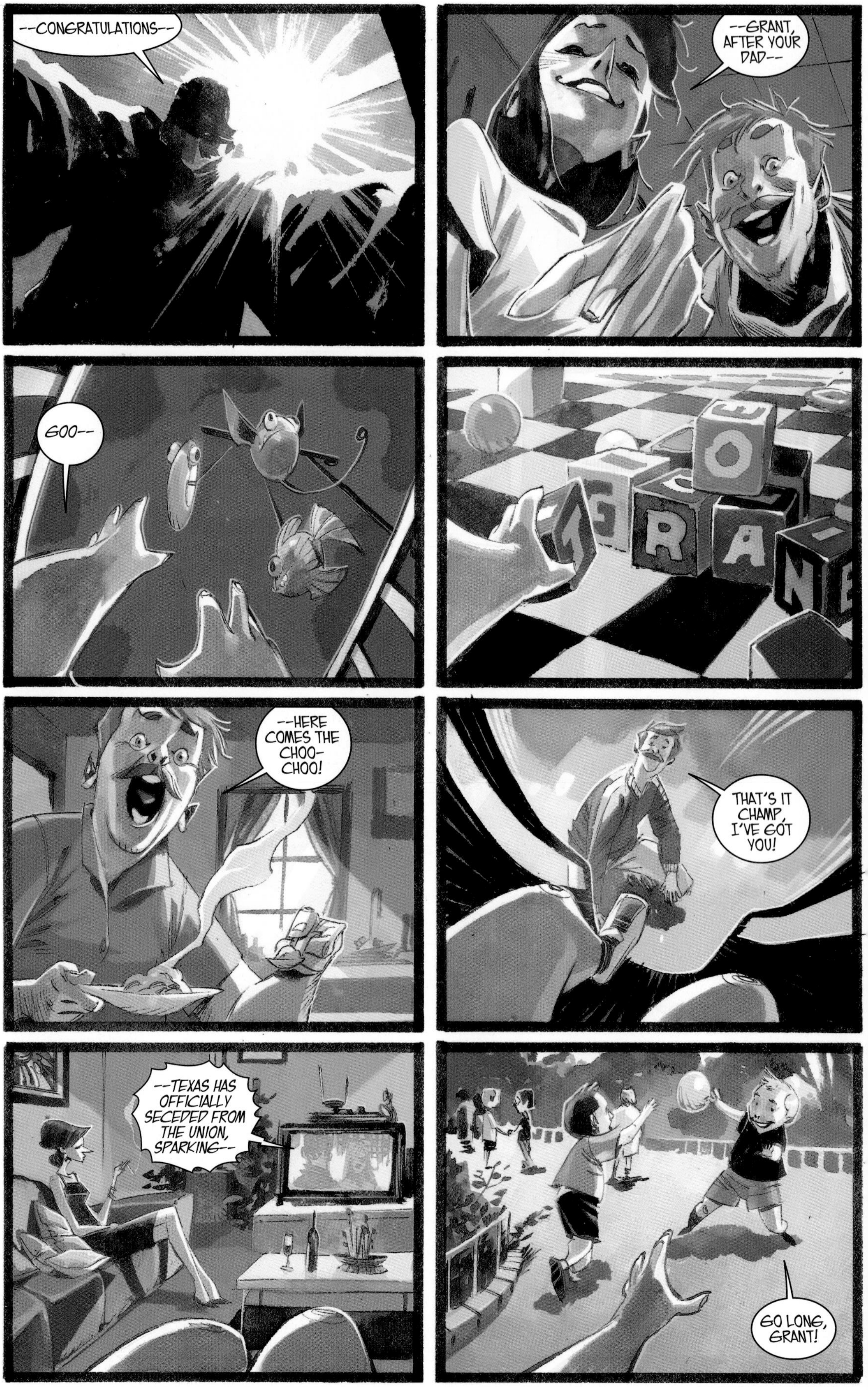
--CONGRATULATIONS--
--GRANT, AFTER YOUR DAD--
GOO--
--HERE COMES THE CHOO-CHOO!
THAT'S IT CHAMP, I'VE GOT YOU!
--TEXAS HAS OFFICIALLY SECEDED FROM THE UNION, SPARKING--
GO LONG, GRANT!

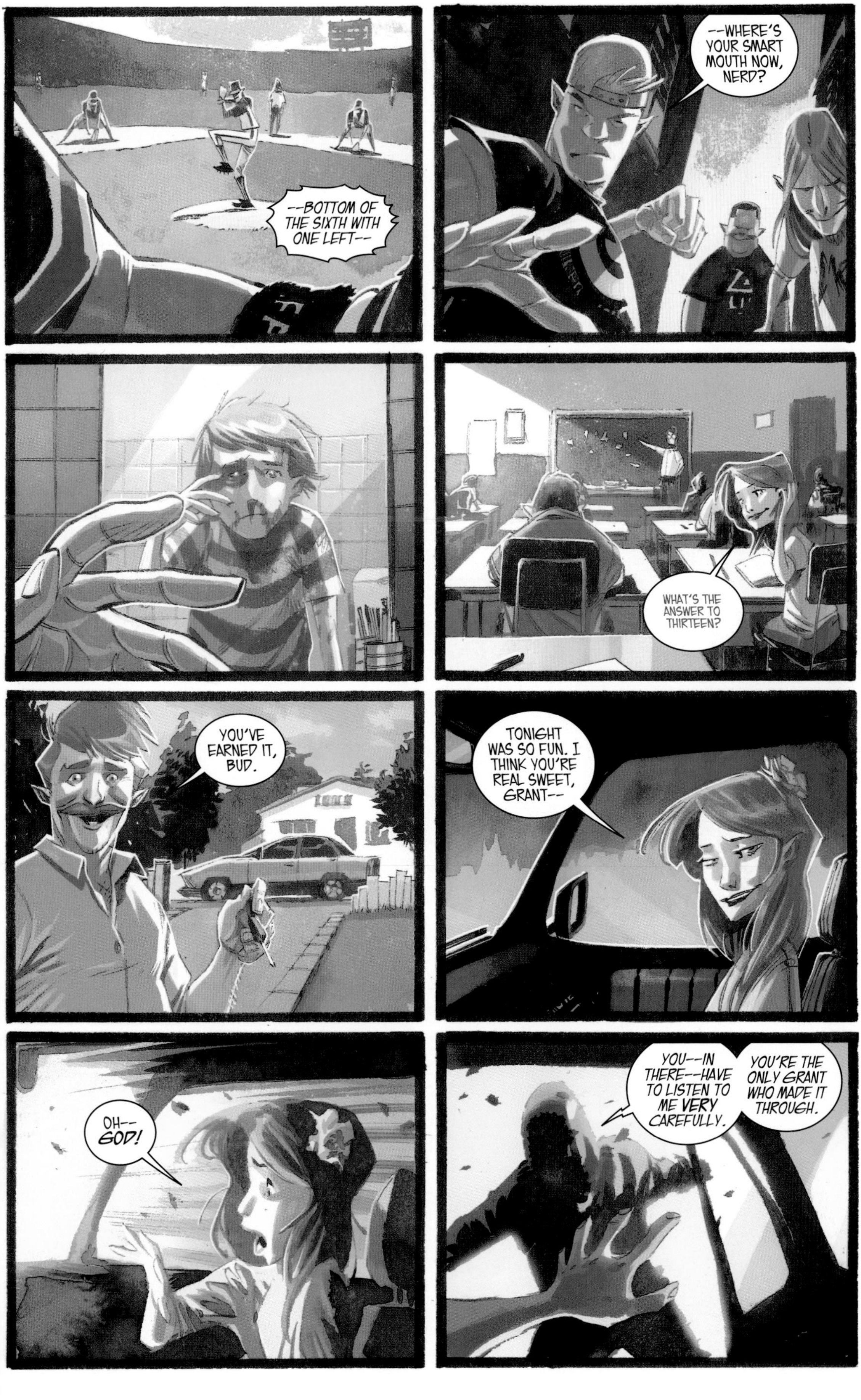
--BOTTOM OF THE SIXTH WITH ONE LEFT--
--WHERE'S YOUR SMART MOUTH NOW, NERD?
WHAT'S THE ANSWER TO THIRTEEN?
YOU'VE EARNED IT, BUD.
TONIGHT WAS SO FUN. I THINK YOU'RE REAL SWEET, GRANT--
OH-- GOD!
YOU--IN THERE--HAVE TO LISTEN TO ME VERY CAREFULLY.
YOU'RE THE ONLY GRANT WHO MADE IT THROUGH.

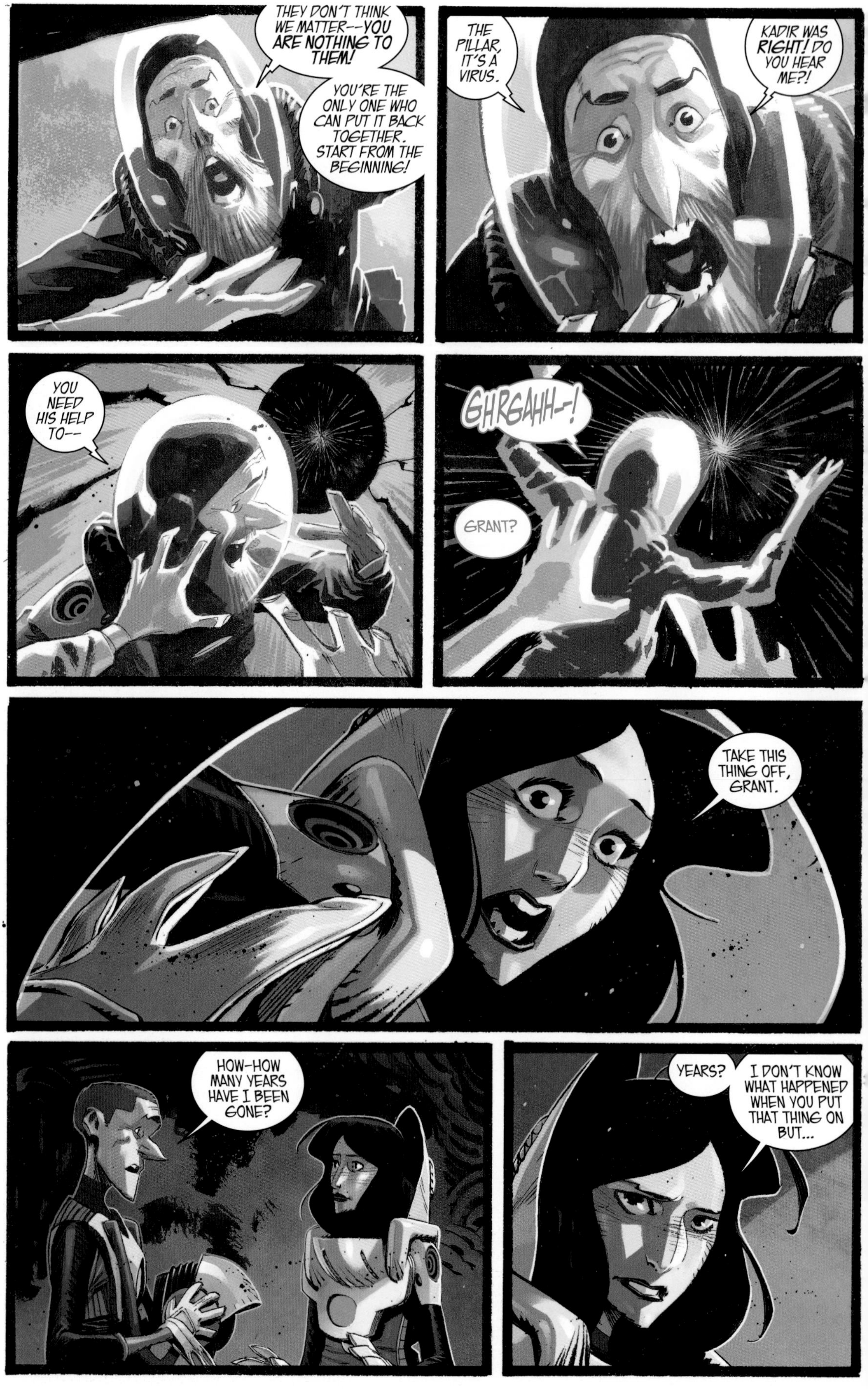
THEY DON'T THINK WE MATTER--YOU ARE NOTHING TO THEM!
YOU'RE THE ONLY ONE WHO CAN PUT IT BACK TOGETHER. START FROM THE BEGINNING!
THE PILLAR, IT'S A VIRUS.
KADIR WAS RIGHT! DO YOU HEAR ME?!
YOU NEED HIS HELP TO--
GHRGAHH--!
GRANT?
TAKE THIS THING OFF, GRANT.
HOW--HOW MANY YEARS HAVE I BEEN GONE?
YEARS?
I DON'T KNOW WHAT HAPPENED WHEN YOU PUT THAT THING ON BUT...

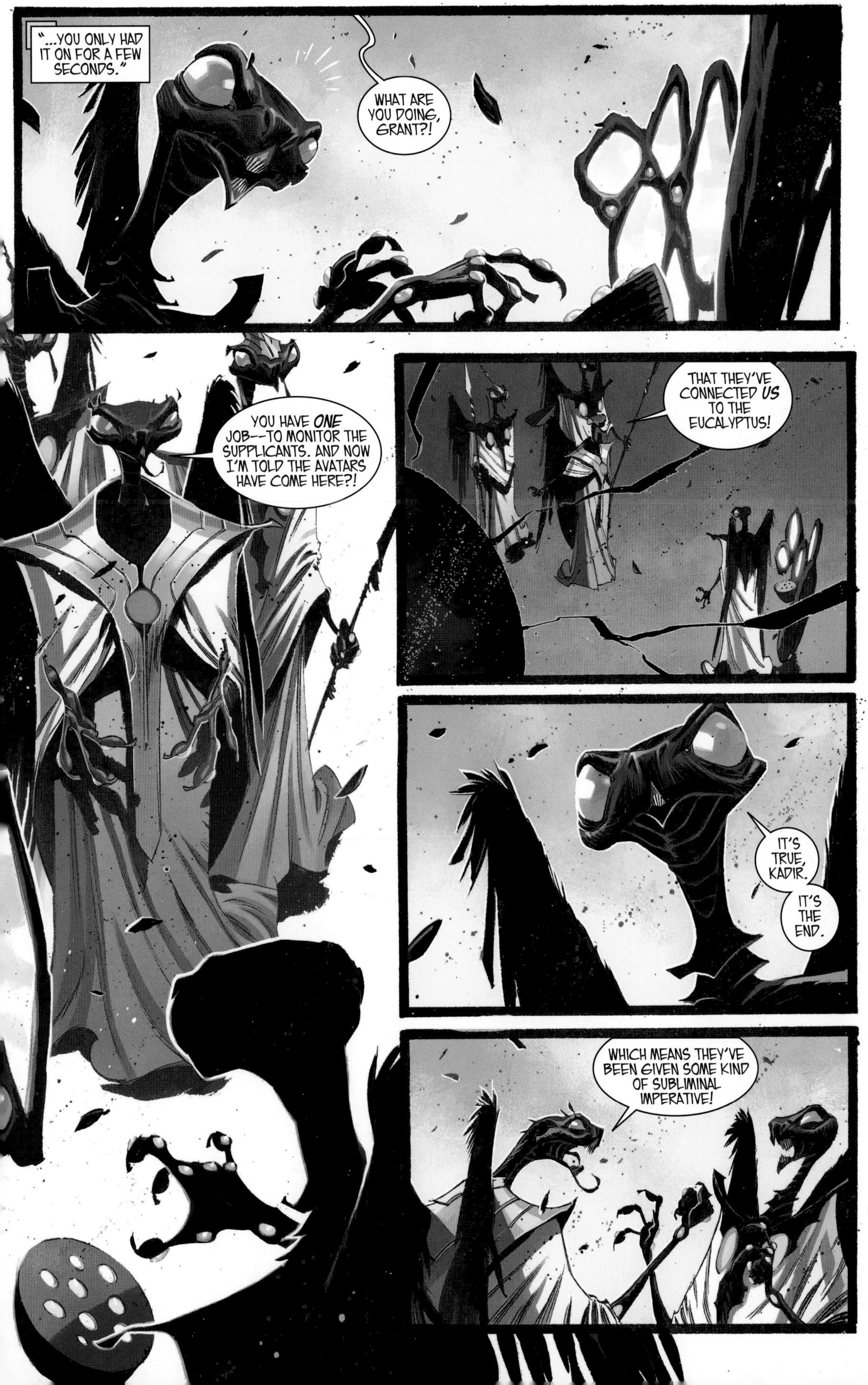
"...YOU ONLY HAD IT ON FOR A FEW SECONDS."
WHAT ARE YOU DOING, GRANT?!
YOU HAVE ONE JOB--TO MONITOR THE SUPPLICANTS. AND NOW I'M TOLD THE AVATARS HAVE COME HERE?!
THAT THEY'VE CONNECTED US TO THE EUCALYPTUS!
IT'S TRUE, KADIR.
IT'S THE END.
WHICH MEANS THEY'VE BEEN GIVEN SOME KIND OF SUBLIMINAL IMPERATIVE!

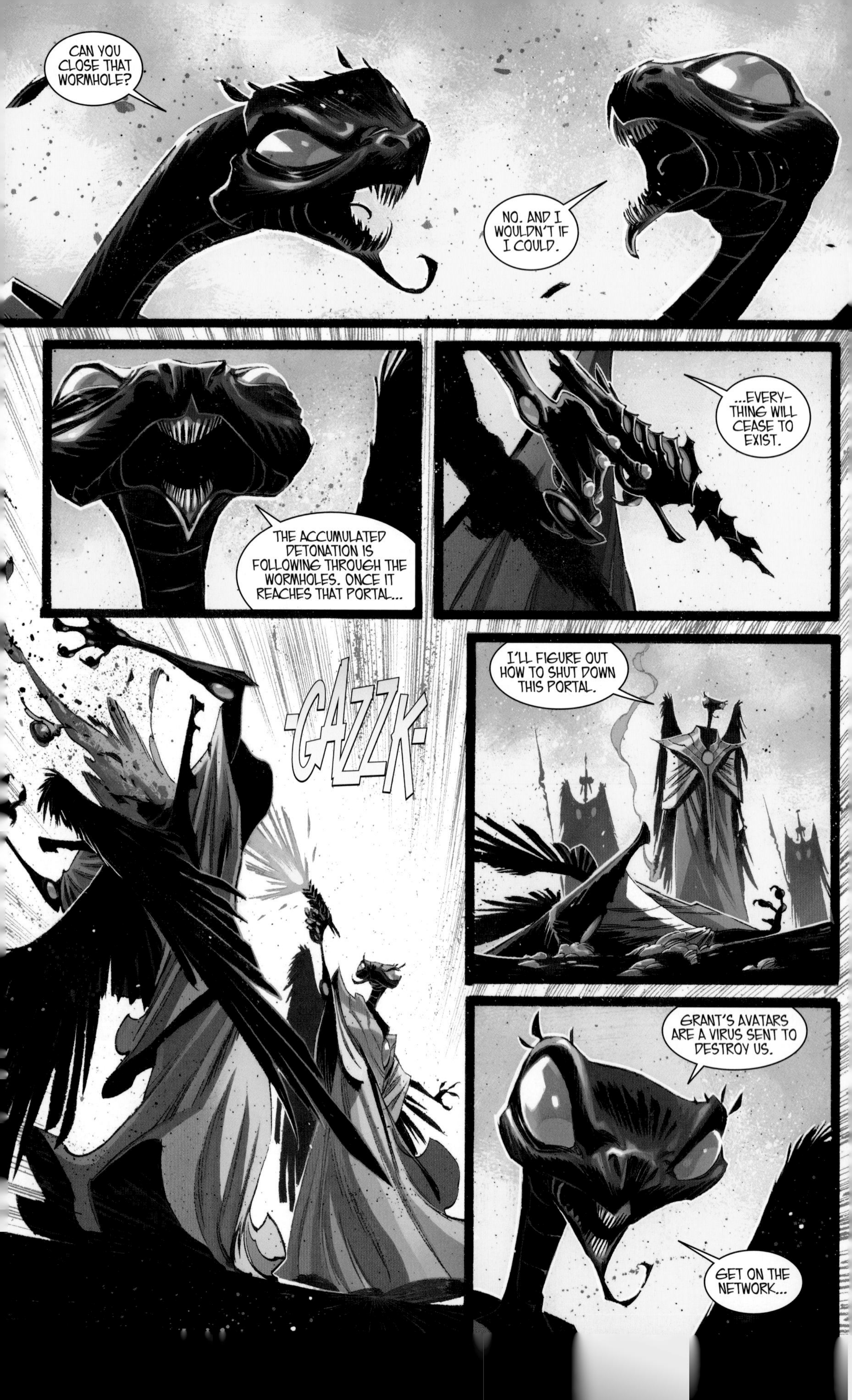
CAN YOU CLOSE THAT WORMHOLE?
NO. AND I WOULDN'T IF I COULD.
THE ACCUMULATED DETONATION IS FOLLOWING THROUGH THE WORMHOLES. ONCE IT REACHES THAT PORTAL...
...EVERY-THING WILL CEASE TO EXIST.
-GAZZK-
I'LL FIGURE OUT HOW TO SHUT DOWN THIS PORTAL.
GRANT'S AVATARS ARE A VIRUS SENT TO DESTROY US.
GET ON THE NETWORK...

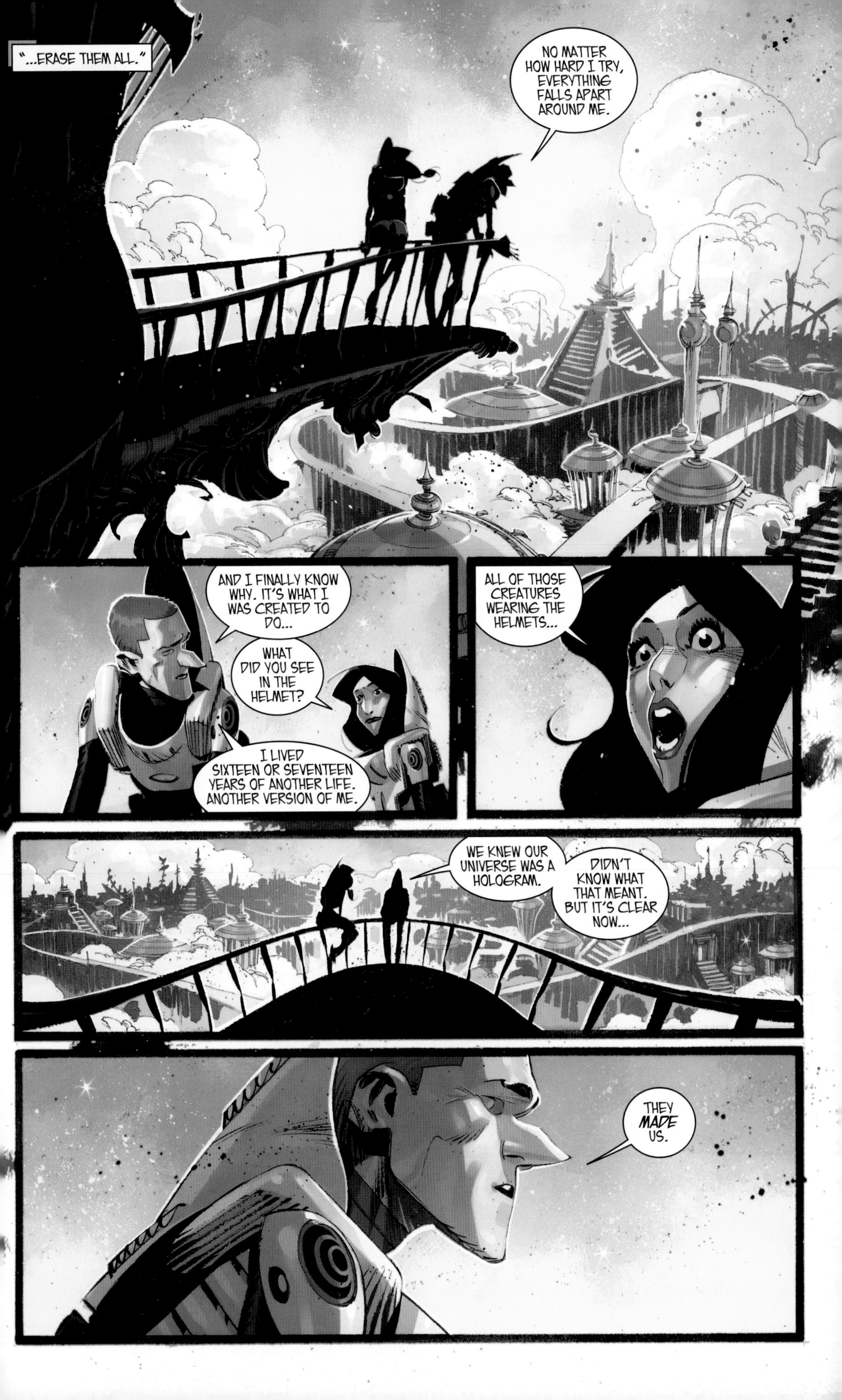
"...ERASE THEM ALL."
NO MATTER HOW HARD I TRY, EVERYTHING FALLS APART AROUND ME.
AND I FINALLY KNOW WHY. IT'S WHAT I WAS CREATED TO DO...
WHAT DID YOU SEE IN THE HELMET?
I LIVED SIXTEEN OR SEVENTEEN YEARS OF ANOTHER LIFE. ANOTHER VERSION OF ME.
ALL OF THOSE CREATURES WEARING THE HELMETS...
WE KNEW OUR UNIVERSE WAS A HOLOGRAM.
DIDN'T KNOW WHAT THAT MEANT. BUT IT'S CLEAR NOW...
THEY MADE US.

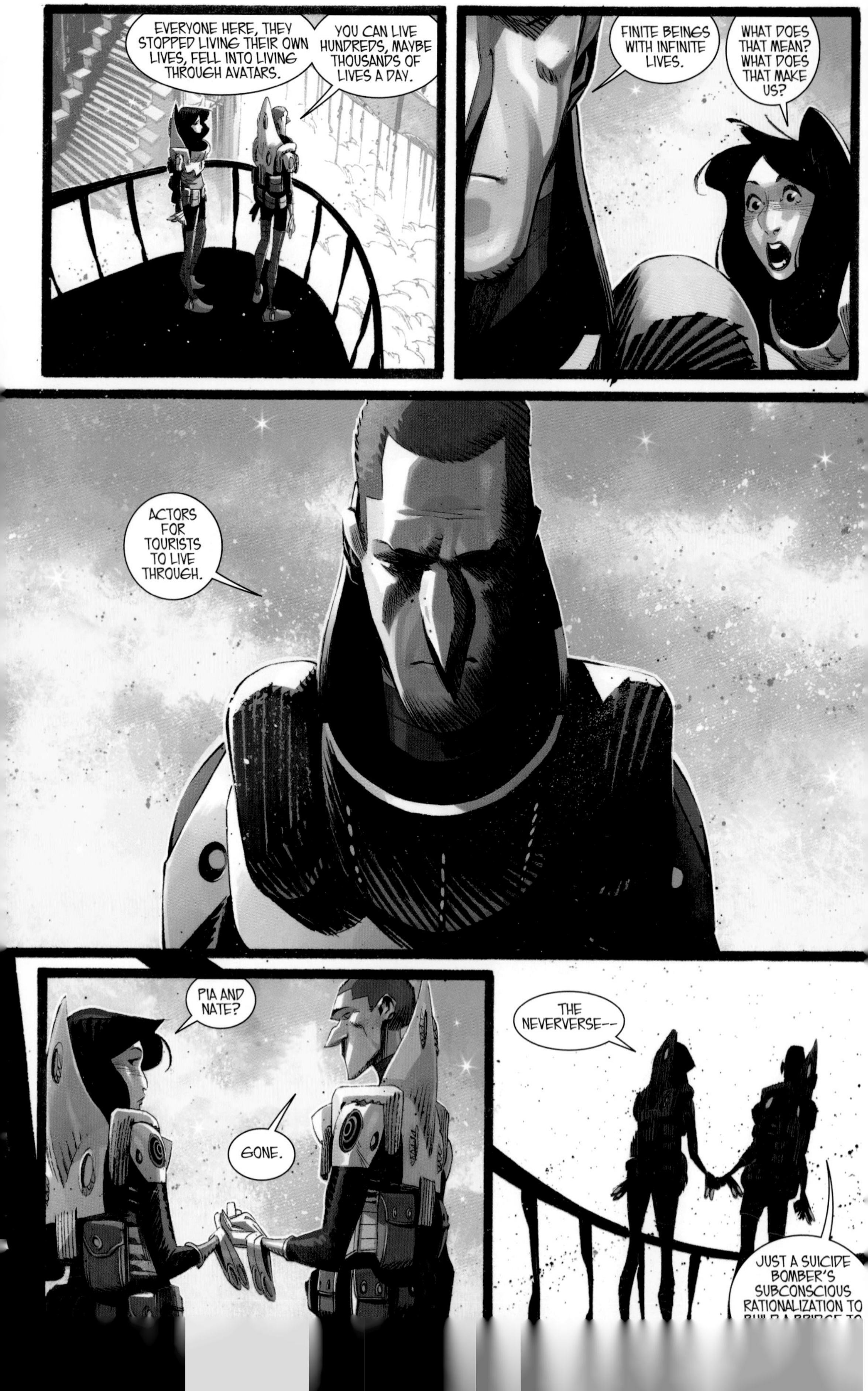
EVERYONE HERE, THEY STOPPED LIVING THEIR OWN LIVES, FELL INTO LIVING THROUGH AVATARS.
YOU CAN LIVE HUNDREDS, MAYBE THOUSANDS OF LIVES A DAY.
FINITE BEINGS WITH INFINITE LIVES.
WHAT DOES THAT MEAN? WHAT DOES THAT MAKE US?
ACTORS FOR TOURISTS TO LIVE THROUGH.
PIA AND NATE?
GONE.
THE NEVERVERSE--
JUST A SUICIDE BOMBER'S SUBCONSCIOUS RATIONALIZATION TO

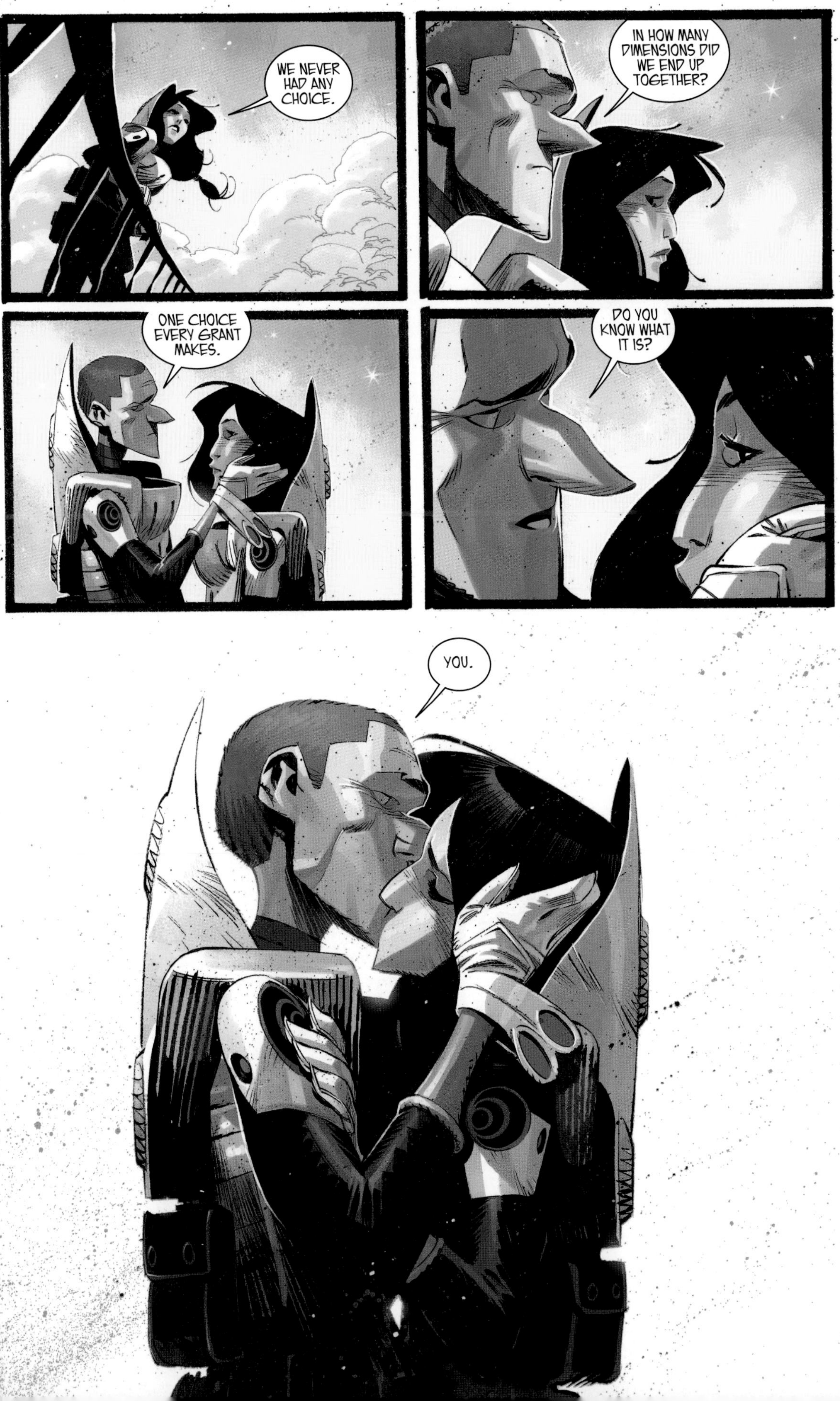
WE NEVER HAD ANY CHOICE.
IN HOW MANY DIMENSIONS DID WE END UP TOGETHER?
ONE CHOICE EVERY GRANT MAKES.
DO YOU KNOW WHAT IT IS?
YOU.

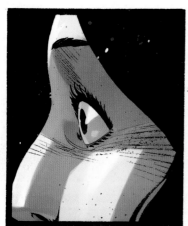

NO!

WHAT I FEEL IN MY HEART IS REAL!

WHAT I FEEL FOR OUR CHILDREN IS REAL--AND THEY NEED US!

THAT'S REAL!

WE'RE LIVING AND BREATHING.

WE'RE NOT SOME SIMULATION!

OR THAT'S JUST WHAT WE'RE PROGRAMMED TO THINK... PART OF THE ILLUSION OF OUR REALITY...

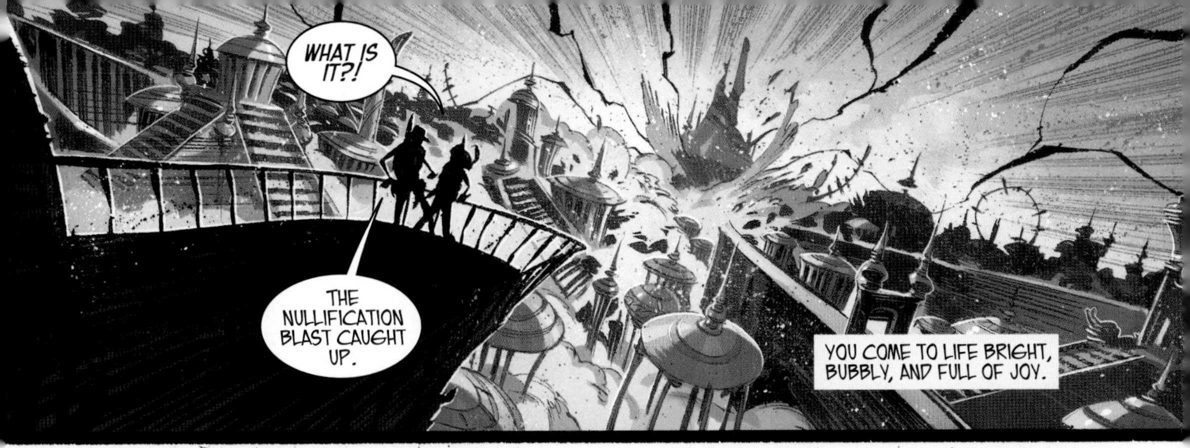
WHAT IS IT?!
THE NULLIFICATION BLAST CAUGHT UP.
YOU COME TO LIFE BRIGHT, BUBBLY, AND FULL OF JOY.

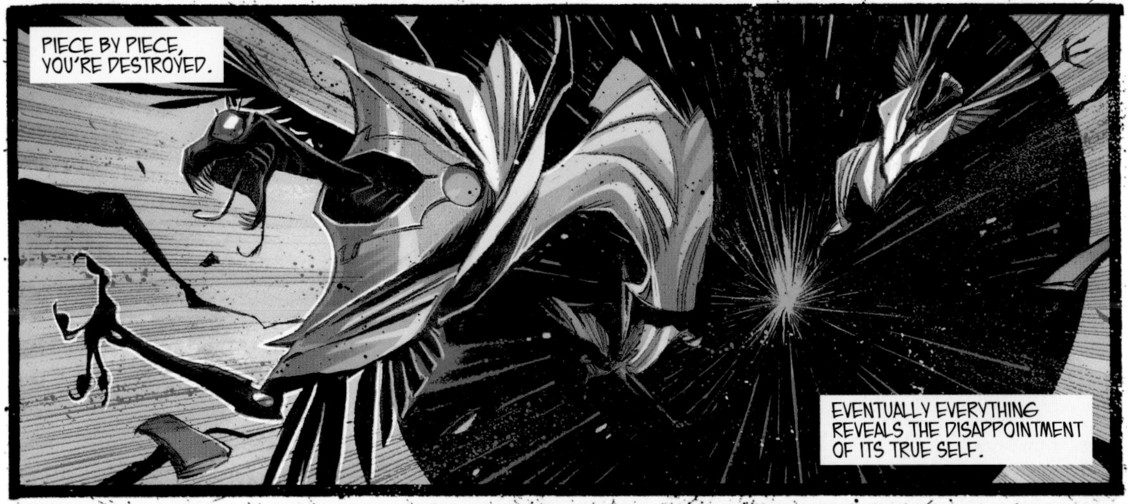
PIECE BY PIECE, YOU'RE DESTROYED.
EVENTUALLY EVERYTHING REVEALS THE DISAPPOINTMENT OF ITS TRUE SELF.

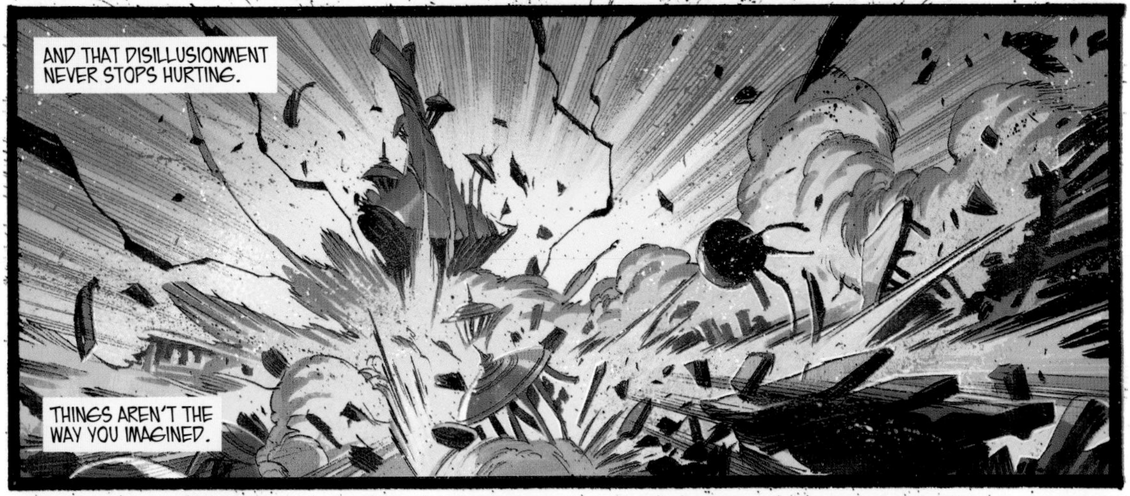
AND THAT DISILLUSIONMENT NEVER STOPS HURTING.
THINGS AREN'T THE WAY YOU IMAGINED.

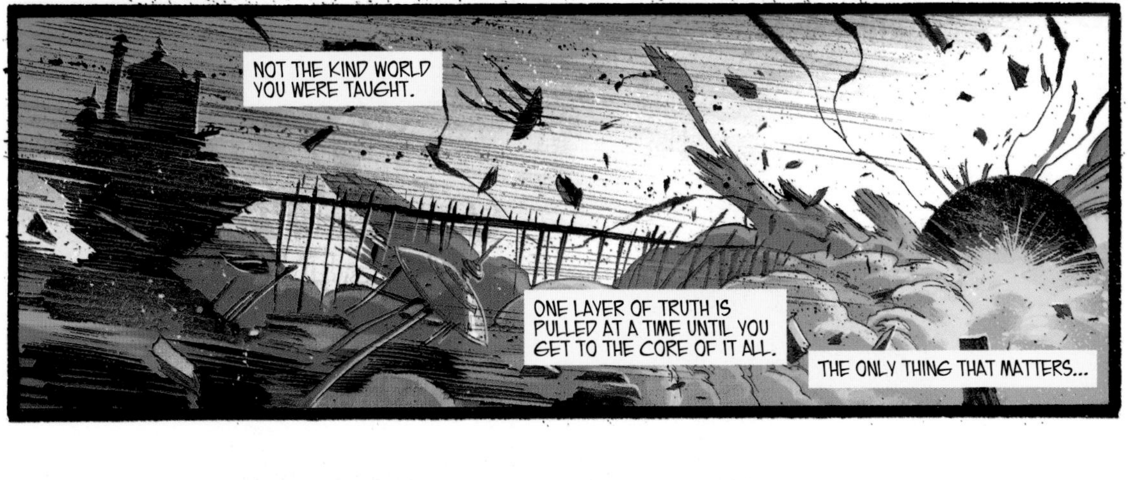
NOT THE KIND WORLD YOU WERE TAUGHT.
ONE LAYER OF TRUTH IS PULLED AT A TIME UNTIL YOU GET TO THE CORE OF IT ALL.
THE ONLY THING THAT MATTERS...

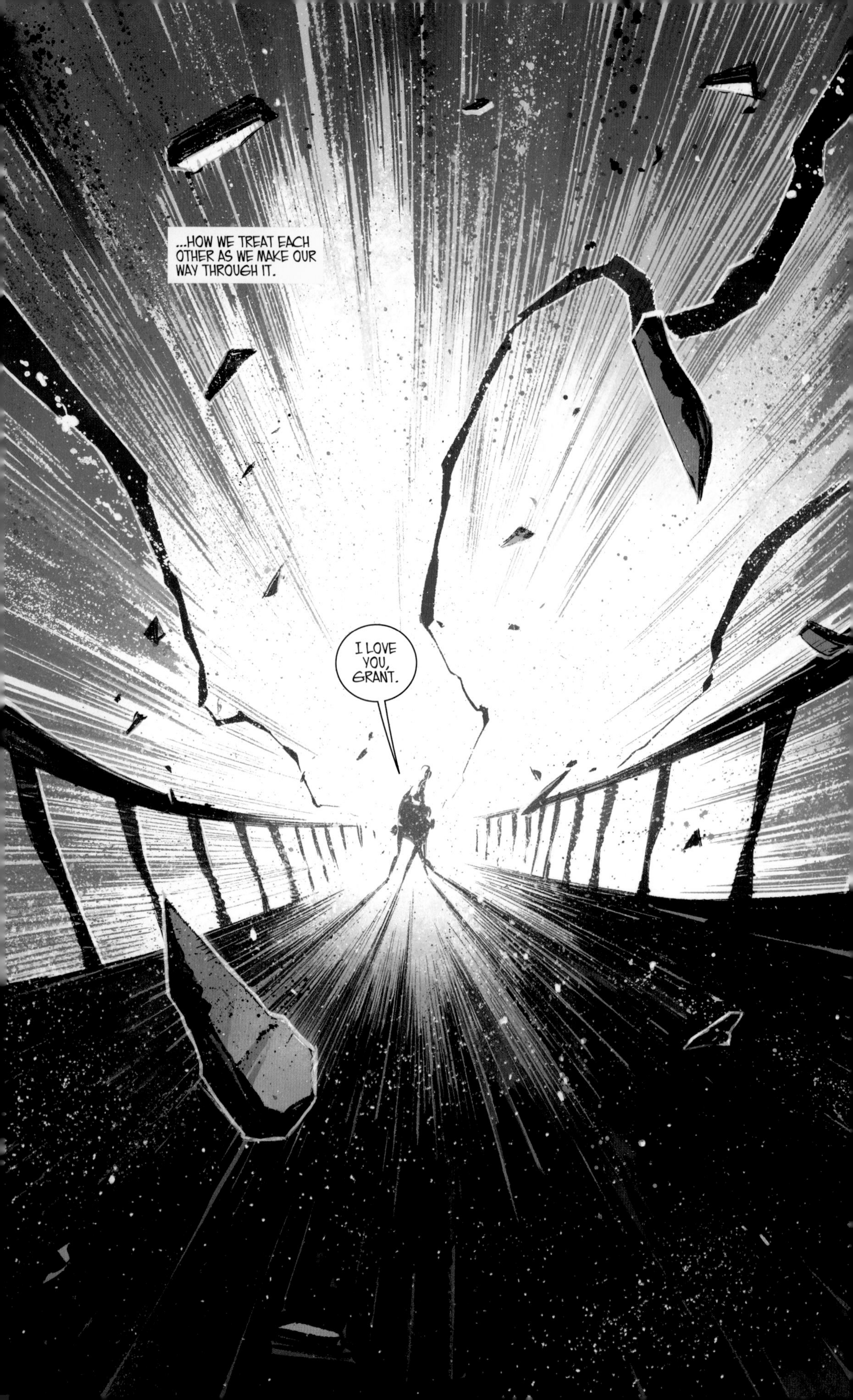
...HOW WE TREAT EACH OTHER AS WE MAKE OUR WAY THROUGH IT.
I LOVE YOU, GRANT.

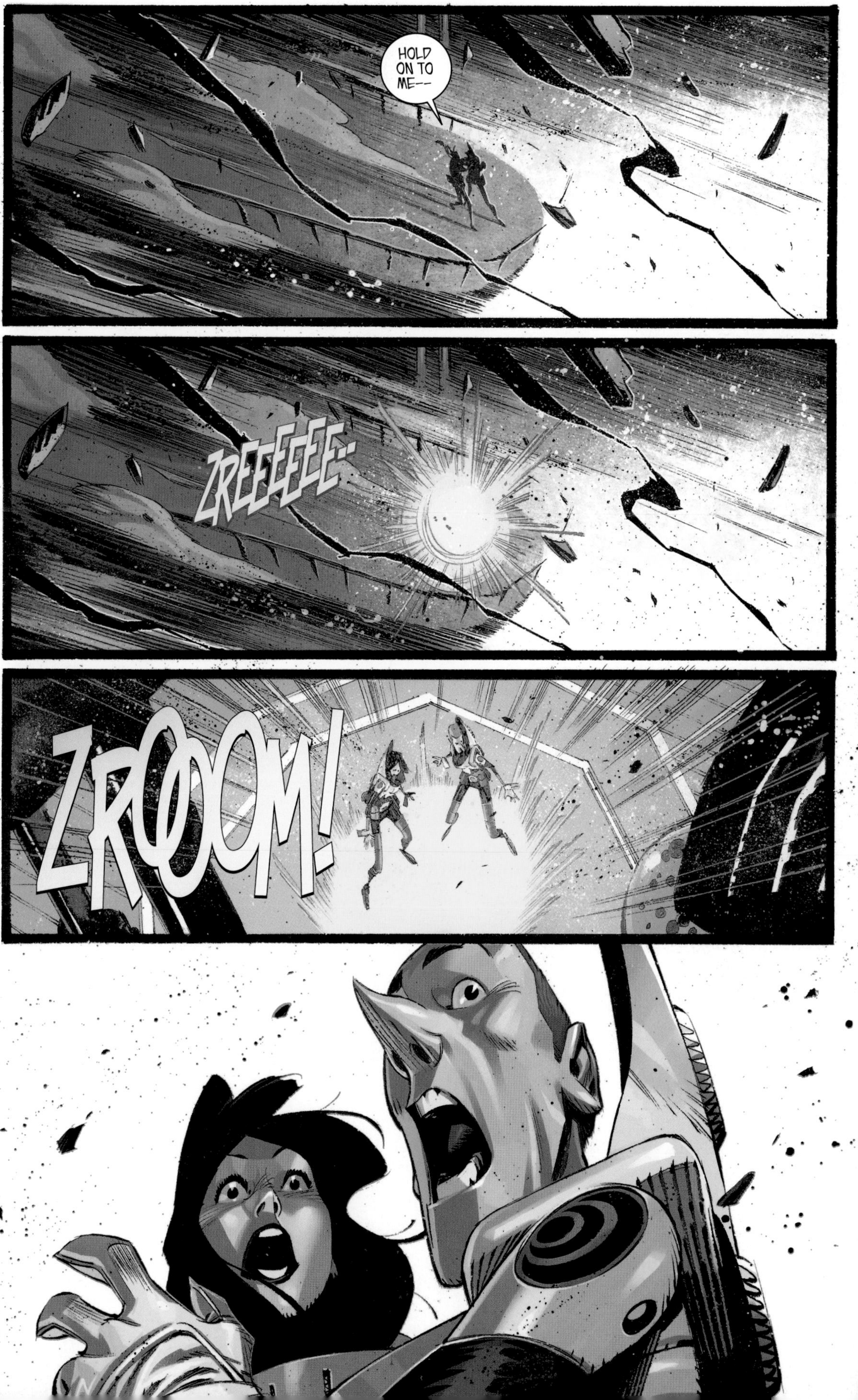
HOLD ON TO ME--
ZREEEEEE-
ZROOOM!

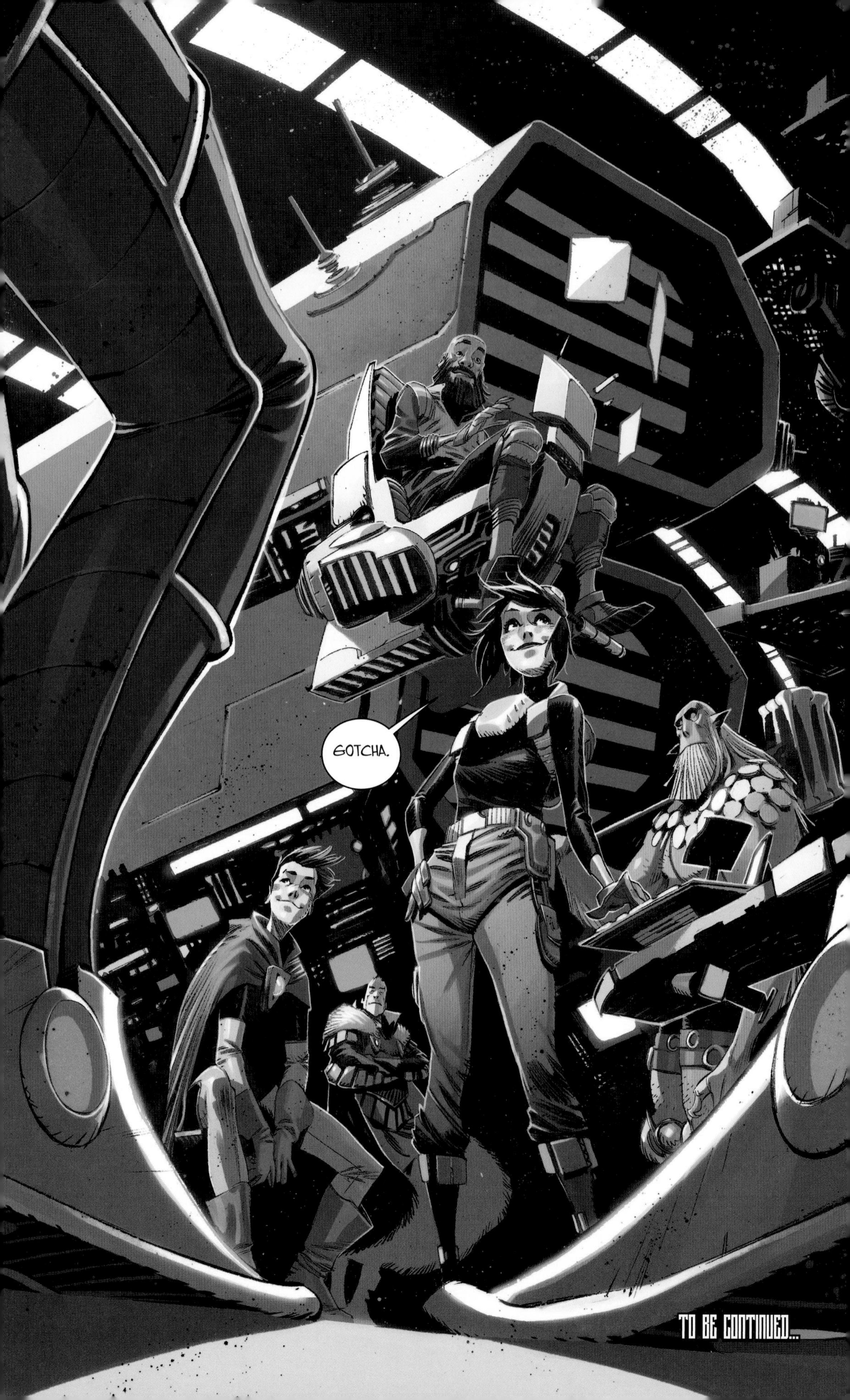
GOTCHA.
TO BE CONTINUED...

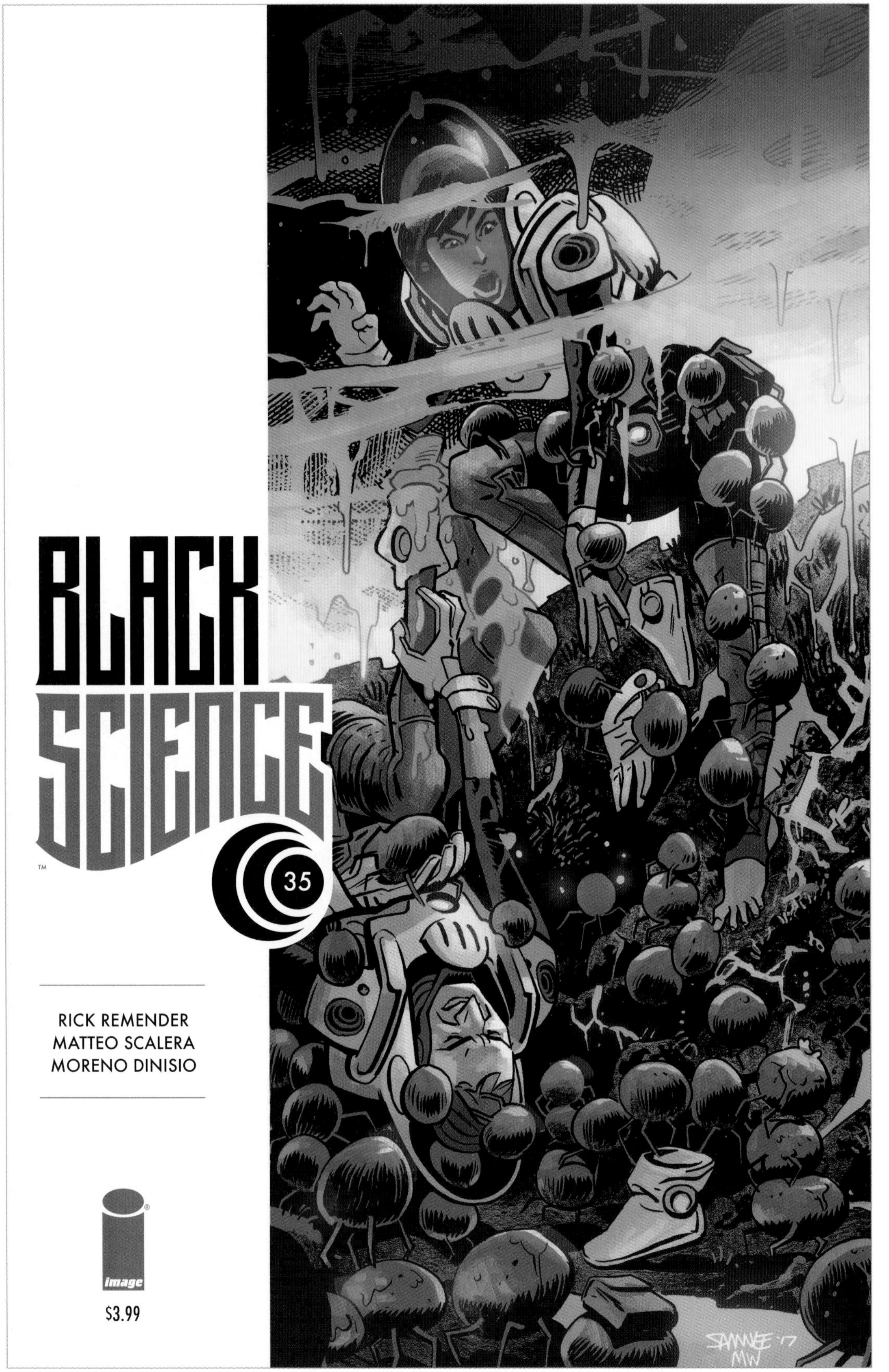
BLACK SCIENCE
35
RICK REMENDER
MATTEO SCALERA
MORENO DINISIO
image
$3.99
SAMNEE '17
MW

#35 VARIANT BY CHRIS SAMNEE & MATT WILSON

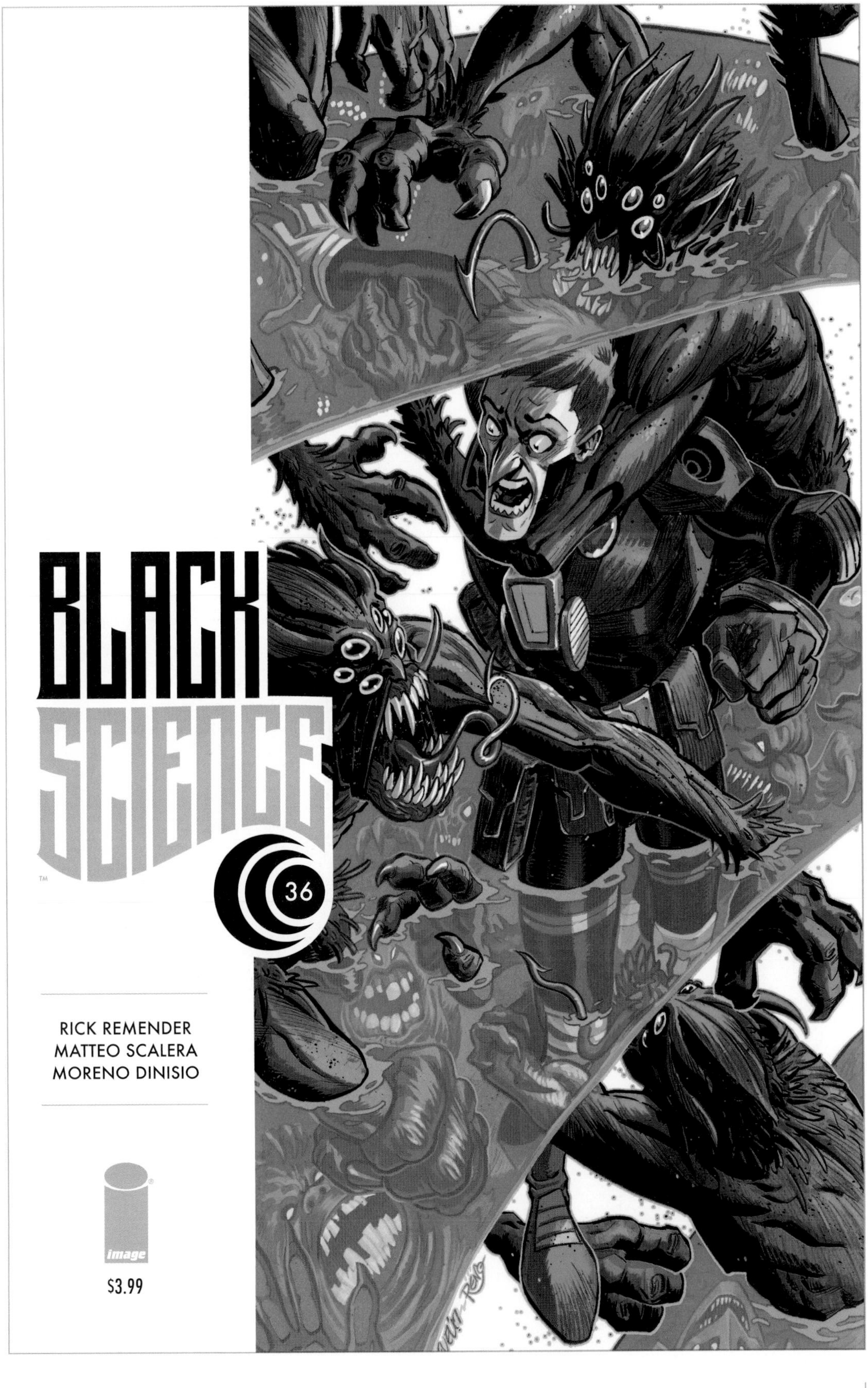
BLACK
SCIENCE
TM
36
RICK REMENDER
MATTEO SCALERA
MORENO DINISIO
image
$3.99

#36 VARIANT BY BRIAN LEVEL & MORENO DINISIO

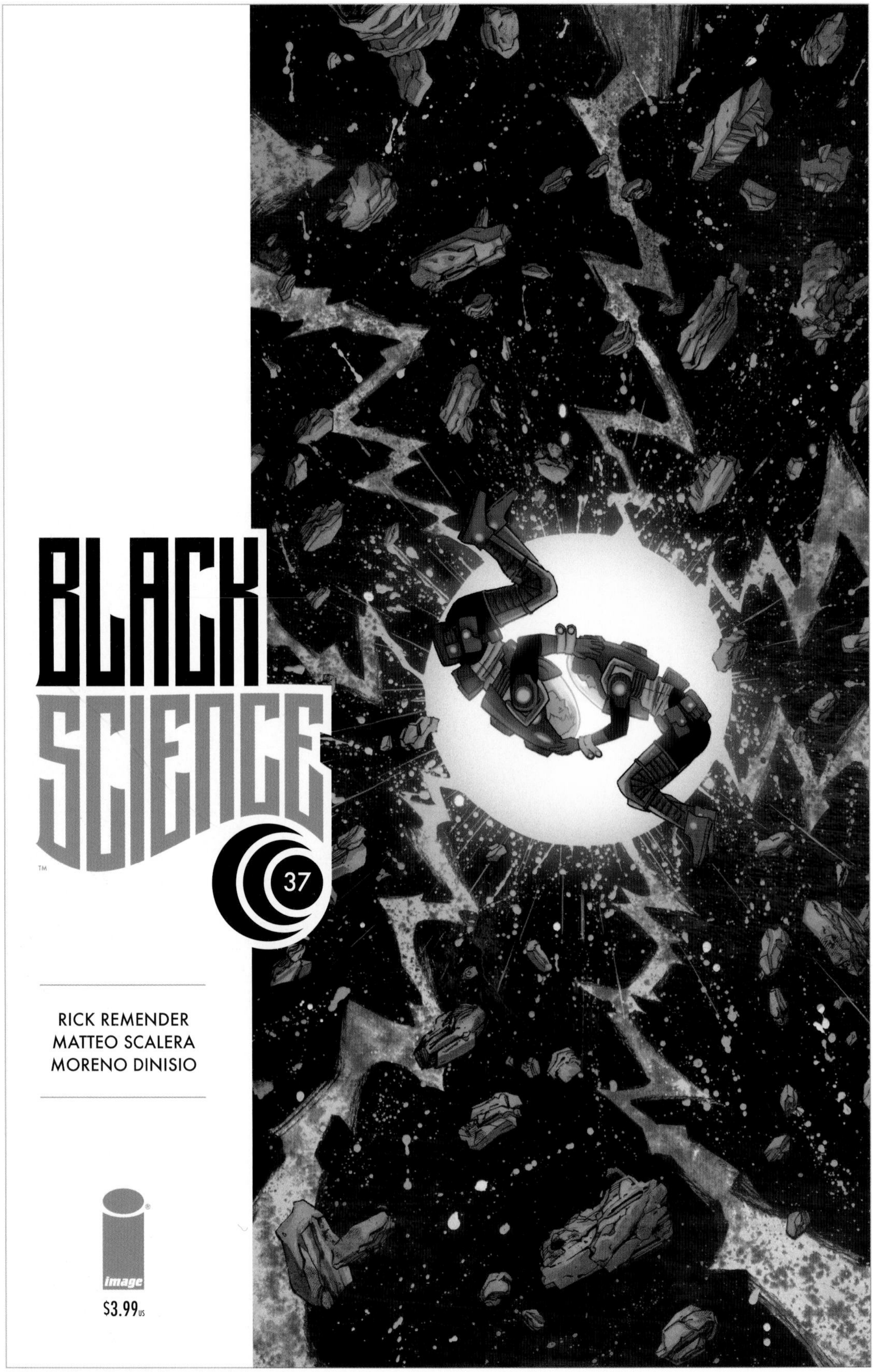
BLACK SCIENCE
TM
37
RICK REMENDER
MATTEO SCALERA
MORENO DINISIO
image
$3.99US

#37 VARIANT BY DECLAN SHALVEY & JORDIE BELLAIRE

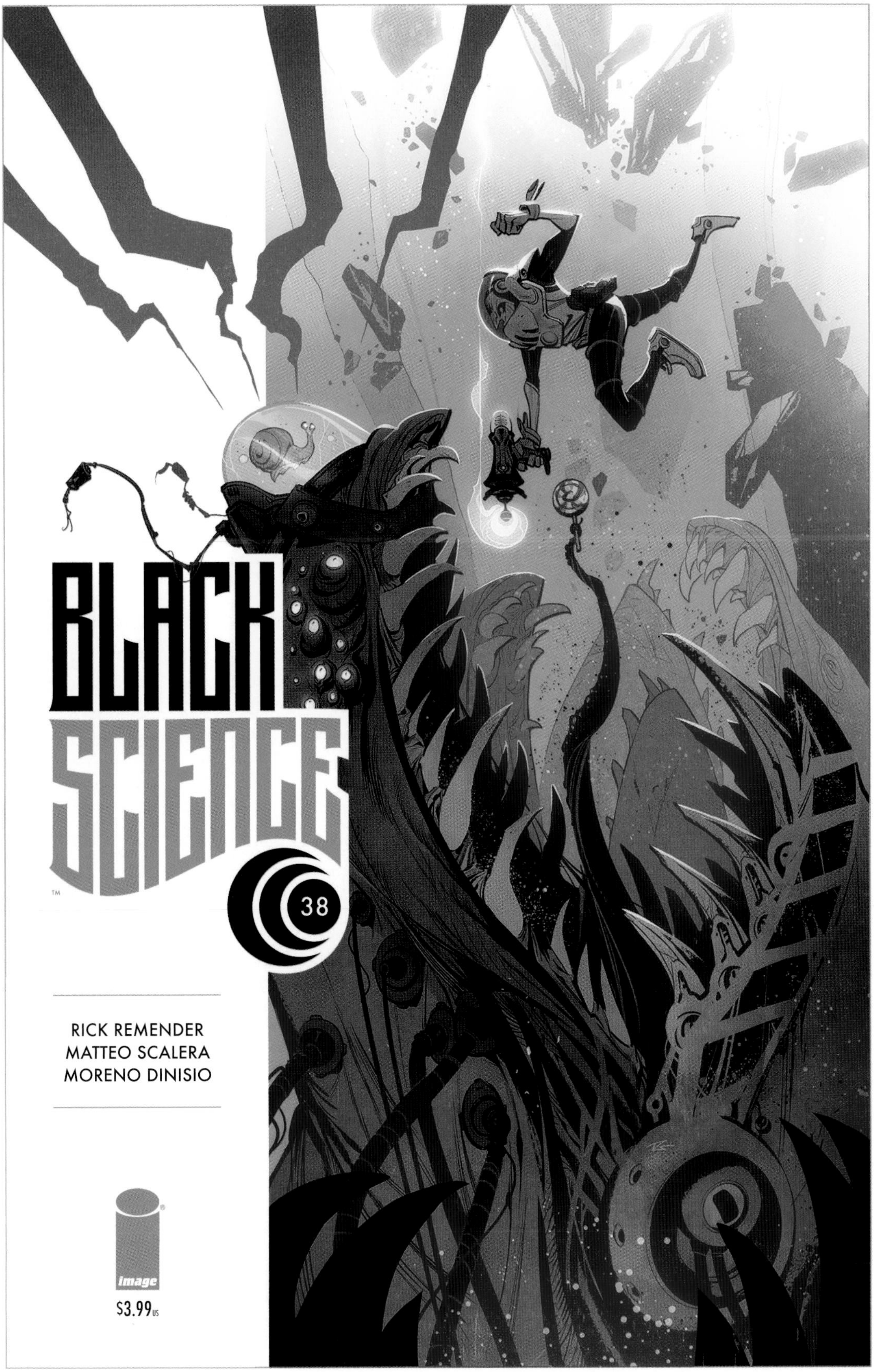
BLACK
SCIENCE
™
38
RICK REMENDER
MATTEO SCALERA
MORENO DINISIO
image
$3.99US

#38 VARIANT BY DAVE GUERTIN OF CREATUREBOX

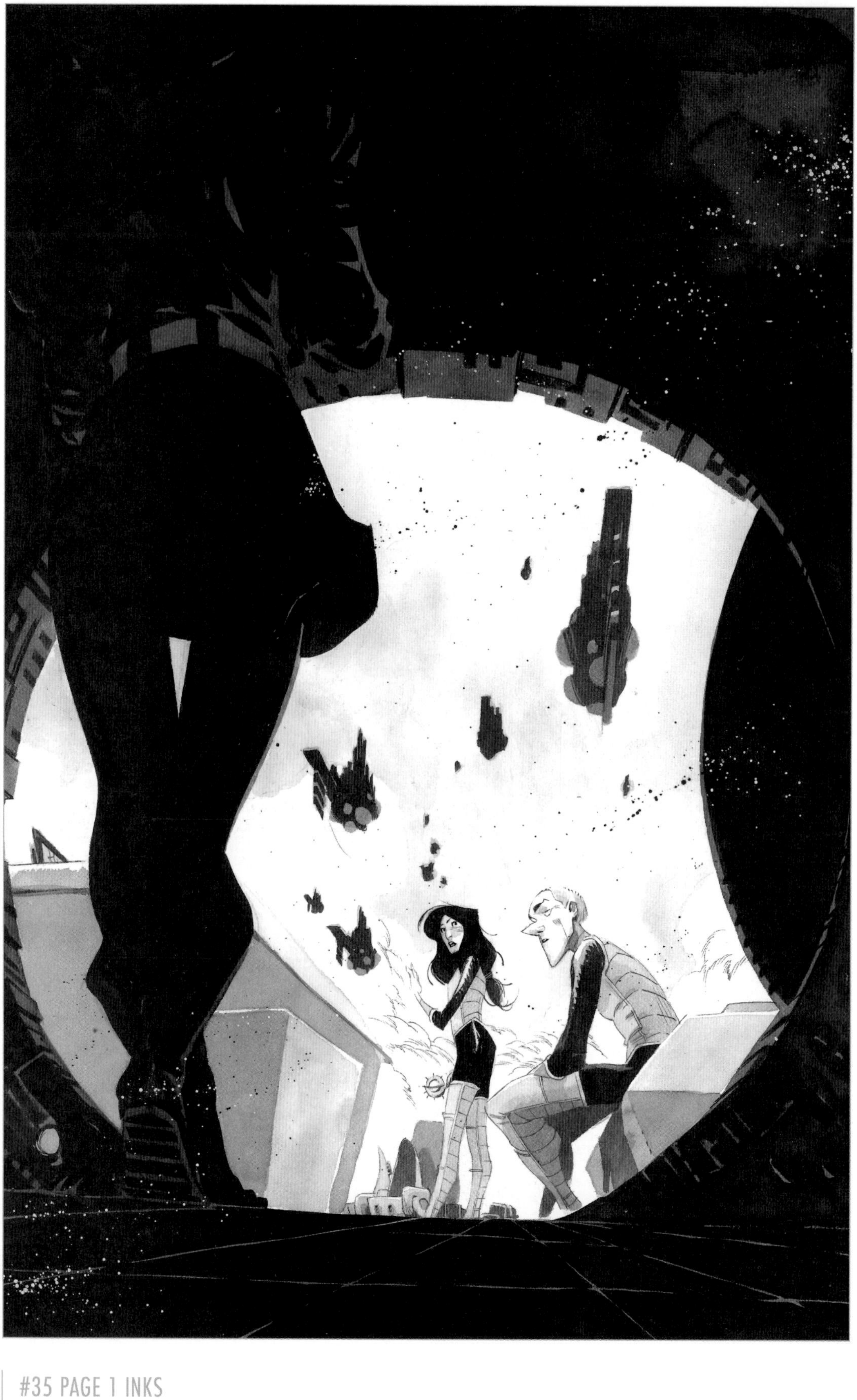

#35 PAGE 1 INKS

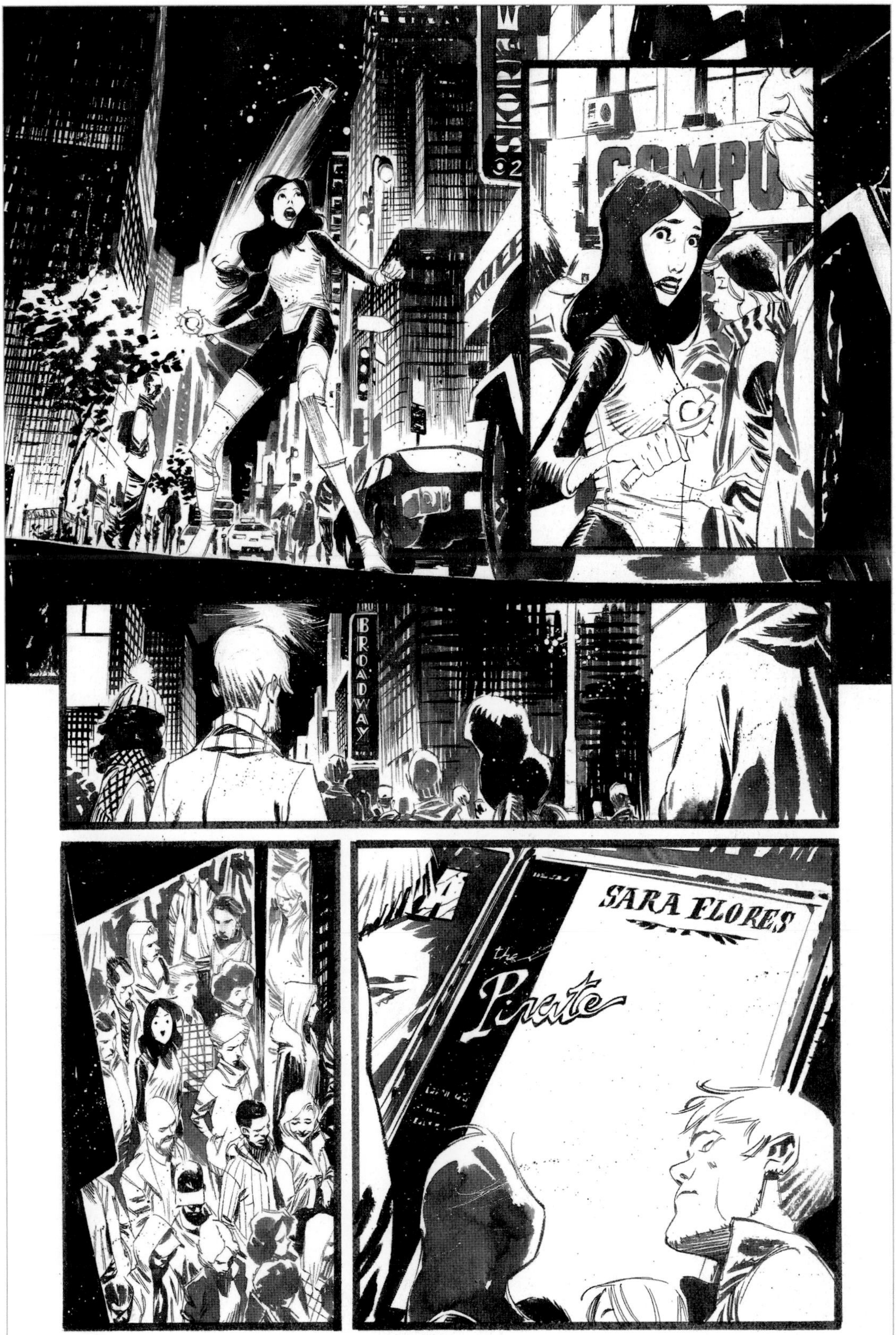
SKORJ
COMPU
BROADWAY
SARA FLORES
the Pirate

#35 PAGE 8 INKS

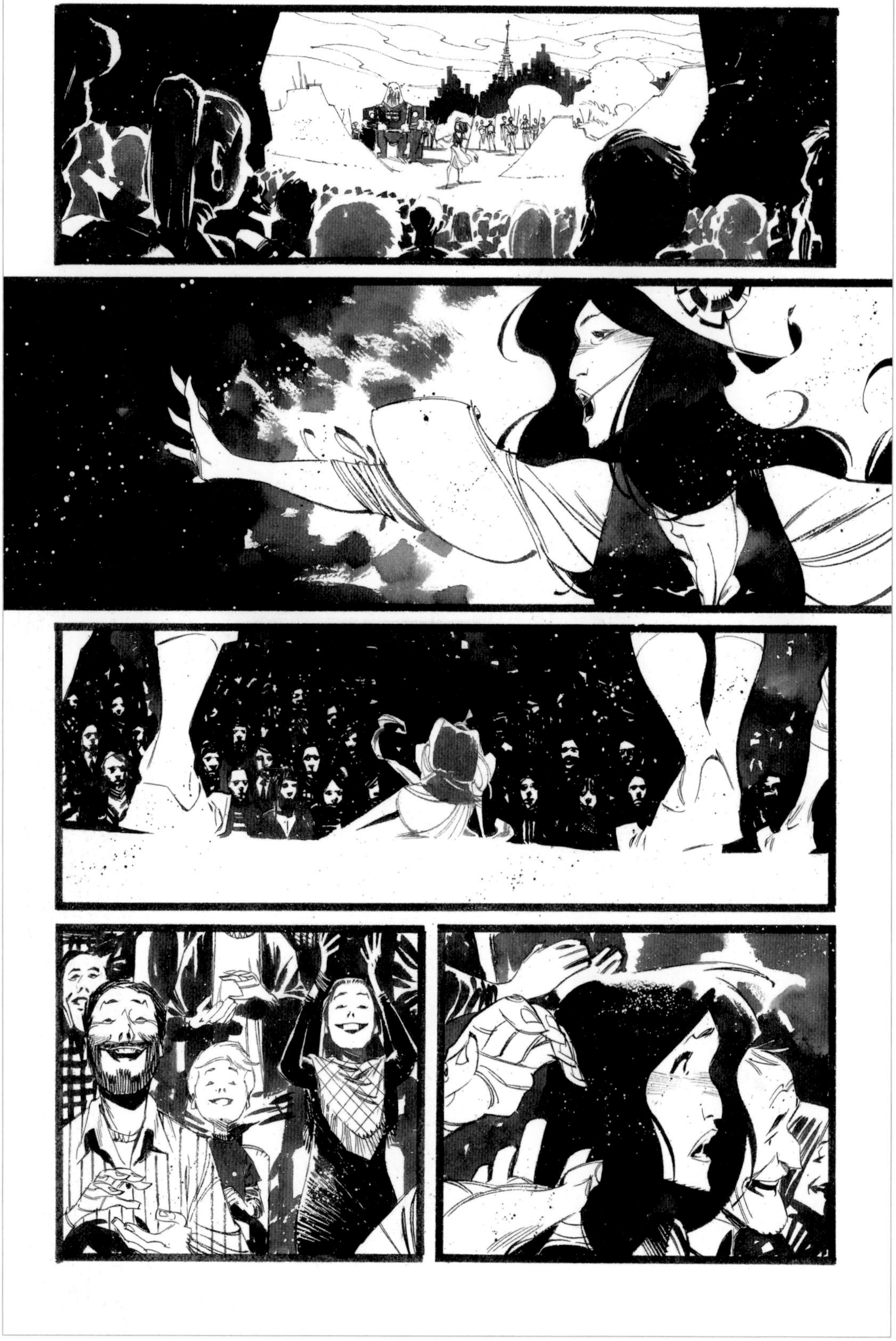

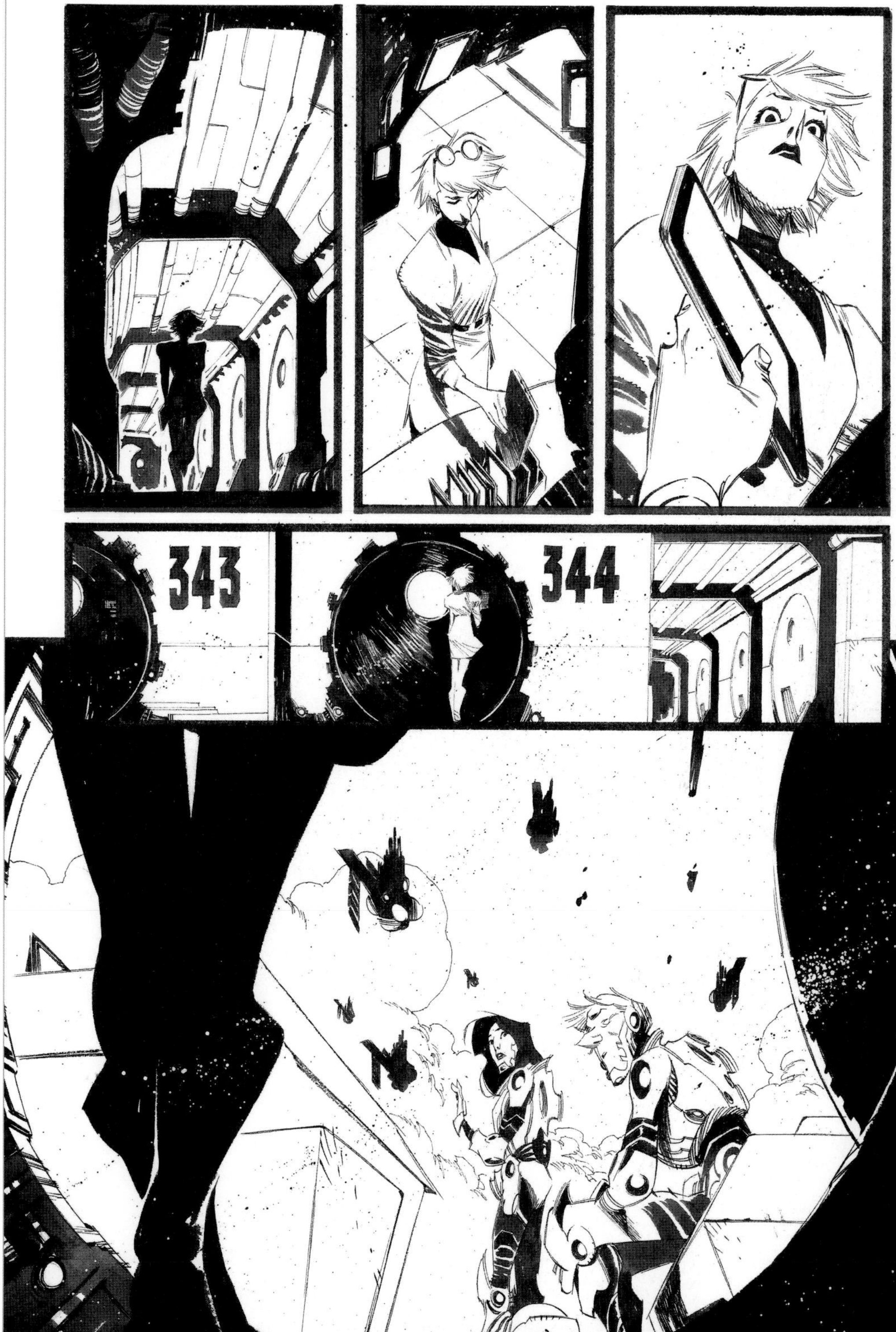
343
344

#35 PAGE 22 INKS

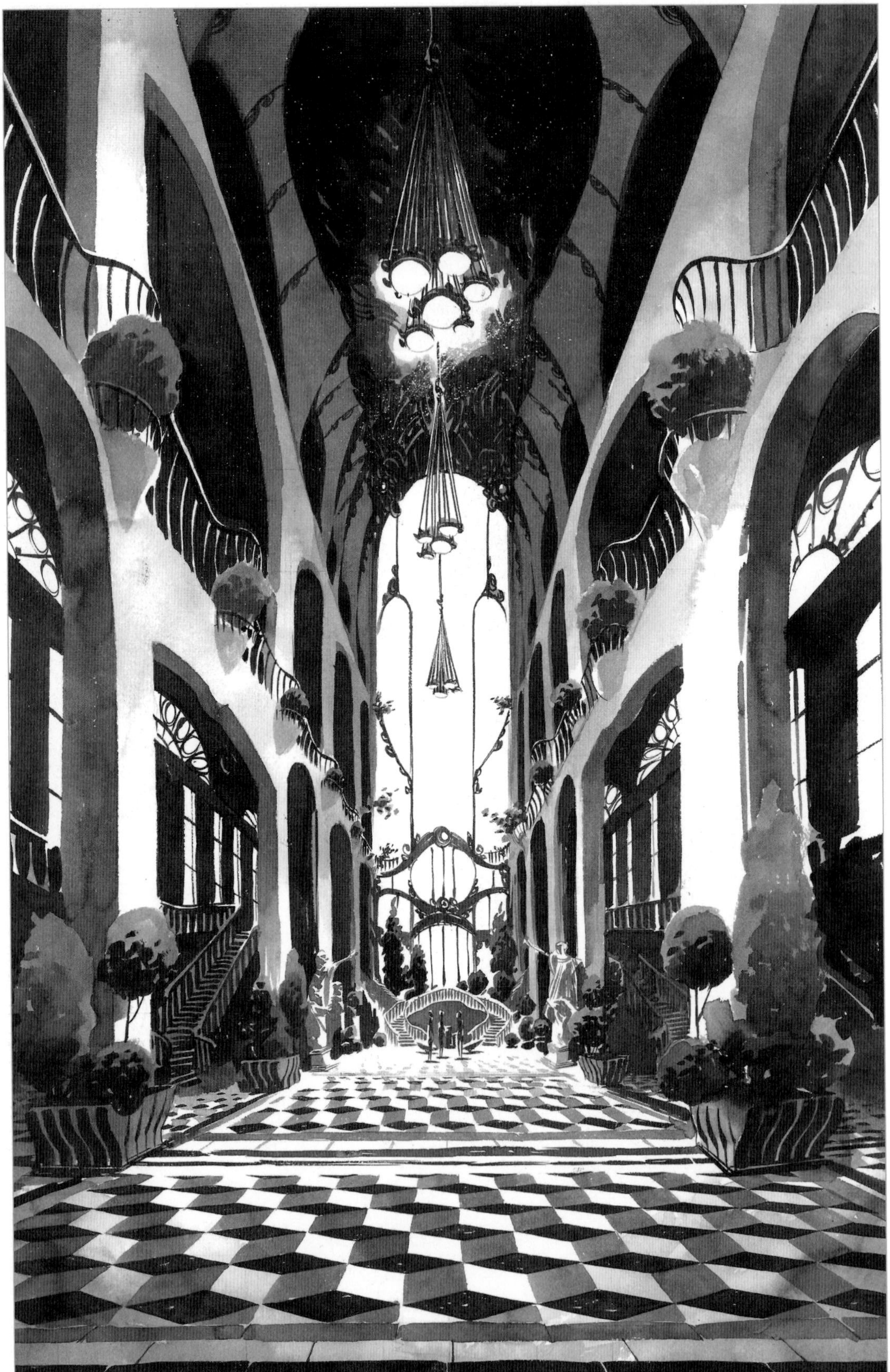

#36 PAGE 1 INKS

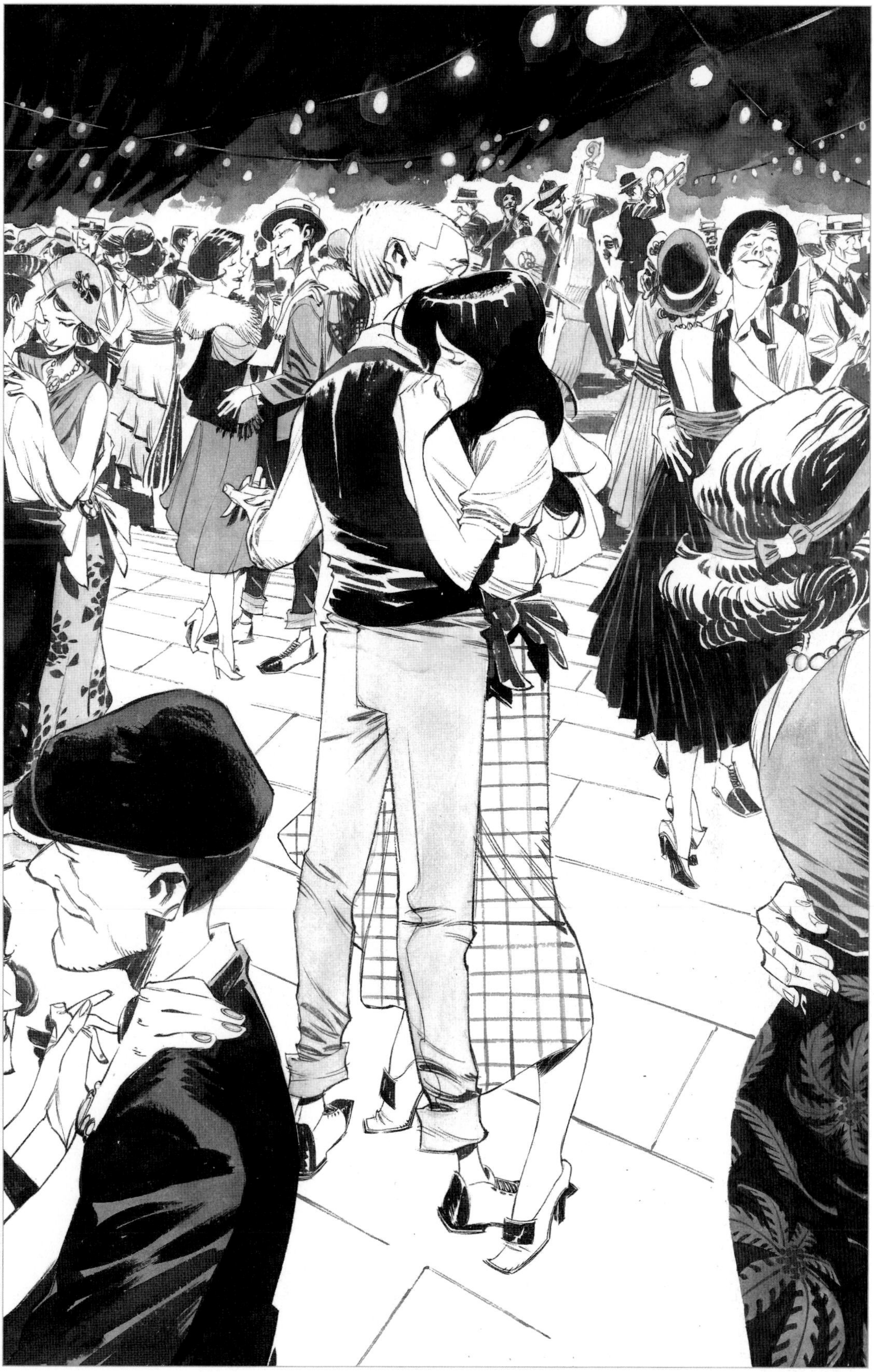

#36 PAGE 12 INKS

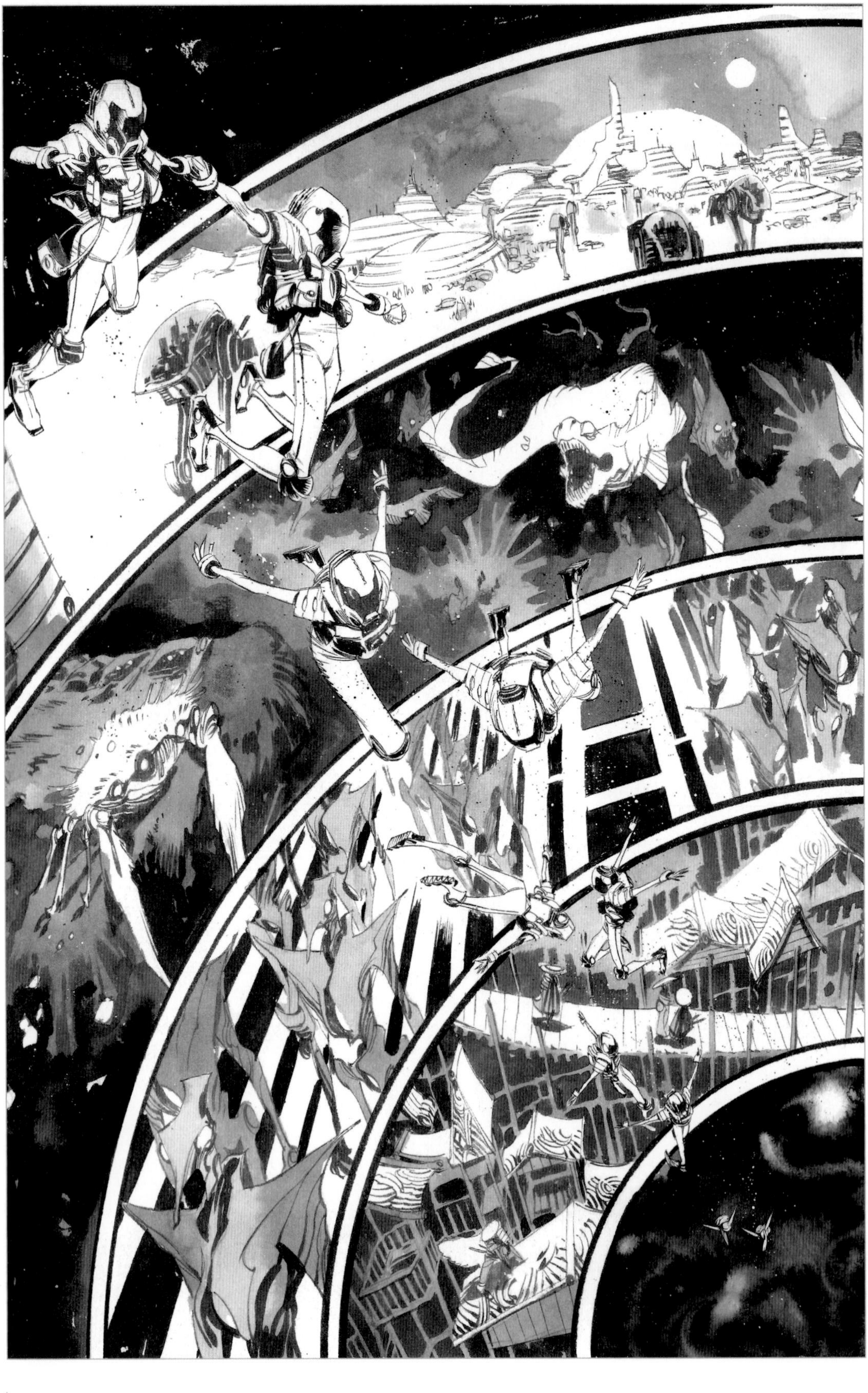

#37 PAGE 4 INKS

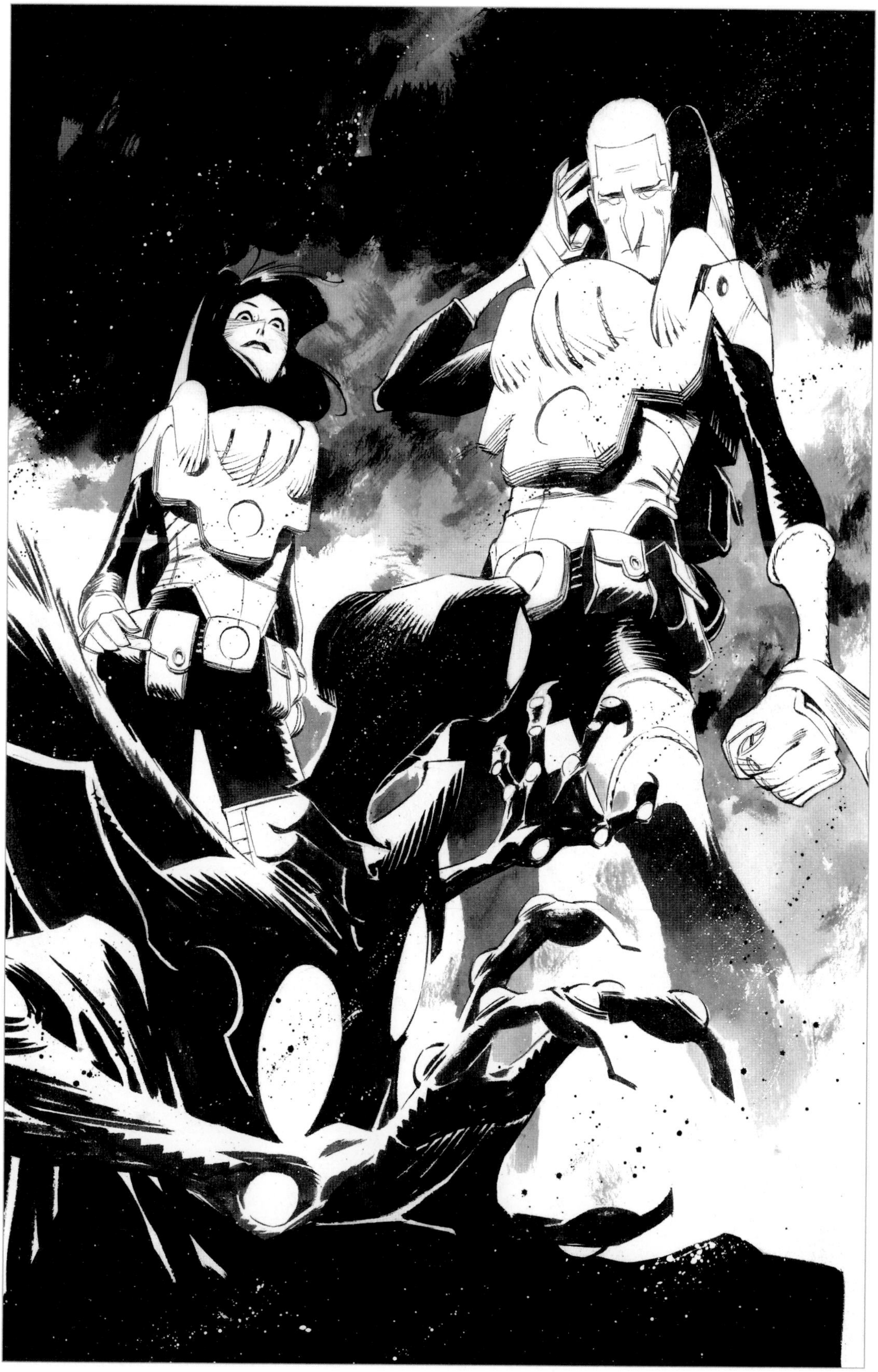

#37 PAGE 20 INKS

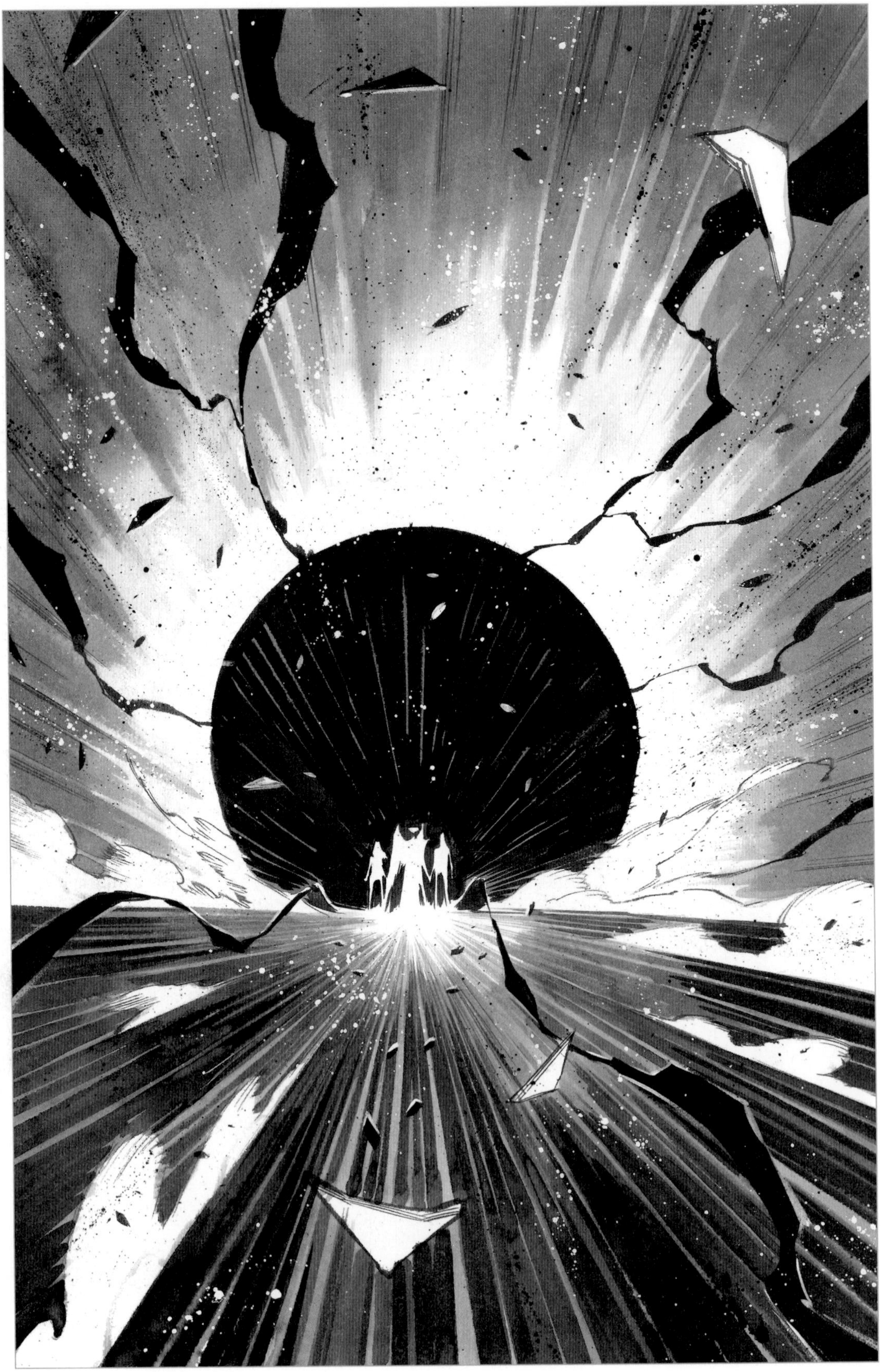

#38 PAGE 1 INKS

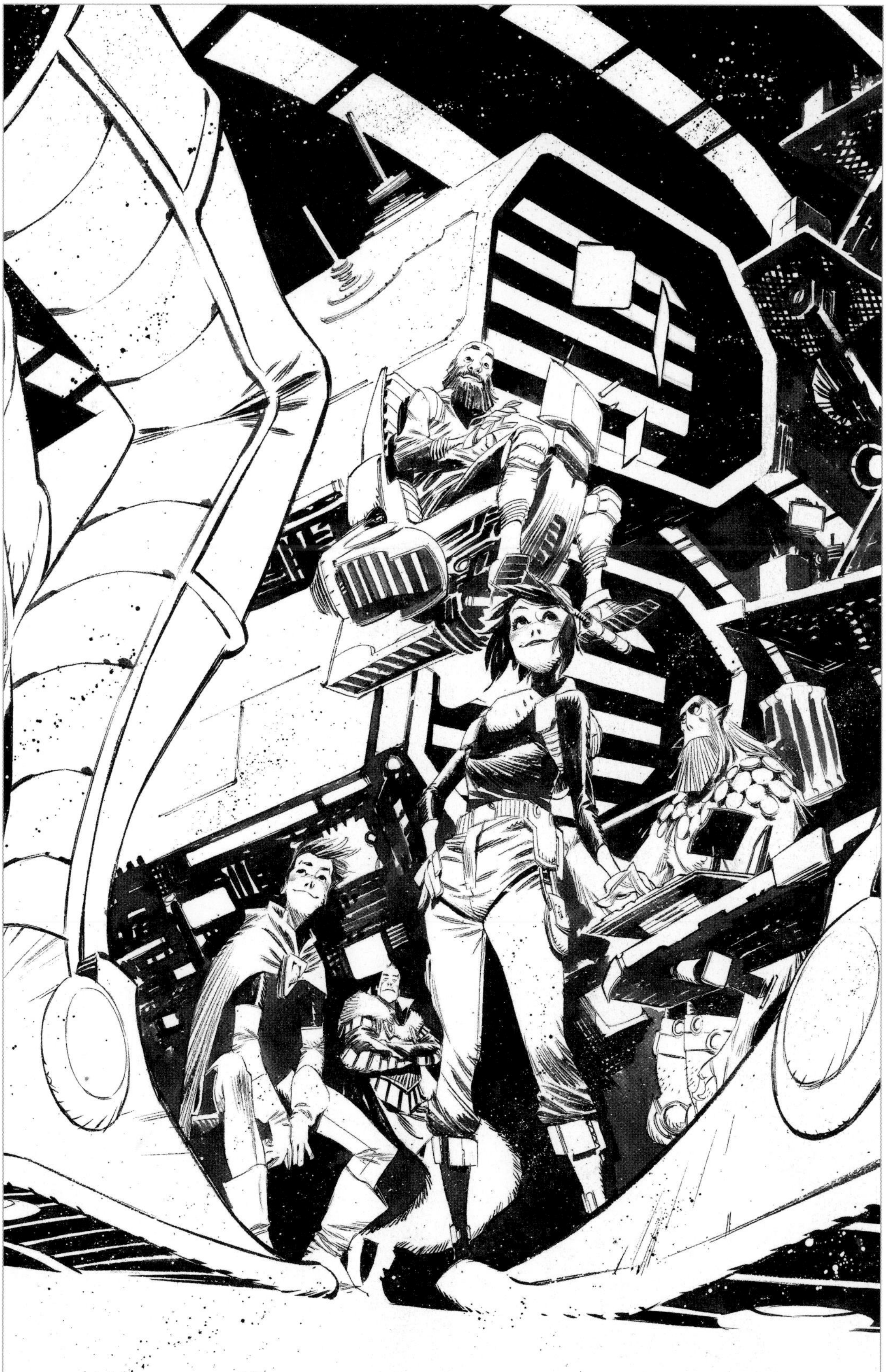

RICK REMENDER

Rick Remender is the writer/co-creator of comics such as *Deadly Class*, *Fear Agent*, *Seven to Eternity*, *LOW*, and *Black Science*. During his years at Marvel, he wrote *Captain America*, *Uncanny X-Force*, and *Venom* and created *The Uncanny Avengers*. Outside of comics, he served as lead writer on EA's *Bulletstorm* game and the hit game *Dead Space*. Prior to this, he ran a satellite of Wild Brain animation, worked on films such as *The Iron Giant* and *Anastasia*, and taught sequential art and animation at San Francisco's Academy of Art University.

He currently curates his own publishing imprint, Giant Generator, at Image Comics while serving as lead writer/co-showrunner on SyFy's adaption of his co-creation *Deadly Class*.

MATTEO SCALERA

Matteo Scalera was born in Parma, Italy, in 1982. His professional career started in 2007 with the publication of the miniseries *Hyperkinetic* for Image Comics. Over the next nine years, he has worked with all major U.S. publishers: Marvel (*Deadpool*, *Secret Avengers*, *Indestructible Hulk*), DC Comics (*Batman*), Boom! Studios (*Irredeemable*, *Valen the Outcast*, *Starborn*), and Skybound (*Dead Body Road*).

MORENO CARMINE DINISIO

Born in 1987 in southern Italy and holding a pencil since year one thanks to a painter father, Moreno grew up with the aim of becoming a professional artist. After studying comic art in Milan, he went on to work as a comic and concept artist and character designer until 2013, when he crossed into American comics, coloring *Clown Fatale* and *Resurrectionists* (Dark Horse). Moreno first collaborated with Matteo Scalera on *Dead Body Road* (Skybound). With the release of *Black Science* in December 2014, he continues their fruitful partnership.